DEADLY INHERITANCE
JEULIA HESSE

DEEP CREEK PUBLISHERS

CONTENTS

Copyright	VI
Dedication	VII
Also by Jeulia Hesse	VIII
1. Prologue	1
2. Chapter 1	14
3. Chapter 2	19
4. Chapter 3	26
5. Chapter 4	28
6. Chapter 5	34
7. Chapter 6	52
8. Chapter 7	60
9. Chapter 8	72
10. Chapter 9	76
11. Chapter 10	83
12. Chapter 11	92
13. Chapter 12	109
14. Chapter 13	111
15. Chapter 14	126

16.	Chapter 15	140
17.	Chapter 16	145
18.	Chapter 17	150
19.	Chapter 18	169
20.	Chapter 19	179
21.	Chapter 20	187
22.	Chapter 21	194
23.	Chapter 22	199
24.	Chapter 23	208
25.	Chapter 24	212
26.	Chapter 25	215
27.	Chapter 26	221
28.	Chapter 27	222
29.	Chapter 28	228
30.	Chapter 29	237
31.	Chapter 30	241
32.	Chapter 31	245
33.	Chapter 32	248
34.	Chapter 33	253
35.	Chapter 34	262
36.	Chapter 35	267
37.	Chapter 36	275
38.	Chapter 37	282
39.	Chapter 38	288

From the Author	291
40. Preview	292
41. Chapter 1	293
42. Chapter 2	296

COPYRIGHT

First published by Deep Creek Publishers 2021

Copyright © 2021 by Jeulia Hesse

All rights reserved. No part of this publication may be reproduced, stored or transmitted in any form or by any means, electronic, mechanical, photocopying, recording, scanning or otherwise, without written permission from the publisher. It is illegal to copy this book, post it to a website, or distribute it by any other means without permission.

This novel is entirely a work of fiction. The names, characters and incidents portrayed in it are the work of the author's imagination. Any resemblance to actual persons, living or dead, events or localities is entirely coincidental.

First Edition.

Cover copy by BlurbWriter.com

For my loving husband

Also by Jeulia Hesse

The Stone House Inn
Deadly Inheritance
Killer Recipe
Soul Sentinel

The Deep Blue Sea Series

Secrets in the Deep Blue Sea
Sins in the Deep Blue Sea
Ghosts from the Deep Blue Sea
Curses in the Deep Blue Sea
Treasures in the Deep Blue Sea
Hearts in the Deep Blue Sea

PROLOGUE

June 2005

She sat in the lawyer's office and pulled on her necklace, straightening it against her crisp, freshly pressed blouse for the hundredth time that afternoon. The chair felt ancient and scratchy through the thin nylon fabric of her skirt, and a bead of sweat trickled down her back between her shoulder blades. The open window was not helping to move the air. Silently, she wished the assistant would flick the switch to the ceiling fan just over their heads.

She was nervous—guilty to be doing what she was doing, but it was her property. The issue was legally buttoned up, her name on the deed. This was what her husband had wanted. It was what he had told her to do if anything ever happened to him. She had brushed him off then, not taking him seriously. What could possibly happen to him? They were young, healthy, and had their lives ahead of them.

But the unthinkable had happened, and now she was sitting in this lawyer's office making sure his brother and his family would never own the family estate. His father had left it to him. He had left it to her, and now she would leave it to her family. The Stone House Inn would never be owned by a natural member of the Stone family again.

Instead of paying attention to the stifling air in the room, both the attorney and his assistant were engrossed in their note-taking of the conversation. "Ada, we just want to be sure we are capturing the specifics in your will. You are saying everything you own, the house, business, property, and any funds are to be left to your daughter, and her heirs. You are naming your niece Christina, and her heirs as a secondary, if your daughter does not survive you."

She nodded.

"And you are stipulating that Daniel James Stone and his son Jeremy William Stone, and any heirs, are to be clearly excluded from any claim to the estate, the business, and anything left to you by your late husband William Brant Stone. Essentially, they are to be left out of any inheritance at all. Is that correct?"

Again, she nodded, eyes cast downward. "It's a family matter..." she began.

"No matter." The bespectacled attorney waved off her concern. "You are the rightful owner of the property and business. It's up to you what you wish to do with it upon your death. It's up to us to advise you in the matter."

She raised her eyes to meet his over the desk piled with files, folders, and loose papers. He had a look that both peered into her and offered comfort and reassurance. She was surprised, but not put off by the clutter in his office. He had come highly recommended by a trusted friend. She had wanted someone thorough, quick, and private; the orderliness of his office didn't matter.

The two-hour drive to Burlington was filled with worry as she wondered if her actions would create turmoil where calm currently resided. It was an uncertain and questioning calm, as far as she was concerned. The sense that something would be ripped from beneath plagued her, disrupting the serenity that her life should be. Her husband gone now for a few years, had left her well off; she should have no financial worries. She worried constantly that someone or something would push her and her precious daughter out of their home. After all, her husband had been torn away from her in a stupid and senseless accident. The risk was real.

She steeled herself. She had to be sure that what she was doing would outlast her own life. Under no circumstances should her wishes be disrupted or overturned. "If I did that...put that in the will.... Can anyone come along and turn this over? Could they take the inn away from my daughter?"

"The people you are specifically excluding?"

"Yes. I want to be sure."

He looked at her carefully. He had seen a lot in the past 20 years; liars, sociopaths, even a murderer or two. Simple estate plans were pretty run-of-the-mill, but they were not in his sphere of expertise any longer. He had taken her case as she was referred by a client and her circumstances intrigued him. The widow wanted to ensure that her will specifically excluded her husband's only remaining relatives from having any claim to her late husband's property. It was a property that had been handed down to the oldest son for nearly a century, and this apparently had been the first time the oldest son did not have a son to hand it down to. He had taken the time to review the available documents on the property to validate that this particular filial donation pattern was not a condition of ownership nor had a legal precedence. Apparently, it was a family tradition, and not a condition of inheritance on the estate.

What also had drawn his attention was the adoption paperwork he had come across while doing his research. It appeared that Mrs. Stone's daughter was adopted by her husband shortly after their marriage. It added a layer of interest to the transaction, but it didn't cast any legal bearings on her wishes.

"Once we have drawn up the final paperwork and sign with the appropriate witnesses, you can file the will in the probate court for safe keeping. That will ensure clarity." He nodded to her. "How old are the heirs? Should they also have copies?"

"No," she answered firmly her tone surprising him, "they are in school."

He nodded unabashed. "Any other relatives or close friends? Anyone you would make power of attorney or executor?"

Surprising him, she shook her head.

He pressed on. "We often create the documents as a package for these items, as part of estate planning."

"Not now," she said firmly. "I just want the issue handled. When the time comes, I'll think about all the other things I need to. For now, I just want this taken care of."

He nodded. She was the client after all.

Something ate at him about her, but he could not put his finger on what it was exactly.

The outer office intercom signaled his next appointment had arrived; it was time to move on. He would see her briefly for the final signatures of the documents in a few days. Beyond that, Ada Stone and her family drama would be out of his mind.

It wasn't until much later, while sitting home with a bourbon after a long day, that the seasoned lawyer remembered what was bothering him about the client in his office earlier. There had been strong suspicions of foul play when both parents of the now deceased Mrs. Stone's spouse had died under suspicious circumstances. He was sure there weren't any charges in the case, as a murder trial in rural Vermont would have been memorable. He vowed to look it up when he was back in the office the next day, just to settle his own curiosity.

As life goes on, and busy lives fly by, the thought from the evening was not revisited the following day and was left without further consideration.

June 2010
Five Years Later

Christina walked through the woods with the setting sun shining brightly through the trees behind her. He was up ahead and from the splashing sounds, had already entered the water. She heard his sharp intake of breath as his body hit the icy water of the spring fed pond. She could visualize the chilly water gradually covering his muscular legs, then his belly, and finally reaching his chest. Her mouth went dry.

She abruptly stopped walking the trail, hesitating from exiting the woods. Was she ready for this huge step in their relationship?

Her heart thudded loudly at the thought of him naked in the water. Her body ached for his touch, but she still hesitated, nervous. Everyone was at the party. Everyone in their small circle of friends would all know where they were, and what they were undoubtedly doing.

Her cousin Annie had promised to cover for her, although she seemed slightly reluctant and distracted. She hadn't been her usual self. Christina had blamed her cousin's moodiness on her recent breakup with her long-time boyfriend, made more difficult during this busy summer-time of social gatherings and activities. They had been having the time of their lives and suddenly, Annie had broken it off with Shawn. They had always had a tumultuous relationship, but this time the breakup felt a bit more serious. The cousins had each been spending more time out with their boyfriends while on break from college, and now Annie was single and on her own.

Ada, Annie's mother, had stopped closely monitoring their whereabouts since their first school break a few short years ago; instead, she had implored them both to watch over the other. As long as they were being smart and safe, she didn't demand to hear the details of their whereabouts. They were technically adults after all, even though they were still dependent on her for tuition and room and board until after graduation.

Christina pushed these thoughts aside and concentrated on the man waiting for her in the picturesque pond.

She loved him, and she knew he loved her. He went to a different school but had stayed committed to her throughout the past few years. Their relationship had blossomed from a high school crush into something deeper, into an intense love. She had never felt for anyone what she felt for Kevin. He was steady, calm and patient with her as their relationship matured, never pushing her for more before she was ready.

She stepped from the woods to the water's edge. It was an idyllic spot; the pond on the mountainside was glinting in the last rays of sun. She could see him swimming toward the far shore. Reaching a spot where he could stand, he turned and looked toward her, their eyes meeting over the length of the water.

All his clothes were tossed casually at her feet on the small beach. As she stared into his eyes, knowing he was naked beneath the water, she felt bolstered. She was ready. She had waited for this moment and was glad to have it now with him and in this beautiful place.

She removed her shirt and shimmied out of her cut offs. He became still, watching her. Slowly and deliberately, she unclasped her bra letting it fall to the ground as she slipped out of her panties. She heard him take a sharp intake of breath and knew it was not from the icy water this time. Her skin tingled as she imagined his eyes moving over her body to places he had not seen altogether bare. She appreciated her build; long legged with a bit of curve to her hip. Encouraged by his reaction. She dove into the water, and quickly met him on the other side.

"You're beautiful." He said with his eyes full of wonder.

She smiled at him, knowing she looked at him with love in her heart. "You're pretty hot yourself."

His hands trembled slightly as he reached out for her in the clear water. Without hesitation, she wrapped her arms around him, kissing him deeply. Her tongue darted into his mouth as he deepened the kiss, his tongue meeting hers. Her silky skin burned where it touched his in the chilly water. They had come close to making love many times, but this time they planned to go all the way. Neither had ever been fully naked with the other, so their hands searched and caressed newly revealed skin. Her nipples contracted from the cold and grazed his chest as his hardness grew against her belly.

Without a word, Kevin lifted her into his arms, continuing to kiss her eager mouth as he brought her to the shoreline. A few steps away, an old hunting cabin stood empty and waiting for the two lovers. He had prepared the cabin earlier that day with sleeping bags in keeping with their plan for the night.

He ended the kiss looking intently into her eyes. "I love you."

She pulled his mouth to hers kissing him again. "I love you too," she breathed as the kiss ended.

He carried her to the cabin, pushing the door open with his broad shoulder. He lay her gently on the bed of sleeping bags, pausing to admire her. With his hands shaking he retrieved a foil packet nearby and ripped it open, applying the condom with clumsy fingers.

She giggled as he joined her on the bed. He kissed her neck and her nervous giggles turned to soft moans.

His dark head moved from her neck to her breasts. Taking a nipple in his mouth, he sucked and gently grazed his teeth across the soft skin. His hands moved down her body and found her hot wetness. They both moaned breathlessly as he shifted and took her in his mouth, she cried out surprised by the sensation. It was glorious, and she wanted him desperately. She had for some time, but was scared and uncertain about having sex. Now she was so very sure, as he gently pushed his hardness into her. He thrust his hips forward as she called out. He stiffened, looking at her face, sweetly afraid that he had hurt her. He held himself still. "Chrissy," he whispered in her ear, "You ok?"

Slowly, she relaxed her face as he watched. She opened her eyes. Passion clouded her vision as she reached for him. "Don't stop," she begged, "Oh Kevin, don't stop."

A thrill rushed through her as he gently and slowly moved his hips. She moaned, wrapping her legs around him. She shuddered beneath him as she called his name. He could hold himself no longer and he shuddered and collapsed on top of her.

Long moments passed as they lay on the sleeping bags entangled in each other's arms. "You brought me flowers," she said, pointing to an old beer bottle with daisies jammed into its neck. It was truly a sweet gesture as the flowers were her favorite, he had picked them for her on their first 'official' date.

"Everything for my girl," he said, spooning her on the makeshift bed.

They dozed, holding each other, and listening to the night fall outside of the cabin. Bull frogs croaked outside in the pond and crickets chirped, filling the night with sound. He rolled from the makeshift bed and fumbled around, finally locating the candle he had brought. He lit it, brightening the small space and creating a gentle light for the lovers to see each other.

He moved back to the bed, kissing her face. "You ok?" he asked with some concern.

She blushed deeply. "Yes," she replied, reaching for him. She surprised herself with her need for more of him.

They kissed deeply as she pulled him onto her again.

"Now you've had me, you can't get enough of me?" he laughed, kissing her neck, overjoyed at her reaction to him.

The hours that followed were as passionate and sweet as the two new lovers discovered and enjoyed each other. Dawn crept into the decrepit cabin and birds began singing loudly, stirring them from their post sex dozes. The air had remained warm throughout the night and a mist rose off the pond as the predawn light filled the sky with pinks and light blues. The young pair marveled at the sky, holding each other closely. "We better get back before everyone wakes up," she said reluctantly, holding him close.

He pulled her on top of him. "Oh no," she giggled and kissed his ear, "no more sex."

"Ever? Maybe a little dip would change your mind."

He rose from the bed, taking her with him. His strong arms and broad chest easily lifted her with him as he ran out of the cabin and directly into the chilly water. She giggled and screamed while teasing her by dropping her into the icy pond. Finally, he submerged her completely, sliding her suggestively down the length of his body. They kissed deeply.

"I love you so much." He said, holding her in his arms as they stood hip deep in the icy water. "I want to spend the rest of my life with you."

She kissed him back. They had had this conversation multiple times. He wanted to remain in Vermont after he was done with school and had begun searching for jobs for the start of the following year. Her career choice in hospitality management opened more opportunities for travel. She would need to build experience which would come if she could get a start in a more metropolitan area. "I wish you would come to New York with me."

"No cities for me. I'd die."

She grinned, knowing full well he would enjoy a visit but would never leave his woods. He loved the undeveloped land and the quiet found in the outdoors. "You'll still come visit me?"

He nodded, grinning. "As long as I don't have to stay."

Kevin loved being out in nature, where he was happiest and most at ease. It suited him that his career choice was biology, forestry, and education. She had been studying hospitality management in the city. They'd known each other for years as friends from her summers spent on the mountain, but it was not until the past few years that their relationship had blossomed.

She shivered in his arms. "Come on. We better get dressed."

They exited the water and in the early morning light, Kevin collected their discarded clothing from the bank of the pond. He handed her clothes to her as he determined who was the owner of each article. As he retrieved both pairs of their shorts, they were barraged with a series of text messages from each of their phones.

"Must have just gotten a signal," he laughed.

"It's so spotty here. You can move a few feet and get a signal, take a few steps and its dead as a...."

"I got ten missed calls!" he shouted. But then his smile faded to concern. "Look at all these texts."

She dug in her shorts for her phone, quickly scrolling through the messages as apprehension built in her gut. "We'd better get back. It's something about Annie. Apparently, she didn't show at the party. Everyone is looking for her."

She grabbed his hand as they quickly made their way down the forest path to his truck. She would call once she had a good signal, away from the mountain. This wasn't good. No one knew where her cousin was.

The last message she had gotten was a call from Ada. Worry and apprehension permeated her voice. Annie had not shown up to the party as expected and had not come home either. The girls had gone out around the same time last night, but no one had seen Annie since she left the inn. The tone of her aunt's voice on the message had her stomach churning with anxiety and guilt. "I hope you know where your cousin is. Your friends said you were with Kevin last night."

Guilt burned in Christina's stomach. She and Annie had always looked out for each other, ever since they were small.

They were best friends. It was that simple between them. Yet here she was, sneaking around with Kevin while Annie had gone missing. Deep dread came over her as the couple careened down the gravel mountain road.

Christina had no idea where Annie could be.

10 Months LaterApril 2011

She pulled away from his attempt at an embrace, pushing her palms flat against his chest. He had expected her dismissal. It was what he had grown used to over the past few months; nonetheless, it still hurt. "Crissy…?" he whispered the question into the air, not anticipating a response.

"I took a job in the city." She said icily, steeling herself for his reaction.

He placed his hands to his thighs and exhaled slowly. He dropped his gaze to his empty hands. Hands empty of her, as she pulled away, reflecting the void he was feeling inside. He could not bring himself to respond to her statement. Deep in his soul, he had expected it. She had been pulling away since Annie disappeared, and it mystified him. Not only was she pulling away from him emotionally, but now this push of physical distance was sealing the deal.

He stood looking at her slender form in the moonlight, waiting for a response. He wanted to take her in his arms, kiss her silly and profess his undying love for her. He wanted to whisk her away to the nearest justice of the peace and make her his. Instead, he remained still, knowing as he knew her that that kind of action would push her away for good. She would be forever gone if he tried to pin her down.

She had a drive to prove herself in the world. A drive she had doubled down on. With Annie gone, all eyes were on her. She felt she carried that responsibility to succeed. He also knew that she carried a horrible guilt, since she was here and Annie was not.

They had all been tortured by Annie's disappearance. There hadn't been a clue, not a single piece of evidence or even a suspect had been unearthed alongside her missing cousin. Now, after a year of waiting for anything, they had begun to slowly move on with their lives. They had all been changed, but most of all, Christina had.

He took a cautious step toward her. He reached out to touch her fingers, just the tips, gently and lightly. He knew anything more would be too much, and she would pull further away from him. "I will always love you," he whispered, his voice husky with emotion.

She pulled her hand away from his and walked toward the path back to the house. She stopped, turning back to him. She tilted her head without making full eye contact. It seemed like she was going to say something, but then she stopped herself. Turning her face downward and angling her body away from him, she walked away, along the path back to the house where her aunt waited. The same house where her aunt would wait forever for her daughter to return.

Watching Christina go, Kevin felt an indescribable burning grow in his chest and his broad shoulders slumped with despair. He knew at that moment that his heart was breaking, cracking his chest open. As the tears coursed down his face, he watched until he could no longer see her figure on the path.

CHAPTER 1

2018 The early spring rain that had held off during the brief graveside service started to pick up intensity as the mourners carefully picked their way back to their cars over the soft sodden ground. Christina stood, watching them staring solemnly while her mind drifted miles away. She wanted to be anywhere but here.

An unexpected squeeze on her arm startled her from her thoughts. The grip was strong and bony. "We'll meet you down at the parish center," said a wiry old woman. Her name was Mabel Brown and she spoke loudly, carefully over-enunciating her words.

Christina smiled to herself, realizing that Mabel was probably accustomed to talking to her husband in that manner. He was a stubborn man who was hard of hearing but refused to wear his hearing aids. "OK great, thank you again for arranging all that..." Christina replied.

"Not sure who will come," Mabel retorted, gruffly shaking her head, "probably anyone looking for a free lunch."

Mabel turned away, walking carefully on the muddy grass. She was one of Ada's oldest friends. They had grown up together in this small town on the side of a Vermont mountain and had known each other nearly 60 years. Ada had a habit of making derogatory comments about her to Christina whenever they had a spat, which was often. Mabel was prone to drama and loved to sensationalize any situation she could. Ada had once said that Mabel could "complicate a two-car funeral."

Christina watched her for a moment, as Mabel walked gingerly down the small hill to her enduring husband who was holding the car door open for her. As Mabel reached the car, both she and her husband turned and looked back at Christina. "Don't stay too long, you'll freeze," Mabel said. "It's getting cold, and those city shoes won't keep you warm."

Christina glanced down at her feet, suddenly self-conscious of her high heels, unlike the more utilitarian shoes worn by other mourners. *Only here could anyone make me feel incompetent*, she thought, shaking her head. The older couple drove away from the grave site in their ancient, paneled station wagon. They both looked back at her, and Mabel's lips were incessantly moving as she spoke to her husband. Self-conscious of their looks, Christina raised her hand and waved in a small gesture suited to the muted occasion. But the wave was not returned.

The rain started to become heavy, and a cold breeze blew through her unlined trench coat, making her shiver. The elderly couple probably wondered why she chose to stand alone in the chilly rain while everyone else left. Christina was used to others thinking that she was different. She had always been the outsider here and never quite belonged. She was the perpetual visitor from out of state. She opened the large utilitarian umbrella she kept in her car, ever the Girl Scout, and was glad she had thought to bring it with her for the brief service.

Kevin had not come to the funeral. She was sure as she was certain she would have sensed his presence if he had shown up. In a way, she was relieved to not have to face him or any kind of an awkward exchange. He had sent her a note after Ada passed; it was a kind gesture. Yet she had kept it, unsure of her reasons for doing so. She had left him behind as much as she had left her aunt. She recognized the old guilt rising in her gut.

She stood looking at the granite memorial. The family name was inscribed at its base in huge letters.

Stone

The memorial held several generations of inscriptions, noting the birth and death dates for those buried nearby. A new marking indicated a date earlier this year – February 1, 2018 – as the most recent. Ada's ashes had already been buried by the funeral home prior to the service, leaving a patch of fresh turf covered in mud splattered flowers. Funeral workers had already removed the few chairs from the service, but their impressions were left in the soft ground.

Christina had not cried during the brief service. Her grief was assuaged by a few months. But coming back to this place after so many years laid an emotional weight on Christina's shoulders that she had not experienced when she was absent. She had avoided trips back, preferring to keep in touch with Ada over the phone. And sometimes, Ada even came to her in the city. Of course, as Ada grew older and became less able to travel freely, Christina had relented and visited her infrequently.

Gravestones covered the ground all around her. Large ones, like the Stone memorial nearby, and many more of varied shapes and sizes, as varied as the lives they represented. Small stones, heart wrenching for the brief lives they represented, were nearly covered by grass as they sank into the cold dirt over the seasons of alternating warmth and freezing temperatures. It was the latter reason why the services were held until today, as Mabel had insisted. Any friends of Ada's that were capable of paying their respects would only attend a burial service when the weather broke. Then the threat of broken hips in the snow and ice was not an issue.

As Ada had no one remaining in her immediate family except for Christina, a brother-in-law and his son, so the delay was not an inconvenience. It had further put off the need for Christina to come back to this spot, which was a plan she favored.

Carefully, using the heels of her shoes to give her purchase in the soft ground, Christina made her way to a unique blush marble headstone nearby. The color of the stone was in contrast to those in the vicinity. She stood for a moment, her eyes moving slowly over the inscription carved into the soft marble. *"Always loved, always missed, gone from our sight but not forgotten in our hearts."*

The first tears of the day began to well in her eyes as she read further.

Anna Margaret Stone
Born September 7, 1988   Lost June 19, 2010

Christina remembered that the last time she had come here was with Ada. It had been emotional torture. She was reluctant to come to the cemetery and could not fathom what Ada had been thinking at the time. "I need a place," she had said, "To come and pay respects, to talk to her, to feel like... I have some kind of closure."

Seeing her best friend's name on a cold gravestone had torn Christina apart. It made her death seem so final–that she was really gone and would never be coming back. Her heart ached with renewed pain as she wept now, just as she had all those years ago. Christina had not been there to help her then, and now, nothing or no one ever could.

She turned and walked away from the cemetery, and got back to her car, tears coursing down her face.

There were no ashes, no casket, and no bones beneath that stone.

CHAPTER 2

Kevin pulled his truck into the parking lot of the parish center, scanning the cars for the Sheriff's cruiser. He was nervous and really needed the moral support to face her. He desperately wanted to see her face, hold her hand and see how she was doing after losing her aunt. He realized that he'd come today, not totally for her, but for himself as well. She was in town, close by and in reach. There was no way he could put off that kind of an opportunity.

He wasn't sure that he could go alone into the midst of old town matrons, all who would be watching his every move. Dammit, Shawn should show up. Ada was his old girlfriend's mother for heaven's sake.

A knock on his car window startled him and he gritted his teeth, suppressing an expletive as he rolled down his window. "Glad to see you made the time in your busy schedule."

Shawn grinned, leaning his bulk down to face his friend. "Wouldn't miss it for the world. My boy needs a wing man to face the town's gossip grandmas. Plus, they usually put on a decent lunch, a good enough reason for showing."

Kevin smiled to himself watching his friend pat his stomach, secretly glad lunch would be available too. It would offer fodder for conversation and something to do with his hands. He had not seen her in forever, except for at a distance several years ago. He was eager and nervous; what would she think of him showing up? He patted his own stomach, mimicking his friend. It was flat and muscled, thanks to his love of the outdoors. Hiking benefited him, easily retaining his physique after many of his peers gained guts that spilled over their belts.

Kevin got out of his car, joining Shawn, who was scanning the parking lot. He knew Shawn was checking to see who was in attendance. He likely knew who owned each vehicle. "So old pal, what is your plan? Will she throw herself at you, regretting all the years she let pass without you?" Shawn held his gaze on one vehicle in particular and furrowed his brow.

Kevin winced at his words. He wasn't *wrong*. That was his dream. That she would come back to him and see that he still held on to hope for them. She would see they were meant to be together. He knew deep down that this was not realistic, but a guy could dream. He was being courteous coming to pay his respects to Ada. He had known her longer than he had known Christina, so it was only right that he come.

The two old friends entered the parish center together. As expected, the wall of elder female eyes fell on them as they made their entrance. He swore he could hear the whispers grow as Ada's lifelong friends took in the two newcomers to the funeral reception. Several shifted their seats to have a better view of the men as they joined the short line to pay respects to Christina. He scanned the room quickly for any of Ada's relatives from the Stone side and did not immediately see any before Christina caught his eye.

She had noticed him. A thrill rose in his chest as he spotted the flush growing on her beautiful face. *Don't get your hopes up*, he thought. He nervously straightened his tie as he approached her from across the room, Shawn tailing faithfully behind. Reaching her, he formally grasped her hand and kissed her smooth cheek. "So sorry for your loss."

Shawn repeated the sequence as Christina graciously accepted their condolences. "Thank you both for coming, I didn't expect to see you."

He noted she was keeping her tone neutral, addressing them both and not him singularly. "Of course, we came. Ada was part of our family. Or I should say, she made us part of hers," Shawn replied.

Kevin noted a shadow pass over Christina's face at his words and she outwardly winced. He didn't understand it at first, but it dawned on him as Shawn droned on about the turnout and the lunch spread, buffet style, on the long tables against the far wall. Evidently Christina did feel guilty about not being around much for her aunt after Annie's disappearance. Her untimely death must have grown that guilt as other non-family members stepped in to fill the void that she and Annie had left. Ada was a kind woman, so it was easy for her to stay connected with her daughter's old friends. She had made it easy for both men to retain their relationships with her.

Christina's expression changed as Shawn spoke, her eyes locking on someone over his shoulder. A furrow creased her brow as she turned her attention to Shawn. "Thank you for coming. Why don't you have a bite to eat before you have to go back out?"

Christina moved them on to speak to the man who had come in after them. Kevin was disappointed in himself for not saying more, but was thankful for Shawn for being there to fill in any awkward moments. He didn't really think through what he would say exactly. Stepping in the door had been half his battle.

He caught a cloud of heavy aftershave. Jeremy Stone grabbed Christina's attention next. He was Ada's nephew from her husband's side, so it was fitting that he should be here. Kevin didn't appreciate that he had Christina by the hand and was talking to her earnestly.

"I don't like that guy," Shawn stated, filling his plate full of food. "Lawyers and law enforcement don't always mesh. I get it, and I have some good friends that are lawyers, but he has always struck me as somebody that is just a bit on the slimy side."

"Oh really? Interesting. Why do you say that?" Kevin took a seat beside Shawn at an empty table covered in a plastic tablecloth.

"No specific reason honestly. I mean he's on the board for the local Bank, he's involved in Rotary and does fundraising for the local non-profits. There's not a run or walk for something or other that you don't see his name or his father's construction company as a sponsor."

"Yeah, I see him involved in a lot. Hasn't he helped some older people with their wills, or with family issues without getting paid? Wasn't he helping Ada out too? I think he took over for her when she went into the hospital."

Shawn sat back in his seat; a crumb of egg salad stuck to the corner of his mouth. He looked as though he was thinking of saying something, but thought better of it. "Yeah. It's almost like he's a little too good."

Kevin laughed to himself. He knew it was ludicrous, that Jeremy was too good. But he knew what Shawn meant–there was something not to be trusted about him.

Plates of cake and Styrofoam cups of hot coffee appeared on the table next to the two men. Mabel Brown smiled at them, her smile widening as her gaze swept over Kevin.

"Nice big slice for you, Kevin. You need a little meat on your bones."

Melodious laughter interrupted the awkward moment with Mabel. Kevin knew the source of that sound; he would recognize it anywhere. "Oh, funeral cake, that looks great." Christina said joining the men. She took a chair opposite Kevin, facing him across the narrow table.

"I'll get you some of your own, dear. Time you got off your feet anyway," said Mabel, leaving the group alone.

"Here, you can have mine." Kevin shoved his piece in front of Christina.

She smiled. "What about the meat on your bones?"

"I'll take the piece she brings back." He smiled back, looking into her beautiful blue eyes.

"Who says I'd let you have it? That one is mine; whereas this was your *special* piece."

"Does that mean you're keeping them both?" Kevin chuckled out loud, elated with the exchange.

Shawn shook his head laughing. "Some things don't change. I wonder how you keep your figure if you are still eating like that."

Mabel delivered three plates of cake to the table. "Don't take that boy's cake, Crissy. Here's yours."

Kevin smirked at Christina, merriment in his eyes. She returned his smile, delighted with the additional cake. Her expression quickly changed to confusion as Mabel moved the large slice of cake away from her, replacing it with a much smaller modest piece.

"You have to be careful; you know issues with sugar can run in families. Your aunt had it all her life and controlled it real well; not like the rest of us. I was on pills and had to go to the shots. Insulin! Don't get old!" Mabel shook her head, but her eyes betrayed her merriment. "Ada was a good friend and helped me with that. Maude too. She just went on the shots last year. Such a shame what happened to Ada though. I guess you never know what's gonna happen when you get up to our age."

Christina's appetite for cake seemed to be diminished by the topic of conversation. She picked at it with her fork, not taking a bite. The shadow from earlier was back on her face and her brow furrowed. "I thought she died from heart failure."

Mabel patted her shoulder. "That's right, dear. In the coma, her heart failed. But the coma was caused by sugar. The Sheriff was the one that found her on the floor. The poor thing, she'd been there all night."

Christina looked over at Shawn. "Is that right, Shawn?"

Shawn swallowed a mouthful of cake and took a swill of coffee before answering. "You knew that, right? I found her that morning and called EMS. Beyond that, I really don't know much more, 'cept it was bad."

"I know you were the one that found her, but did you know if it was caused by her diabetes?" Christina asked.

Shawn pulled his vibrating phone out of his pocket and looked at the screen. "Well, duty calls, folks." He rose wiping his mouth unceremoniously with his sleeve.

"Good to see you, Crissy. Safe travels back to the city," Shawn said, exiting the parish center with long, purposeful strides.

"I never knew Ada to have too many ups and downs with her counts, but I guess you never know. Anyway dear, sit and enjoy your cake. We'll start cleaning up in a bit," Mabel said addressing the pair. Then she turned to Kevin. "Did you get a break from school?"

"Lunch break. I have to head back shortly," Kevin replied.

Mabel left them alone at the table. The mood subdued as Christina picked at her cake.

"When do you have to go back?" he asked.

She looked up at him, her gaze melting his heart. He reached out to touch her hand, but pulled back at the last second, unsure of himself.

She noticed.

"In the morning." She held his gaze; he could feel his face was warming. "I have to meet with Jeremy before I go."

"I hear he's been taking care of things, at the inn and all." He cleared his throat. This was uncomfortable. He didn't know where to go with the conversation and he needed to get back to work.

The shadow passed over her face again. She stood, gathering the plates from the table. "I should really..."

He stood as well. "Yeah, I need to get back."

A forced smile came on her lips, but didn't rise to her eyes. He knew he'd said something wrong. She must feel badly that Jeremy was taking care of things and not her. But Jeremy *was* an attorney, so it did make sense. She had always harbored guilt about her aunt and the inn. It was what broke them apart. Acid built in his gut, and not from the church lady luncheon food.

"Thank you for coming. It was good to see you," she said.

He nodded to her and walked out to his car. He was glad to have seen her, but it seemed like any chance they had was still weighed down by her conscience. If only that terrible night hadn't happened all those years ago...

CHAPTER 3

He clutched the steering wheel of the car, knuckles turning white. Bone deep hatred for them all was churning in his belly. He knew he had to go through the motions for the funeral and the other niceties. It was too much to bear. He had to get out of there.

Watching that little city slut parade around like a queen as everyone paid homage really made him burn. She needed to go the way of the others. He would see to that. He would get what he wanted.

It had worked in his favor for a while. Even though they didn't get what they had wanted from the beginning. It was rightfully theirs! They were smart and he had figured out some better ways to get the money that they needed and deserved. It was so nice to have the ease of available cash. Life was pretty easy.

The old bat had suspected they were up to something. It was too easy to deal with her.

He was feeling pretty proud of himself. No one suspected a thing. Not one thing.

People were starting to trickle out of the parish center. He ducked down in his seat, not wanting to leave yet, but knowing that he really should.

Loads of old biddies came trailing out of the building. Done with their free lunches, now they needed to go home to sleep it off. They got nothing else to do, damn lazy freeloaders.

It dawned on him that all of these people were here because of something he had done. All of them.

A feeling came over him. He recognized, welcomed and relished it. It poured into his veins and warmed his skin.

Power.

He had taken another human life.

Again.

He hadn't been caught, not for this or for the last one.

He needed to keep it that way.

His hands shook as he gripped the steering wheel. A drink, he needed a drink. He craved the burn that would slip down his throat and the warmth spreading over his body. The thought aroused him. Maybe he would take advantage of that. There were a few women available, eager to be with him for the money he offered. He knew he helped to fund their drug habits, but didn't much care, as it fed him in other ways.

He slipped his car out of the parking space and onto the main street and headed to the local bar.

CHAPTER 4

"Are you serious?" her friend Gina asked astonished, plopping herself down in the chair opposite her desk, "this isn't some twisted late April fool joke, is it?"

Christina shook her head. "I wish it was some warped joke, but as far as I can tell, it's real."

She was still stunned at the revelation that Ada had left anything to her in her will, and was even more astonished that its contents included the Stone's family home, which was currently set up as an inn. Ada had given her the entire business and everything she had left. Ada's attorney, Jeremy Stone, had spoken to Christina at the parish center after the funeral service. He seemed in a rush, anxious to be sure that he caught her before she left for the city. The two of them arranged to meet with her in his offices the next day.

Christina had known Jeremy since she could remember. He was Annie's cousin on her father's side and was a few years older than them. The families were not close. Christina remembered him as a quiet, studious type, who was not part of her intimate group of friends. Though Christina hadn't known much about or spent much time with him, he had done his best to ensure she was comfortable in his office. He was attentive and gracious, but his efforts made her feel awkward.

As she sat in his law office, she remembered that he had been questioned in Annie's disappearance. Most of the boys in their group of friends had been queried as well. The police were adamant about leaving no stone unturned to find out what happened to the missing girl.

Nothing had ever turned up. It was if Annie had just disappeared off the face of the earth.

The details in Ada's will were complex, containing information about the family home that had been converted to an inn in the 1940's, after WWII. The inn had not been operational as a business for several of the past few years, though it was cared for by resident caretakers. There were additional details of the acreage, land use, stables, property abutments and historical society correspondence. Christina had been totally unprepared to absorb much of information presented.

The contents of Ada's will was a complete and total surprise. Jeremy had understood her incredulous response. He had recommended that she take some time to absorb the whole idea of the inheritance, but said that she needed to return to see to legal details and the future of the property. He explained that there were matters that needed the new owner's attention, including the inquiries of a real estate developer. His tone had made her feel there was an urgency to the situation and her anxiety began to rise.

Ada had made Jeremy's firm the executor of her will and her power of attorney in Christina's absence. In that role, Jeremy was also overseeing the continuance of the property and managing any issues, like paying of the bills. It was at that point in the conversation that Christina's brain began to kick in. "Jeremy, Ada has been gone for months," she said.

"Why are you bringing this to me now, and not in February, right after she died?"

Jeremy stood up at her question, cleared his throat and came around the desk, taking her hand in his. "Because, Christina, a person cannot be officially declared deceased until they have been missing for over seven years. We needed to verify legally that the original heir that had claim to the property would not appear. Once we declared her dead, we moved forward to the contingent heirs to carry out the wishes of the deceased."

It took Christina a moment to process this information. Her heart rhythm began to pick up, thumping loudly in her ears as Jeremy gazed into her eyes, imploring her to comprehend his words. When his meaning registered, she felt as if she had been physically struck. Her stomach plummeted, as if she was plunging down the highest hill of a roller coaster. Her silent nod to Jeremy indicated her acknowledgement of this stunning information. She was speechless.

Annie had been gone for over seven years last spring. She had just now been legally declared as dead. Christina was to inherit what was rightfully her dead cousin's legacy. The pain and guilt that had pushed her to never return to this place came raging back as Jeremy held her hand and delivered this solemn news. It was an emotional gut punch. She had left Vermont to start her own life after Annie's disappearance and to escape the constant grief and guilt. But the pain that had diminished with years and absence came roaring back.

Christina did not recall much about the remainder of the conversation, except that she promised to return soon to lay out the plan for the estate. She recalled bolting from the attorney's offices, eager for a quick exit and hoping to leave all this information and pain behind her. It was too much to absorb all at once. She stopped quickly at the local hotel for an immediate check out and got on the road, desperate to be back in the city.

The few weeks after that meeting had been a blur of calls and emails from the attorney. Christina was bombarded with requests to coordinate the best time to be on site to take care of the details and to meet with an interested investor. Now, as she sat at her desk at work, across from her closest colleague, Gina, in the back offices of the hotel, she realized how surreal this inheritance was. "It's true. But I wish it was and April Fool's Day joke."

"You are out of your mind!" Gina exclaimed, banging her hands on the arms of the chair for emphasis. "You have just inherited a house! More than that, it's a historic inn in the country! It's like winning the lottery for someone in our business–a ready-made dream come true!"

Christina sat back in her office chair and looked out over the view of the city. She had worked hard to get to where she was in the world and had put in the time to advance her career. She had done well and felt proud of her own accomplishments and aspired for more. "Well... not so fast. The inn is an old place, and it needs a lot of attention and upkeep. And, it will be difficult to manage the four-hour drive with my work schedule...."

"There you go again, Crissy–putting this place before everything else...." Gina scoffed, getting up from her chair and closing the office door for privacy. "Even after all that happened with the good ole boy club passing you over for the last promotion...."

Christina started to object, but Gina cut her off. "You know what I am talking about–the same thing happened to me two years ago. I am the best chef and you are the best Resort Manager this place has ever seen... but who is running the show, and who gets the promotions? Men... all of them! White, straight men to be exact!"

Christina started to speak and was interrupted by her phone intercom. "Ms. Wade, your two o'clock is here...."

"Thank you. I'll be right out," she replied, shutting off the intercom and turning to her friend. "All right.... I'll be on my way to deliver some delicious meals for our patrons tonight." Gina said, getting ready to leave. With her hand on the office door, she turned back to Christina. "When are you going to Vermont?"

"I leave Monday. I have two weeks' vacation saved and it sounds like I am going to need at least that to get things squared away," Christina replied. "I have to figure out what is what. And I also want to get a clearer story of what happened to my aunt to cause her death. It all sounds very sketchy. Was it heart failure or her diabetes? It won't make a difference, but it feels like I really SHOULD know. The woman left me everything she owned in the world; I at least owe her that." *Especially after I failed her at the end,* she added in her head.

Gina looked at her. "I could use a few days away. You want company? I am especially useful in these situations."

Christina looked a little more closely at Gina. She looked tired, with defined circles under her eyes. Something was off with her friend, she noted. Gina quickly covered the bruise on her arm, pulling the sleeve of her blouse lower. Then she covered the area with her hand for good measure. The women looked at one another; the unspoken communication was clear to them.

Gina opened the office door to leave. "I'll pick you up around seven o'clock Monday morning," she replied to her friend. Crissy responded with a silent cheerless smile and nod. As she watched Gina make her way down the hallway toward the kitchens, she felt worried for her. Obviously, Gina's ex-husband had made an appearance again. Christina had known that there was a chance they would cross paths at some point, since they both worked in the same profession.

Gina's ex was a famous French chef with a cable show in the US. They'd filmed a series of his shows in the city earlier this week and he must have sought her out. Thankfully, his career kept him mostly in the California region when they were not traveling for the show. But nonetheless, Christina knew that no restraining order would keep the famous Jacques Moran away from Gina. He was above the mere common people. And after what happened the last time, Gina was reluctant to press charges.

Christina walked down the hallway to retrieve her appointment, trying to shake off the feelings of stress and worry for her friend's situation with domestic violence. She would be glad to have Gina with her, because if Gina was away, she'd be hard to find. Selfishly, Christina also thought Gina could be a distraction for her. Up in Vermont, Gina would be the only one who knew nothing of her past and the incident that cost her friend her life.

CHAPTER 5

Christina pulled the rental car off the main road in Wardsboro and onto a picturesque dirt road. Gina stirred in the passenger side as the car turned the corner and bumped from pavement to dirt, but she didn't fully wake. Christina chuckled to herself. The few miles up the mountain between here and the inn would take them over a narrow road with high embankments and through thick woods with few views. Then they'd finally arrive at the base of the inn's long driveway. There, the trees opened and showcased the beauty and views of the inn. She found she was looking forward to seeing the property where she had spent so many happy times until it stopped being happy altogether.

It had been several years since she had seen the inn. Remembering Ada's challenges with the upkeep of the historic property, Christina had tried to prepare herself for the reality that the building may not be in good shape. Even though Jeremy had assured her that the inn was being cared for, Christina was prepared for a dilapidated structure in need of much TLC. She couldn't imagine that in her ailing health and mind, Ada would have been capable of managing the upkeep. *Just as well,* she sighed to herself, *more of a reason to plan to sell it and put this place back into the past permanently.*

As she drove the meandering road up the mountain, she glanced at her dozing friend. As she turned the final curve in the mountain road, Christina nudged her. "Hey sleepy head! You are missing the best part."

Gina woke, frowning and stretching out her cramped limbs. "You didn't say how long a drive this would be..." She paused and gaped past Christina, "Wow! Look at that view!"

Christina turned to look where Gina was pointing. She'd seen this view a million times, but it surprised her to see its beauty with fresh eyes. She gaped at the sight, taking her eyes off the road in front of her. It was truly stunning. The tree line opened at the field below, framing the view of the valley and the neighboring mountains. It was beautiful.

A car horn got her attention. Startled, she swerved to the right side of the road to avoid the on-coming car. The narrow road barely allowed the passage of two cars, but their slow speed on the dirt road spared them much risk from an accident. Nonetheless, Christina gripped the wheel tightly as her tires crunched the gravel, careful to avoid skidding on the loose stone. The oncoming car pulled alongside them, and Christina stopped the car. It was a Sheriff's vehicle! Damning her eagerness to show off the local sites to Gina, she sighed. It was just her luck that she'd start her trip off with a ticket.

The driver-side window rolled down in the Sheriff's car, and Christina rolled hers down as well. "You lost?" a man with a friendly set of brown eyes asked, pulling off his sunglasses.

"Shawn?" Christina asked.

The policeman frowned back at her for a second before he broke into a wide grin. "Well, what a surprise!" the Sheriff shouted. "I heard you were coming back."

"Just pulling in now." Christina replied.

Noting Christina's passenger, Shawn leaned further out the window, "Who's your friend?"

Gina smiled tentatively at Shawn, a little taken aback with his overt friendliness. He was so unlike the New Yorkers she routinely interacted with.

"This is my friend Gina," Christina replied. "Gina, this is Shawn, an old friend."

Gina nodded hello shyly from the car.

Christina turned back to Shawn, who had shifted his vehicle to begin to pull forward. "Trouble on the mountain?" she asked. She wondered if something was happening at the inn. That was the last thing she needed.

"Long story," he replied. "And I've gotta get rolling. I don't like being out of range too long. But I'll catch up with you later." He pulled the sheriff cruiser away, waving. "Nice to meet you Ma'am!" he shouted at Gina as the cruiser pulled away.

"Who was that?" Gina asked with interest. "He was hot!"

Christina chuckled to herself. Shawn Taylor had turned out nice, but she would never have thought in a million years that he would have ended up on the police force, not with all the outrageous things he had done and claimed to do. Annie used to break up with him regularly over each stupid thing he was planning to do or had admitted to doing.

Moments later, they pulled down the long driveway to the inn. The late afternoon sun glinted off the windows, making the whole place seem on fire. The trees surrounding the large house were neatly trimmed, along with the shrubs against the front of the building. Spring flowers were in abundance, with the front gardens overflowing with bright colored tulips and daffodils. The inn gleamed in the sun, white and colossal among the trees. Beyond, through the portico area, the wood of the red horse barn was visible, creating a charming pastoral setting.

Christina sat in the car a moment, taking in her arrival back to this place that had been so significant in her life. Her emotional response, at least initially, was not what she was expecting. She anticipated grief and sorrow had consumed her the last time she had been there. But now, she felt glad to see this place again. She had spent so many happy times here during her summertime visits.

It had been here that she felt most at home and part of a larger family, in contrast to the silence of her stepfather Victor's house. After the death of her mother, Victor had done his best. He undeniably loved her, but being suddenly thrust into single parenthood after a lifetime as a bachelor, left him flat footed. They had a stiff, but warm functional relationship. Boarding school and summers here at the inn with her aunt and cousin had been Victor's plan of action for Christina. But when she had begged him to let her graduate high school with Annie and spend her senior year in Vermont, it had caused strain on their relationship. Luckily, Victor had eventually relented.

The exterior appearance of the inn was well-kept and appealing, just as she remembered. She waited for grief and guilt to appear, snaking their way into her psyche. After all, that was the way she felt the last time she sat in this driveway. Curiously though, what she felt was delight and excitement to be back here. This was unexpected and a pleasant surprise. Thinking that maybe this would be a tolerable trip, she exited the car.

"Come on, Gina," she said to her friend, "Let me show you around."

Gina opened the car door, gawking at the stately surroundings. "Damn girl," she exclaimed, "You didn't tell me you were rich! This is not at all what I had in mind from your explanation of this place."

Gina moved around the car to help Christina hoist their bags from the trunk. "Let me get a picture of this." Gina took a few shots with her phone and started to send them via text message.

"Oh yeah, I forgot to mention that cell service can be spotty at best up here. I am not sure it's gotten better since I've been here last," Christina explained to Gina as she made her way to the front door, loaded with her luggage.

"What? Why didn't you tell me?" Gina asked comically, holding her phone up in the air searching for a signal. "What kind of hellish place have you brought me to?!"

Christina felt her anxiety dissipate as she stepped into the foyer of the inn. She was expecting to be assaulted with the feelings she'd pushed aside long ago, since she'd experienced sorrow, fear, and the pervasive guilt last time she stood in this spot. Instead, the lemony scents of furniture polish, ammonia glass cleaner and a distant delicious smell of something baking brought pleasant memories of home back to her senses.

The two women stood together in the doorway, taking in the scents and the classic New England entryway with the large staircase leading to the upper floors. The wooden banister was gleaming from a recent polishing. To their left was the library. The walls covered in bookshelves, except for the large, front-facing windows and the field stone fireplace. To their right was the main living room with its walls covered in paintings and old photographs of the area. Cushy chairs and a large sofa framed the center of the room. Directly in front of the women was a vintage hotel reception desk with a wall of antique room keys hanging behind it. A vase of fresh flowers sat on the top of the counter and Christina's name was visible on the note card stuck into the stems.

A shuffling and mumbling sound was coming from behind the lobby desk. The top of a worn baseball cap covering a snow-white head was just visible over the top of the counter. "Everything has to be perfect," the figure mumbled unhappily, "always on my tail..."

Abruptly, the figure stood, laying a screwdriver and a greasy rag on the top of the counter. The elderly man stood and looked at the two women, surprised to see them standing there. He smiled kindly at them. "I am so sorry, ladies," he started to say, coming around the desk toward them. He swept his arms, as if to herd them out the door. "We aren't opened for guests. I guess I left the door open...."

"Jim?" Christina questioned, laying her bags at her feet. "Is that you?"

The older man stopped what he was doing and looked intently at her, frowning, and wiping his greasy hands on his jeans. After a beat, recognition passed over his face and his broad smile deepened. "Well, look at you!" he exclaimed, coming forward to greet her. "I'm sure glad to see your pretty face again."

He opened his arms and Christina easily stepped forward and embraced the old man. "Oh Jim!" she said. "It's great to see you! How have you been?"

He nodded, smiling, "We're doing all right. 'Least that's what she tells me!"

Still holding his arm, Christina turned to Gina. "Jim, this is my friend, Gina," she said, introducing her traveling companion.

Jim's eyes glinted as Christina knew he was taking in her friend's beautiful dark complexion and petite shapely figure. He reached out and shook her hand.

"Pleased to meet you, Jim." Gina greeted him smiling.

"Jim has been working here since I can remember," Christina explained. "Both he and his wife live here, and care for everything you could imagine. Maude cooks and does housekeeping. Jim takes care of the general maintenance and the gardens, and whatever else needs to be done."

"And there is a lot to get done in this old place," Jim added smiling. He continued to wipe his hands on his pants.

Christina waved her hands. "Well, it looks great. Looks just as I remember."

Jim nodded. "Good," he replied, "Maude wanted everything to be perfect when we found out you were comin.' I've been working non-stop," he said, taking off his cap and wiping his broad forehead with his hand. "Course, we can't do everything all ourselves. 'Specially since we're gettin' up there," he said.

Christina tried to fathom how old they were. She had considered them old when she was a teenager, but that assessment had been relative. Back then, everyone over forty seemed ancient. But Jim did seem a bit more bent in his stature and more weathered since she last saw him.

"Jeremy has been helping us to keep things straight. God bless that boy." Jim mused, "After Ada went in the hospital, he's been keeping things going."

Surprised, Christina asked, "you've been open? I thought that there haven't been any guests for years."

"Right, right," Jim replied. "We haven't been running like regular season or nothin.' But we do host guests here and there. Mostly for private guests from Jeremy's firm. He lets us know when they are comin' and how many, and we take care of things for 'em."

This information puzzled Christina. She was working under the understanding that there had not been any guests for years and that the inn was not functioning. Maude and Jim had remained on the property to caretake only. They provided maintenance and the security of someone living there. There was an arrangement in the estate trust that had provided for these expenses. Much of it came from the reciprocal housing arrangement that had always been part of the agreement with the caretaking pair. Christina mentally filed this information away. She would follow-up with Jeremy the next time they spoke to go over the operations.

Jim reached down to gather their bags, but each woman took their luggage from him before the elder man could lift them. "Let me take your things upstairs," he stated. "She's got your room all made up." Gesturing to Gina, Jim continued, "We can get you a spot all made up. Let me get her on it."

Feeling a bit guilty for having the older couple wait on her, Christina replied, "Gina can take the made-up room, and I'll make up another."

Jim nodded his agreement as the two women headed for the stairs.

"Come on up, Gina," said Christina. "Let's drop off our bags and then I can show you around."

Gina nodded, following her up the gleaming wooden stairs. "Something sure smells wonderful. I didn't realize I was hungry until now. Someone must be baking something delicious!"

Christina laughed. "Smells like Maude is in the kitchen. It will be wonderful. I bet it'll be some nice down-home cooking."

The women made their way upstairs with Gina marveling at the classic surroundings and Christina at the memories. Christina led Gina down the hall and to a second set of smaller stairs. "I'm sure Maude would have made up my old room. You can take that, and I'll take the old guest room. The family rooms are up on the third floor."

"Don't you want to sleep in your old room?" Gina asked of her friend, knowing she would defer.

The third floor had a narrower hallway from the second's open and airy feel. Christina opened the door to a room facing the back of the house and let Gina step in. An antique four poster bed greeted them. It was covered with a beautiful, floral quilt. The room had a small, attached bath with a tiny modern bathroom and shower. Christina blocked herself from feeling the emotions expected from stepping into her old room, where her summers were spent.

"It's beautiful!" Gina exclaimed, walking in and depositing her bag on the floor. She immediately picked up a photograph beside the bed, looking questioningly at her friend. The photo was of a young girl and two adults.

"That's me, Victor and my mother," Christina answered, taking the framed photo from Gina, and looking at it. "Before she died. I think this was taken right before their wedding."

"That's you?" Gina asked. "What a smile!"

Christina glanced back to the photo. "Yeah, those were happy times. They were so in love."

Gina clucked her tongue, taking the photo and setting it back on the bedside table. "Look at all these pictures," she said, pointing to a bulletin board hanging over a small desk.

Christina openly winced. Noting her reaction, her friend took her hand. "You going to be all right? You want to stay in this room?"

"Surprisingly, I'm ok," she replied, reassuring her friend. "But that class picture…" She pulled a small classic school photo from the corner of the bulletin board. The small photo was of Christina in her early teenage years. Her face was spotted with blemishes and her smile was accented by a mouth chock full of braces.

Gina took the picture from her hands, shaking her head. "Oh honey," she laughed, "we all have one of these…"

Christina laughed. "Gina, I can't believe you would have a picture like that," she said leaving the room. "I am going to put my stuff down. Meet you downstairs in a few? Make yourself at home."

Gina laughed, taking out her cell phone again to snap a picture of the photo. Christina shook her head, laughing. The cell service was so bad here that she was not worried that those pictures would be shared anytime soon. That gave her a chance to get them deleted from Gina's phone before Gina sent them to their other co-workers at the hotel. She laughed to herself.

Heading down the hallway, she found the guest room where her mother and countless other family guests had stayed. It was a neutral location for her to spend the next two weeks. It didn't have any personal items or many memories, so it would suit her needs. She located clean sheets and blankets and set to making the bed.

She heard Gina's steps on the stairs and knew she had headed down for some exploring. *She was not shy and would find things to entertain herself,* Christina reflected of her friend. This made her a great choice for this trip, as she offered some distraction, but also didn't require planned entertainment for every minute.

After settling in the guest room, Christina started to head downstairs, and then changed course. So far, she had not been besieged by the sorrow she expected by coming back to this place. Perhaps since Ada was no longer in residence, making it clear that something had changed, she didn't long for the past. Or maybe because of the length of time of her absence, the hurt had healed over a bit. Christina felt heartened this visit would not be as emotionally challenging as she expected.

She opened the door to Ada's room. The mattress was missing from the large bed, but the room was largely as she remembered. She closed the door to Ada's room, and then placed her hand on the next room's doorknob. Directly across from Ada's room and down the hall from her old room was Annie's bedroom. Christina steeled herself and opened the door.

The room had been recently cleaned, because the smell of furniture polish hung in the air, but the space was remarkedly familiar. It was like stepping into her teenage years again. Posters and pictures hung from the walls and Annie's favorite bright yellow bedspread gleamed in the midafternoon light from the tall windows. It looked like she could have walked back in time. She could imagine coming into her cousin's bedroom as her 17-year-old self, and Annie would come out of the bathroom with her hair in a towel.

Ada had left the room just as Annie had it the day she disappeared. It seemed nothing was changed or out of place, except it was a bit cleaner of course, without all the teenage girl clothes and general debris of life. The police had been through here, and she knew Ada had spent weeks sobbing in this room, waiting, and hoping for her only child to come home or make contact in some way. Christina knew her own sorrow was benign in comparison to what Ada had experienced with the disappearance of her only child. The depths of her despair were unfathomable.

Christina walked slowly around the room, taking in the objects left behind by the missing girl. There were pictures on the bulletin board of happy high school days, including a bunch from the photo booth at the fair and several of Annie in prom gowns. She had been asked to a prom each year, ever since she was a freshman in high school. She was a beautiful girl in the sparkling dresses, smiling in each photo with several different boys, until the more recent ones kept featuring Shawn by her side. Christina smiled to herself. Annie had said that the guys had all asked her as a friend or simply as someone who would make it a fun night, instead of one besieged by teenage love dramas. Christina had not been around for these events. She was either staying in the city with her stepfather or away at boarding school, but she heard about the details from Annie directly in their frequent calls.

One picture caught her eye. It was a shot of them both together, hugging each other tightly posing for the camera. They were probably sixteen at the time, and Ada had snapped the picture of the two laughing girls. Christina smiled, remembering the time before tragedy pulled them apart. It was a happy memory. She tucked the picture back into its place, noting to herself to save this photo and perhaps some of the others before she put the inn on the market. Preserving the good times was desirable.

Christina came down the front stairs, finding Jim back behind the lobby desk. "Find everything you need all right?"

He was crouching behind the desk with tools in his hands. "I hope it's all right with you, but Maude picked up some of Ada's things. Don't like to leave medicine and such layin' around the place. I think they both were on the same shots anyway, so Maude's using them. Those shots for the sugar. Ya know what I mean?"

"Insulin? I didn't know Maude was taking that. And of course, it's totally fine. Why let it go to waste." She approached the desk and leaned over its top to see what Jim was working on. "What are you doing back there anyway?" she asked.

"Oh, I am trying to get this darn drawer to open. She insists that I need to fix everything in this place–make it all work, just like it did two hundred years ago." Jim stood up from behind the desk, wiping his greasy hands on a cloth. "But yeah, she had to go on the shots last year. The sugar pills weren't workin' anymore, I guess. Ada showed her how to do it, and there was really nothin' to it. Ada made it look real easy anyway."

It was curious to recall that Ada had been diabetic her whole life. She had dealt with the condition gracefully, smoothly integrating her blood sugar checks and insulin injections into her busy life. She had been meticulous. That was why it was curious that her diabetes caused her death. Christina stepped behind the desk with Jim as he pulled on the lowest drawer that was not budging despite his efforts to open it. She pulled on it also, but it did not move. "That is tight," she said, "not even a shimmy when you pull on it. Was it opening before? Did Maude need something in it?"

Jim looked at her and laughed. "Darn if I know if it worked before. I can't remember. It's been so long since we've been runnin' around and usin' this desk.

"Before I forget agin.' These are for you, came this mornin.'" Jim said gesturing to the flowers in the vase on the desk.

She took the card from the bouquet. They were sent from Jeremy. She noticed an uncharacteristic feeling of annoyance rise in her gut as she read his note. He had been very persistent in contacting her daily to discuss the inn, bringing forth new details in each conversation. The last few calls had included discussions that were heading into a more personal nature. Sending flowers indicated something more than a relationship between an attorney and client, and Christina didn't like it.

She took one last tug on the drawer in her irritation. "Let's forget about it for now," she said. "Let's go see what smells so good in the kitchen."

The older man eagerly agreed. They started walking toward the back of the building, until they stopped in their tracks upon hearing raised voices coming from the direction they were heading. "Uh no," Christina muttered to herself.

She had completely forgotten what Maude could be like in the kitchen. It was purely her domain, and most people were unwelcome visitors, unless you came to eat. Ada and Maude used to get into some tangles in the kitchen. Now, it sounded like Gina, as a professional chef, had found her way to the kitchen and territories were being crossed.

Christina pushed open the swinging door, finding Gina and Maude glaring at each other over a plate of cookies. Noting they were her favorite, snickerdoodles, Christina swept in and placed herself purposely between the two women. She snagged a cookie on her way.

"Mm mm, so good," she muttered through a full mouth. "Maude, so nice to see you again."

The older woman was a giant compared to the two women in the room with her. Standing well over six feet, she was a formidable figure, even at her advanced age. And her scowl made her terrifying. She broke her frown when she recognized Christina, and her face lit up. "Well, well, still stealing cookies before your dinner, I see," she said smiling. Her voice was deep and gruff, but her smile lit up her features.

"I see you've met my friend, Gina." Christina started, waving her cookie filled hands toward the smaller woman, who continued to frown at the older woman. "How have you been?" Christina pulled up a stool to the counter in front of the plate of cookies and took in the bright kitchen.

Maude moved to pour a glass of milk, placing it in front of Christina. "You want some?" she asked Gina gruffly.

Gina tentatively sat next to Christina, accepting the milk and taking a cookie from the plate.

"Ada told me about the renovations here in the kitchen. It looks great in here. How do you like it?" Christina asked Maude, her mouth full of a second cookie.

Maude looked around the kitchen and shrugged, going back to the butcher block where she had been working. She picked up a meat cleaver. She had apparently been chopping up meat when Gina interrupted her. "It's nice," she replied curtly. "It was done about five years ago, I think." She turned and scowled meaningfully at the two women before turning back to her work.

Christina realized her meaning. Maude was saying that she could have visited during that timeframe, but she hadn't. Maude had always been blunt—a no holds barred kind of person.

"Ada had some big plans back then," Maude continued. "She wanted to expand the dining room and the menu."

"I remember," Christina replied.

Maude turned back to her work, chopping on a carcass of meat. The hacks from her knife banged ominously on the wood block.

"It's dead already." Gina whispered, giggling to her friend as she watched the viciousness with which Maude was attacking the meat.

Maude turned abruptly back to the women, knife in hand. "You say something?" she asked. Both women silently shook their heads, repressing their smiles at the comedy of the situation.

"What's for dinner?" Gina asked, planting an innocent look on her face.

"Pork chops," the older woman answered. "Oh, and Jeremy is coming to dinner. Said you and he talked."

Christina could not recall that conversation, but there had been many over the past few weeks. It was kind of convenient that he was visiting tonight, because they could get started on the details of the inn operation and review the options for the property.

"Ok," replied Christina. "What time is dinner?"

"Six o'clock sharp," Maude replied.

Both women nodded. "I'm going to go to show Gina around a bit," Christina said, getting up from the kitchen stool gesturing for her friend to follow her.

"Let me know if you need any help," Gina offered as they stepped out of the room.

Christina pulled her friend's arm and ushered her from the kitchen quickly, as Maude muttered under her breath. "So sorry about that," Christina offered to her puzzled friend.

"What is up with her?!" Gina said with her hand on her hip, "I was just being nice and friendly, and she growls at me."

Christina smiled. "Yeah, she is pretty territorial in the kitchen. No one can do anything for her in there. She feels like she must do all the work, unless she specifically directs you to do something. She insists on it.

"She and my aunt used to get into some fights over who was doing what in the kitchen. They ended up setting up a specific schedule for the two of them. Ada would stay out of the kitchen entirely when Maude was working."

"Weird way to treat an employer," Gina replied. "Anyway, forget it. It'll be nice to have a break from work. We'll work it out if I feel the need to cook."

Christina agreed. "All right. I am sure we can figure it out. I can't see her wanting to wait on us hand and foot the entire time. Anyway," she said taking her friends hand, "come and let me show you a secret staircase."

The two women explored the old inn and the secrets that she recalled from her childhood. Through the tour of the house, Christina explained the history of the inn from what she remembered. "The inn was actually built in the early 1800's as a summer home for the Stone family, which was Ada's husband's family. They had made their fortune in the lumber business and had intended to entertain guests here. That's why they ended up having so many bedrooms. The building is considered historic due to its age." Christina continued, "Well that, and also because Daniel Webster and other historical figures have spent the night here as a guest of the family. Webster gave political speech a bit further down the road to 15,000 people who came from all over the area."

"Fifteen thousand people?!" Gina exclaimed. "But aren't we in the middle of nowhere? Where did all of those people come from?"

Christina laughed. "I know. I used to think it was just an old tale, but I looked it up a few years ago, and it's true. There is, or was, a plaque on a rock in a clearing near here. Some kids stole it a few years ago. Actually, that sheriff we met earlier was one of those kids."

Gina laughed. "It's always the criminals that turn into cops."

CHAPTER 6

They concluded their walk through the house in the dining area. It was a small sunny room that Ada had planned to expand outward by adding a three-season large sunroom off the current dining area.

Christina described the plans to Gina who was interested, given her professional experience. "I like the idea. It looks like if you added on here, you would bring the dining area into those gardens. Show me around out there. It looks like it would be really great."

Christina opened one of the back doors leading out to the gardens. "Don't get too excited about this. I may not be keeping the place. If there are no guests, there is no way we could afford to put on an addition."

The two women walked out into the gardens. The flowers and bushes were gorgeous and obviously well cared for. The landscaping included terraced gardens with intricate stone walls. "Wow these are really well cared for," Gina remarked, "stone walls can be expensive and a real pain to maintain. My grandparents had them around their home in Italy. They were always fixing them, it seemed."

"These were rebuilt a while ago, actually. Jim had a construction company from town fix them up," Christina replied. "Actually, I can remember when it was being done. It was the summer that my cousin went missing."

"They are in good shape," Gina replied.

Christina recalled a memory from that summer. She'd been so upset with the equipment and the noise they made. Annie hated it more than she did. It'd wake them up early during their summer vacation, and it made her physically ill to be woken up that early. Of course, the wine coolers the night before probably had something to do with that as well. But they both blamed it on the construction crew.

Christina checked her watch. There were still a few hours until dinner. "Want to take a stroll down the old stagecoach road?" she asked Gina.

"Stagecoach road?"

"Yup," she replied. "It's the old road that used to go past the house and over the mountain. It used to be the main road in town, a long time ago. Now, it's a great trail for walking, biking, and cross-country skiing."

"Intrigued." Gina replied. "Lead the way!"

The two women headed across the lawns to a trail that led across the mountain ridge, almost like an extension of the driveway. It was a beautiful afternoon, and they were enjoying the sun and the scenery as they leisurely strolled down the gravel path. The sun was shining, and the birds were singing. A gentle breeze moved branches of the trees and the grass in the field. "I could get used to this," Gina told her friend. "This is well worth the long drive and the kitchen lieutenant."

Christina smiled. "Yeah its nice and peaceful. I..." Her next words were interrupted by a dog's bark. Surprised, the women looked around for another person nearby. A large black dog burst from the bushes and ran toward them.

Startled, Gina grabbed Christina's arm. "What *is* that thing?"

Immediately concerned that it was a wild animal, Christina's heart bounded in her chest. She urgently tried to recall what to do when approached by a wild animal. Should she run or stay put?

The dog bounded up to them and sat down in front of them, tongue lagging out the side of its mouth. Its expression was eager and happy to see them. Taken aback, the women stood, looking at the dog and searching for its owner.

"Is that thing *smiling* at us?" Gina asked.

Indeed, the expression on the dog's face made him look like he was grinning at them. Its long tongue hung from its mouth as it waited expectantly in front of them.

"I think it wants us to do something," Christina said. "Where'd you come from, boy?"

The dog barked once in reply.

The women both laughed. "Seems friendly," Christina said. "Are you lost?"

The dog barked once in reply, making both women laugh again. "I think he can talk!" Gina exclaimed.

Christina approached the dog, who happily put his head under her hand. She patted his head, and the dog pushed his head on her hand, appearing to thoroughly enjoy the contact. "Oh, you are a good boy," she said, continuing to pat the dog. At the same time, she inspected his neck for a collar or a tag of some sort. "No tag or collar. Poor guy must be lost."

"Are you lost, boy?" Gina asked tentatively, reaching out to pat the dog as well. At that the dog rolled onto its back and exposed his belly. Both women reached out to give him a rub and a scratch. The dog's tongue hung out further and its apparent smile gaped more widely.

They petted the dog for a few more minutes. "All right now, boy," Christina said. "We need to go, and you need to go home too."

The dog made no move. She shooed him away, "Go on. Go home."

The dog stood his ground. The women started to walk back from where they had come. "Poor thing. If he is lost, he must be hungry and thirsty," Gina worried aloud.

"There is a spring-fed pond close by, so he has access to water," Christina said. "But you know, he does seem a little thin. I'm fairly sure I could feel his ribs when we were petting him."

They continued to walk down the trail. The dog started to follow them, falling into step behind Christina. They stopped and shooed him away several times.

"Maybe we should call animal control later–maybe someone is looking for him?" Christina said. "If he follows us back, I'll see if Jim has an idea about what to do. He may know the dog from the area.

They returned to the back door of the inn with the dog closely following them. He found shade under the tree outside the kitchen and appeared to make himself at home. They retrieved a dish from the kitchen and gave the dog water.

Christina located Jim to ask his advice, and he came out back to inspect the dog. "Nope, not a dog I have seen before," he said, scratching the dog's ear. "Looks like a nice fella. Collie Shepard mix, by the look of him. I can call the Sheriff to see what is up."

"The Sheriff?" Gina asked. "Not animal rescue or something?"

"Around here that's who takes care of all that. He'll know if someone lost a dog and is looking for 'em. I'll give Shawn a ring."

Jim went back in the house to make the call, while the women stayed sitting in the shade with the dog. He seemed at ease and stretched out between them on the grass to have a nap.

The sun had heated up the midafternoon, making the shade from the tree the women sat under sweetly refreshing. Christina lay on the soft grass near the panting dog, refreshed with the water they had provided. She was laying her head back in the grass, as the shadows of the leaves above danced on her eyelids–it was so peaceful, she reflected lazily. The sounds of Jim and Gina talking about the gardens, the flowers and their upkeep faded as the pair moved away from her spot in the grass. Her breath lengthened as she drifted off to an afternoon doze with her new companion by her side.

"Looks like he's made himself comfortable." A male voice spoke over her prone form on the grass, casting a shadow over her face.

She startled from her snoozing, covering her eyes with an upraised hand. A weight on her chest shifted as the dog removed its head from her torso. She sat up, rubbing the sleep from her eyes.

She knew it was him before their eyes met.

She had known it would be a possibility to cross paths with him on this visit, so this moment could have been avoided. The inn was a destination, so no one coming this way would be simply passing through.

Their eyes met and they held each other's gaze for a heartbeat before he turned his regard to the dog. Her pulse picked up. She took the opportunity to appraise him. He had matured over the years. His body had filled out with lean muscle. "Sure, looks comfortable," he said, bending down to rub the dog's ears as he checked for tags under the thick fur. "Sure he's stray?"

He was tanned, even this early in the season. He knelt on the ground, close enough to her so she could feel the warmth of his body in contrast to the cool grass. His dark eyes were shaded by his thick black hair covering his eyes. A grin was on his lips as he took in her figure laying on the lawn. "No tags," he said, hands running over the dog's torso, half petting half inspecting. "He's skinny, but no injuries."

"He followed us back from the stagecoach road," she said, finding her throat dry as she spoke, so her voice came out croaky. "We didn't see anyone around. Why are you here? I didn't know lost dogs were your thing."

He nodded, standing up and patting the dog's head, "Shawn asked me to stop by."

"Oh. Are you working for the Sheriff these days?"

He laughed, reaching down to offer her a hand getting up from the grass. She took his offer and he supported her as she rose from the lawn, attempting to do it as gracefully as possible. Once on her feet, he held her hand longer than she intended, looking down at her face as she stood in the sunshine. "You look good, Crissy," he said briefly, squeezing and then releasing her hand just as quickly.

Her stomach jolted and her heart rate accelerated as she reacted to his touch and his words. The back door from the kitchen banged open and a man wearing a three-piece suit emerged. "Supper in ten minutes," bellowed Maude from within the kitchen, "Kevin, you're staying. I've set a place."

Jeremy approached the pair under the tree, smoothing the sleeves of his jacket. His eyes were intently fixed on the couple. "Kevin," he said with disdain while he greeted the other man.

He reached out to greet Christina with a kiss on her cheek. Just as his hand touched her arm, the dog uttered a low, menacing growl. "What the hell is that?" he exclaimed, stepping back and gesturing to the dog.

Christina reached down to pet the dog, reassuring the animal. "It's all right boy. Jeremy's a friend."

Jeremy stepped back and looked disapprovingly at the dog with thinly veiled disgust on his face. "I didn't realize you had a dog."

Kevin knelt by the dog, patting his head. "She's watching out for this one." He rubbed the dog's ears, telling him that he was a good boy. "We're trying to see if we can find out anything about him."

Jeremy's gaze turned to Kevin, the look of derision not leaving his face. "I didn't see your car out front."

"I walked." Kevin retorted, smiling widely at Christina as she looked at him with a puzzled expression on her face.

"Never mind." Jeremy said, cutting off her question for Kevin. "Let's go inside, Christina. We have a lot to discuss, since you're only here for a few days."

He took her arm. The dog stepped forward toward the pair, but Kevin gently restrained him. "It's all right boy," he said, reassuring the animal in a whisper. "I don't like him either."

Then Kevin called after the couple, "Be right there."

Christina turned back to Kevin with a smirk on her face as Jeremy pulled her toward the house. They shared a brief exchange. They both knew he really had no choice but to stay for dinner. It was Maude's command, and they were all still a bit scared of her. Additionally, Kevin knew that it would annoy Jeremy to no end if he remained present. And so, he would happily stay for dinner.

CHAPTER 7

Dinner that evening was a curious event, with Gina and Maude glowering at each other over yet another kitchen territory infringement and Jeremy outwardly annoyed at Kevin's presence at the table. The scowls and frowns simmered over the steaming serving plates and bowls heaped with delicious smelling food.

Christina was starving. Her stomach growled loudly at the sight of the meal and the scents of home cooking. Both Gina and Maude glanced in her direction, hearing her loud stomach. Christina shrugged, taking a seat at the table next to Maude.

"Some things don't change," Maude said to the group, "I can hear that rumble without my hearing aids."

Everyone at the table glanced Christina's way and she bushed deeply, shrugging her shoulders, while serving herself a hearty portion of potatoes.

"Geez, in all the excitement, I don't believe we even had lunch. Luckily, Christina didn't start World War three..." Gina muttered over the table.

Maude guffawed loudly, coughing into her napkin stifling a laugh. "Live dangerously with this one, when it comes to being without food."

The table erupted in laughter and teasing as they all agreed earnestly with each other's assessment of Christina's low blood sugar behaviors. The mood at the table lifted as they exchanged stories of her hunger-driven outbursts. She was used to this kind of loving abuse from friends and shrugged it off, smiling and laughing with the group.

Kevin joined in the ruckus, while Jeremy remained largely silent, glowering across the table. "One time, she was full-on shouting at me. We were hiking somewhere in the white mountains, I think and it was way past breakfast. I was begging her to eat a snack or to take a bite of *something*, and all the while, she was screaming, 'I'm not hungry!!'" The table erupted in laughter with head nods and agreement all around.

"Second breakfast!" Maude and Gina shouted in unison, both pointing and laughing at each other as they said the same thing. The ice was visibly cracking between the pair.

It felt good to have the group at the table laughing and talking, even though Christina was the butt of the jokes. Her appetite and thinness had been a source of great comedy all her life. She looked around the table, and even though there were missing faces and new ones—she had missed this easy camaraderie. She looked at Jeremy thoughtfully. He was the only outsider at the table.

She had not expected to see Kevin so soon, and his presence on her first day back left her a bit off kilter. What surprised her even more was her response to him being there, it was not emotionally tumultuous as she would have expected, especially with the way that they had left things between them all those years ago. There had been so much left to say, but she had *needed* to leave.

She had imagined a brief interaction, sterile and painless, perhaps on the street or in a store. She would have never expected a full-fledged interaction with him sitting at the dinner table as he had so many times before, chatting amiably with his table companions.

He had always had a knack for conversation and could fit right into any situation. Kindness and patience exuded from him. He had been certainly patient with her own challenges over time, always as a friend and then, as more. Her mind drifted as she gazed at him across the table.

"Can we talk this evening, Christina?" Jeremy asked, trying to get her attention by leaning over the table in her direction. He attempted to raise his voice over the lively conversation.

She nodded her reply, her mouth full of food. She had much to discuss with Jeremy, who was overly eager to meet with her. There was so much information she needed to make some serious decisions.

Jim and Kevin spoke loudly as they exchanged local information, drowning out Jeremy's further attempt for conversation. "How's the trail holding up with all the rain?" Jim asked, reaching for the basket of biscuits. He enthusiastically piled up his plate with the abundant food on the table.

"Wet in spots and slippery," Kevin replied, copying Jim's enthusiasm for the meal. He piled his plate full of food. "Hope it clears up a bit for the solstice, or it'll turn into a mess with all the increased traffic."

Maude reached in front of Jeremy to hand Kevin a heaping serving bowl of mashed potatoes. "Here boy," she smiled at him, "You must be starved."

Jim enthusiastically agreed with her. "He must be. You know, Kevin, I saw your dad today when I was in town. He's lookin' pretty good. Said he feels stronger every day. He asked if I'd seen you lately."

Kevin nodded; his mouth full of food. He caught Christina's concerned look when Jim mentioned his father and swallowed, stating, "Cancer. He's fine now and is in full remission. It knocked his socks off over the winter though."

"So sorry to hear that," Christina answered softly. "I always liked your Dad. Tell him I was asking for him the next time you see him."

"As I was saying, Christina, there has been some interest in the property..." Jeremy continued, trying to get Christina's attention.

She nodded to him and assured him that they would talk after dinner. He remained eager to jump into the conversation, and she started to get irritated with his persistence.

"There's pie for dessert, and I'll make you up a doggie bag," Maude interrupted, talking over Jeremy with her deep booming voice. "You need calories with all that walking."

"Hold on," Gina piped in, shaking her head in disbelief. "You said you *walked* here?"

Kevin laughed. "That's right. I hiked."

"I've been living in the city too long," Gina said, smiling with him.

"I have one of those summer jobs that you'd think would be really cool when you are younger. You know, just getting to spend your days and nights in the woods, with no people around. And you get *paid* for doing it!" Kevin continued hungrily eating whatever was in his reach.

In between bites, he was able to answer further questions. "I generally pick up trash or help hikers who are lost or get hurt. Sometimes I do repairs that I can handle on my own or I work with the forest service or the rangers."

"Do you camp out all of the time?" Gina asked, intrigued by his story.

"Yeah–that was my question too. I thought you went into teaching," said Christina.

Kevin laughed loudly, obviously enjoying the attention from the women. Jeremy shifted in his chair, evidently displeased with the turn of the conversation away from Christina's inheritance. "Yup. I teach Biology. I do most of my trail work when school is out. The trail doesn't get busy until late spring or so. It works out all right."

"I suppose it helps to pay the bills." Jeremy offered into the conversation, smiling snidely at Kevin. "Life can't be easy on a teacher's salary."

Kevin smiled widely at Jeremy, refilling his plate once again. Reaching past Jeremy while purposely flexing his biceps, he said, "I do all right. At least it's honest work, that's more than some can say."

The pair stared at each other across the table. Their differences were stark. Kevin was the gorgeous, tanned, and fit outdoorsman and Jeremy was the pale, bespectacled, yet somehow handsome lawyer across the table from him. The tension in the room began to build.

"Heard there's been some trouble up there," Jim supplied, seemingly oblivious to the exchange between the two men.

"Yeah," Kevin answered, the tension magically broken. "There always seems to be more traffic on the trail after a book or movie comes out."

The locals and Christina all nodded their heads in agreement, resuming their meals. Gina looked around the table. "A book or a movie about what?"

Jim reached out and patted her hand. It was obvious that he had taken a shine to this exotic beauty. "Oh, there are some old tales around here. One's an old Indian story that the mountains here are sacred ground. If the mountain's spirit didn't want you there, it would swallow you up. Its why the natives didn't live on the mountains at all."

"Too damn cold and windy," Maude mumbled. "They were probably the smart ones."

Jeremy eagerly jumped into the conversation, anxious to get back the floor. "They call it the Bennington Triangle from here to the other side of the mountain. Hunters and other people have gone missing over the years. People walk into the woods and don't come out." He looked fervently at the two women, hoping to have sparked further interest and attention.

Gina, instead, was intent on watching Christina's response to Jeremy's words. Christina had stopped eating and placed her utensils on the table with her focus downward. She rose slowly from the table, collecting a few plates along with her own before she went into the kitchen. Noting her exit, Kevin followed her, bringing his empty plate with him.

He paused shortly next to Maude. "Let me get that pie for you."

"All right then, and also bring out the ice cream." Maude smiled. "But you can leave those plates. I'll take care of them later."

Christina stood in the kitchen, gazing out of the window not focusing on anything. She felt suddenly tired. She'd feared that the weight of being back here would cloud their visit, and it appeared to have been triggered by Jeremy's words. "They call it the Bennington Triangle. People go into the woods, and they don't come out."

Annie had disappeared in a comparable manner. And Christina remembered how some people in town chose that theory to explain what had happened to her.

Kevin quietly entered the kitchen, carefully placing the dishes on the kitchen counter and interrupting her thoughts. She turned and looked at him. He reached out a hand and lightly touched her fingers with his, loosely taking her hand. "They don't realize how saying those things might hurt you," he whispered gently.

She turned her face up to his, her eyes cloudy with unshed tears. For a moment, they stood hand in hand, gazing into each other's eyes. The years fell away, and she felt like no time had passed. She was back in the kitchen of her aunt's home after all, gazing into Kevin's eyes as she had done many times before. She could feel his breath on her face. His lips were full and close to hers. Her eyes fell to that mouth, and she imagined it pressed against hers. She leaned towards him.

The kitchen door banged open and Maude entered, her broad arms full of dirty plates and dishes. "Thought we lost you," she said, addressing Christina. Then she turned to Kevin, demanding, "Find the pie?"

He gave Christina's fingers a quick squeeze and let them go, returning to the business of pie. Christina exited the kitchen, her mood now subdued. Emotions swirled in her gut. Loss and longing were battling in her psyche. She felt a headache begin to rise from deep in the base of her neck. There was business to take care of, so she opted to focus on that. It felt like one of the few things she could control.

"Jeremy, let's go into the parlor so we can talk," she said tartly in front of the group at the table.

Kevin entered the dining room with pie, plates, and ice cream, and Maude tailing behind. The group all admired the pie. Maude served the remaining group at the table, supplying Gina with a heaping plate and ignoring her objections.

Jeremy retrieved his computer from the lobby entrance and eagerly joined Christina in the front room of the inn. She was sitting on the deep couch surrounded by antiques.

He sat so close to her that their legs touched, claiming that it was the best way for both of them to easily view his computer screen.

Jeremy enthusiastically filled Christina in on the details of the inn, going over a presentation he had created about the inn and its surrounding property. It was professionally completed with photos and maps of the area. The overview surprised and irritated Christina, as it felt over-the-top. She wasn't expecting a formal PowerPoint presentation on the inn. She simply wanted to take control of the accounts and review the operations.

"Thanks for putting this together, Jeremy. It looks like a lot of work went into this presentation. I really only wanted to get into the records and accounts." She chose her words carefully, sensing that Jeremy would not respond well to her criticism. "With my background and experience working in the field with multi-million-dollar hotels, I feel pretty prepared on my own."

At the revelation of her capability to simply take over, he became agitated. "Yes, but while you've been so busy with your *multimillion-dollar* projects, I have been overseeing the operations here. That's what Ada asked me to do if she was ever not able to manage on her own." He abruptly snapped his laptop shut, shoving it into his briefcase.

"That PowerPoint looks like a sales pitch. That's all I am saying. I would prefer to get into the overall expenses to get a feel for where we are financially."

He looked at her incredulously. "I assumed I would still oversee the operations here, just like I did for Ada. I had planned to show you the potentials for the property. There are some opportunities for development...."

This was not the reaction that she was expecting. How could he think that he would still be overseeing the operations? She was now the owner and would therefore be the main decision maker.

"Jeremy, thank you for all that you have done. Please don't think that I am not grateful for taking care of things for my aunt when I was... not available," she said, raking her hands through her hair. "It's been a long day and I am a bit more tired than I expected. If you could just let me have access into the books, that would be really helpful. I'm assuming there is some sort of software that you've been using. I can hop in and find my way. All I've been able to work with so far are some older books from when the inn was fully functioning. I've been projecting out a business plan for operating based on those numbers."

He was taken aback. "You aren't thinking of *operating*, are you?"

She wasn't sure if it was his tone of voice or the vibe she was getting from him, but it seemed as though he felt confident that he knew better than she. She has dealt with that kind of attitude throughout her whole career, and she wasn't about to put up with it when she was finally the one in charge. Her blood vessels constricted in her temples and her head started to pound. She could feel an old familiar headache rising as she tamped down her response to a civil tone. *Be nice,* she said to herself. *He **did** help Ada when she needed him to.*

"I need to make some decisions, obviously," she said through gritted teeth. "I need to work through all the details. If you would just let me have access, then we can talk further about your ideas. I'd like to do my own analysis before we collaborate."

She rose from the couch. He reluctantly followed her lead, standing and gathering his things. "I'll email you the access in the morning. I went through and automated all the books. Ada had handwritten ledgers and manual accounts. They were quite a mess, actually."

She recalled the cluttered small office just behind the lobby and made herself a mental note to go through it. Jeremy prattled on in his irritated tone. "I'll stop by tomorrow with a history of everything I have. I think you will find what you are looking for in Ada's office, but seriously, Christina, don't expect much. She wasn't very consistent with her books."

Christina led Jeremy to the door, seeing him out. She sensed that he had expected a later evening and more in-depth conversation. He leaned down to kiss her cheek. They were both surprised to hear a low growl on the front step. The new dog had made himself at home and was watching Jeremy carefully.

"There you are," Christina said to the dog. She opened the door to let him in. "Come in and sit."

Surprising them both, the dog entered and sat at Christina's feet, panting, and looking up at her. She laughed, at least one man would do as she wished.

Jeremy left in his Lexus, pulling out of the driveway so fast that he sprayed loose gravel everywhere. She knew he was perturbed at her response to his planned discussion. She shut the heavy front door and turned the lock. It had been a long day and she was tired.

Voices and laughter emerged from the dining room. It sounded as if Kevin was still entertaining the group.

She looked down at her feet where the dog still sat expectantly, waiting for her direction. She smiled at the animal's eager expression. "Ok, come on. Let's find something for you to eat."

The dog bounded up, following her civilly into the dining area. There, he joined her friends, as if he had been doing it his whole life. On her way to the dining room, she passed the door to Ada's tiny office. The door was closed, but she tried the knob. It was locked. She would need to follow up with Jim in the morning to ask for keys to the room.

She felt a twinge in her gut that something had been off during her discussion with Jeremy. It was indiscernible, but it still made her uneasy. Maybe she was only tired and overreacting. Jeremy had other plans for the inn and the rest of the property, and he had expected Christina to easily agree to them. He had certainly kept things up, because everything appeared to be in great shape; but he had apparently also been using the property for private guests and had garnered interest from real estate developers.

Jeremy had been making serious plans. And she wondered how involved Ada had been in those decisions.

His surprised reaction to her request for the financial records added to her unease. She decided to give him the benefit of the doubt. He had inadvertently upset her at the dinner table when he'd mentioned the Bennington triangle, and maybe she had been harboring resentment toward him because he was helping Ada when she had not been around to do so.

Still, she knew she would need some back-up as she navigated the complexities of some of the decisions she faced. Her stepfather, Victor, was in London for the summer, so giving him an early morning call would work out nicely with the time difference. He would be able to assist her in uncovering any unsavory business plans that were afoot at her aunt's inn. Lord knows he had experience in that area.

CHAPTER 8

Kevin was elated when Christina came back into the dining area. They were just wrapping up dessert. He had refrained from licking the plate–Maude's pies were that good. Gina had taken note of this and was in deep discussion with Maude over her recipe. She was especially intrigued by how Maude had prepared the fruit before baking.

Kevin refrained from commenting on the fact that Gina and Maude were interacting as they had been lifelong friends. Maude even allowed Gina to help her with the dishes as they continued with the conversation. She was apparently pleased with the topic of discussion and was distracted. Kevin did not want to interrupt that balance.

Jim excused himself to go take another try at the stuck drawer in the reception desk while he waited for Maude to be done in the kitchen. The pair would go back to their caretaker cabin hand in hand.

Kevin's thoughts drifted to Christina. She was more beautiful than she had been the last time he had seen her. He wanted to touch her, and hold her. He knew she had avoided coming back here because she carried a heavy burden of guilt about this place. She had shouldered it herself, but that didn't make it any less real. And it had torn them apart as she'd fled away from here, and from him.

Yet here she was in front of him. He knew she reacted to him earlier in the kitchen. He had seen her eyes glaze over when he had stepped closer. It thrilled him to know that she still had an attraction to him. Even after all of the years that had passed between them.

He hadn't exactly been without companionship in the years they had been apart. But he hadn't had a serious relationship either–it had mostly been half-hearted dating. The half-hearted was on his part, not on his female companions. Several had been eager to go beyond friendly dates and sleep overs. But he hadn't had any interest.

It was because of her.

Christina sat at the table, helping herself to pie before it was whisked away. After a few bites, she dropped her fork on the plate with a loud clatter. "Do you know much about Jeremy?" she asked.

Kevin became cautious at the edge of irritation in her voice. He remembered that tone well. He knew to be cautious as to where he stepped. It must have been a long day for her, driving up from the city and seeing her old summer home again. "We don't hang out, if that's what you are asking," Kevin replied carefully.

She snatched up the fork again and began to forcefully eat her pie, rapidly shoving forkfuls into her mouth until the slice was gone. She sat back and shoved her chair away from the table. "It's still a nice evening outside. Do you want to take a stroll or sit outside on the patio?" she asked.

He followed her outside as she crossed the patio to sit on the stone wall, facing the inn. He sat next to her, pleased to be alone with her. He hoped he didn't screw this up. Clearly, she was irritated. "Why do you ask about Jeremy?" He asked carefully. "Isn't he technically your cousin?"

She sighed, trailing her hands on the cracks between the stones. "No, he's Annie's cousin. Her father's side. Jeremy's not a blood relation, since her father adopted her when she was little, right after he married Ada."

Kevin recalled that. It had not been a relevant factor in their lives. It was just a piece of information.

"He's pushy and he has a lot of ideas about development. I guess he has been helping Ada out for a while." She left out the fact that Ada had to rely on Jeremy, as her only other living blood relative was not around to help out.

Kevin realized where her mind was going. The guilt really burdened her, even still. "Ada was quite capable of getting things done on her own. She had a lot of friends and was able to access what she needed when she needed to get things done." He stopped himself there. He could go on to say, *you need to stop thinking of her as though she was a frail old woman. She was not,* but he kept quiet.

Kevin was afraid of getting into the conversation about the very thing that had broken them apart on her first day back. Christina's guilt. It was difficult to restrain himself, but deep down, he knew if he pushed her in any way, she would pull back. It had just been Jeremy's experience with their exchange. He did not want to have the same fate again. He didn't want to ruin any chance they may have.

"Gina seems nice," Kevin said.

Christina looked up at him, a surprised expression on her face. Clearly, she sensed that he was turning the conversation in a neutral direction. The smile that broke out on her face melted the apprehension he felt.

She held his gaze for a moment. After a beat, she reached out and laid her hand over his on the cool stone wall. Her soft skin burned the rough skin of his trail-worn hands. He resisted the urge to change the position of their hands to hold hers in his.

She smiled widely at him, her eyes glistening. "I've missed you," she said.

His heart soared. There was hope! It wasn't a passionately whispered statement; it was more like a friend than a lover sentiment. But he would take it!

"You must be tired, after that long drive." He smiled back at her. "I'll let you have your evening." He gave her hand a sociable squeeze, got up, and walked off the patio.

Kevin knew he had left her hanging. But he also knew he had her attention.

CHAPTER 9

She had woken up early, with the sun's first rays streaming into her bedroom. Her sleep had been fitful. She had been restless from the unfamiliar bed and the irritating conversation with Jeremy the night before. Maude had made coffee already and was baking something in the ovens that wafted a delicious, sweet scent through the inn. Christina grabbed a mug of coffee and quickly exited the kitchen to the covered porch. The dog followed closely on her heels.

The sun was burning off the early morning mist. She settled into one of the deep rockers to watch the sun rise over the valley below. It was peaceful in the quiet morning as she sipped her coffee, patting the dog's head as he sat close by at her feet. The headache from the night before was a distant thought.

The dog's ears perked up and he turned his head to the back path from the gardener's cabins. A tall figure appeared on the path. As he walked toward her, she immediately knew it was him, and wondered how, after all this time, she was so in tune to his presence. He had changed from a beautiful specimen of youth to a handsome man. His dark hair and eyes, chiseled chin and muscular athletic build would have won him any magazine cover, but instead, he had chosen the solitude of the woods and the beauty of nature over fleeting fame.

As she admired his approach, a disconcerting thought crossed her mind. *Was he married or in a relationship?* He hadn't mentioned anyone over dinner last night, but they had been out of communication for years. She had assumed that he was single, but what if he had someone else? The thought was disturbing. Even though she knew she was not planning to stay, the idea of someone else having him was surprisingly upsetting.

The dog leapt up to greet him, sniffing his feet and wagging his tail. His hair was tousled and wet, and his beard a thick scruff. Recognizing that he must have just showered, she wondered where he'd done it. The fire tower was miles away, through the woods, and without plumbing. His house or rather, his father's house, was miles away down the mountain. "Did you stay here? At Jim and Maude's?" she asked, puzzled.

He smiled up at her as he rubbed the dog's ears. "No," he said with a perplexed expression. "I slept in one of the guest cabins...." She looked at him, still not comprehending.

"Oh, that's right. You wouldn't know.... Jeremy redid all the cabins. They're pretty swanky really, with granite baths and such. I stay in one of the smaller ones all season, or at least, I go between there, my father's, and the trail. Works out well for me."

This roused Christina's interest as the coffee stimulated her mind, prodding her synapses into function. There were several cabins in disrepair, if she recalled correctly, scattered all around the property. It would have taken considerable investment to bring them up to a habitable state, never mind turning them into something 'swanky.'

Kevin entered the porch, standing close by her feet as he continued petting the dog's head. He always seemed to stand too close to her or perhaps, she was simply sensitive to his presence. Sensing her reaction to his proximity, he smiled at her in a slow deliberate grin. He reached over her thighs to take the coffee mug from her hand. She was mesmerized by his closeness and did not immediately respond to the liberation of her cup.

"I hope you won't be uncomfortable with me being here," he said, sipping leisurely from her coffee. "You know, so close by. You're apt to see me quite a bit."

She snapped out of the trance that he was putting her under and grabbed back her mug. "Hey, get your own," she snapped. "I just didn't realize Ada had taken on tenants. I'll have to consider that in my calculations when I sell."

The smile left his face abruptly. "You're selling?"

She stood and the dog bolted to his feet beside her, ready to follow. "Nothing for sure yet, but there's the possibility. I have to get into the books and see what's what before I can make any kind of a decision."

"That's right, you're an expert." He took a step toward her, so they were now standing toe to toe. They were so close that she could feel his breath on her face as he spoke. "It'd be a shame if you sold. Ada worked her whole life to preserve this place in order to hand it down. She wanted you to have it, you know. She trusted you."

He stepped even closer, wrapping a muscled arm around her waist. Every inch of her body instantly responded to his touch, tingling with anticipation. She relaxed against his muscled chest, allowing him to pull her closer. His breath was warm in her hair.

Abruptly, she pulled back, she couldn't fall into these old patterns. She wasn't staying, no matter if she sold or not. He dropped his hands, stepping back from her. His expression was stony. "Still trying to leave," he stated, finishing off the remainder of her coffee.

The physical contact left her aroused. She was surprised her body had responded so easily to his touch. It was like the years hadn't passed and she was still a teenager. He affected her now, just as he had all those years ago, and he knew it. He had intended to do so.

She couldn't let herself get distracted when there was work to be done. She would get it settled and then she could head back to her career in the city. Back to her life and away from here, where the world seemed to be standing still, waiting for Annie to return.

A noise on the far porch startled them both. Sheriff Shawn stood on the steps, clearing his throat. "Mornin.' I didn't want to interrupt, but..." He shuffled his feet, gesturing toward the dog. "I came up to see if you heard anything about the owner."

The pair of them looked down at the dog, who approached Shawn. He immediately started to lick his hands and wag his tail as if he had met a long-lost friend. As the Sheriff rubbed his ears, the dog jumped up on his hind legs, placing his paws on the man's shoulders and enthusiastically licking his face.

"Ohh, down boy," he responded, pushing the dog back down to be on all fours. He continued to pet his head. "I'll be damned. Annie used to have a dog like this when we were kids. Used to jump on me the same way. He'd single me out, and never did it to anyone else."

Kevin laughed and nodded his head. "Oh yeah! That dog *loved* you!" he replied, looking down at the dog. He joined his friend in patting the furry head. "You know, he kind of looks like Annie's dog. You remember, Christina? He used to follow her everywhere."

Christina didn't respond, and she didn't need to, since the men were oblivious to her response. They were completely lost in the details of their memories.

"I swear, it looks just like that dog," Shawn said. "There's got to be a picture somewhere–I think in Ada's office maybe. Anyway, we don't have any leads on anyone missing a dog. I came up to see what you wanted to do if the dog had stuck around. I can take him to the shelter if you want."

At that, the dog broke from the men and went to Christina. He sat on her feet, looking soulfully up at her. The chestnut brown puppy-dog eyes seemed to plead with her. She laughed patting his head. "Actually, he's been no trouble so far. If it's all right, he can stay with me. I am planning to stay here for a couple of weeks, so I can keep him at least until then."

Shawn shrugged. "That'd be better than the shelter, anyway. It's the time of the year where they get crowded with stray puppies and kittens. I'll take his picture and put it on the town website and Facebook page, so if his owner is looking for him, they might be able to find him."

They all laughed together, making jokes as they posed the dog for the photo. The dog seemed to like the attention. Kevin joined her on his knees, petting the dog's head as Shawn snapped a photo of the trio. After he was done, he made his way to leave. "I'll send these to you when I get down the mountain. Better let me have your number."

They exchanged phone numbers as Jim joined them on the porch, carrying a broken plastic box in his hands.

The small group greeted him, and then Christina said, "Oh, I was going to ask you if you had a key to Ada's office? The door is locked and I need to get in there."

"Gee honey, I don't think I ever had a key to that. Jeremy might. He locked it up a while back," Jim replied.

"Whatcha got there?" Shawn asked the older man, taking the box from his hands. "What happened to your camera?"

"Damned if I know," Jim replied.

The Sheriff inspected the broken game camera with a serious expression as he looked over the damage.

"This is the second broken security camera I've come across. I can't figure out why they keep falling off the trees. It's a real shame, because this one is the last one, I have. Never had this kind of trouble during deer season."

"You looking to jack a deer or something? It's out of season for deer," the Sheriff questioned the older man, smiling.

Jim guffawed. "Not doing much of that these days. I was trying to see what was digging in the back garden. It's ruining my roses, and you know they have gone crazy these past few years over by the stone walls."

The Sheriff continued to inspect the damage as Jim talked, turning the box over in his hands and running his fingers over the damaged sections. "Jim, you mind if I look at the footage? Maybe we can see what happened."

"Sure," Jim agreed. "Let's get the office door open for Crissy, and then we can have a look."

All three men worked on the lock to the office. Shawn surprised them all with his lock-picking skills, a carry-over from his less than stellar days as the wayward youth of their group of friends. Christina was surprised by the state of the office once they gained access. It looked like it hadn't been touched in years; it was dusty with scattered ledgers, receipts and statements. They were all strewn across the small desk. The filing cabinet was stuffed with overflowing file folders. It was chaos, and her heart sank as she realized the challenge she faced. She would have to piece the financial records together to be able to make any kind of informed decision. By the looks of the office, she'd be spending quite a bit of her vacation time weeding through its contents.

The men left her to her own devices. Jim and Shawn went off to review the contents of the game camera and Kevin headed toward the trail. At least he would be gone for a few days before she had to interact with him again. She was off kilter with him around and she wasn't sure she could handle that kind of distraction. She needed to stay focused on her reasons for being there.

With the dog laying at her feet, she sat alone in the office, shuffling through dusty papers. After her initial perusal, she dialed her stepfather in London. He would be up, and she needed to talk to someone with his business acumen and no emotional connection to this place. He would know the best course of action for her to take, and where to start in all the mess.

CHAPTER 10

Victor took her call immediately; it was early afternoon in London, and he was in between meetings. He was always eager to help her out in business matters. It was here that he found his footing with their relationship. He had been a loving support to her after her mother died, as well as with Aunt Ada's illness and death. It had been a challenge for him to meet the emotional needs of a young teenage girl when he joined her life as a life-long bachelor who was British to boot. Instead, he exceled at providing her with an exceptional education at boarding school and college and gave her solid career guidance. It worked; he'd given her the structure and education she needed, and the summers with Ada and Annie further fulfilled her emotional needs.

They had bonded over her career goals in business, and he became a valued and trusted advisor as she entered the work force. It was he who she called when things got rough at work or if she needed guidance on advancement opportunities. From the looks of Ada's filing systems, she needed help to figure out where to start to piece together the financial state of the inn.

"See if you can locate the name of her bank and her banker. Email me when you find it. I will set my team on it," Victor directed. "And who is this Jeremy guy?"

"He's Ada's attorney. He has been overseeing things, apparently well before she died. He's interested in developing the property. I got a very well-prepared presentation last night; it appears he has done quite a bit of research on the property's potential for sale."

There was a silence on the phone. "Estate planning is not my area of expertise, but this seems like an extension of the role of an executor," he stated. "How well do you know this attorney?"

She nodded in agreement. "Yeah, I am trying to feel that out. He was Ada's nephew on her husband's side, so there is a relationship there. I do know him from growing up, but only peripherally. He wasn't part of our group of friends because he was a few years older, so I really don't know him well. I need to wade through that a bit. I'm not fully sure of how he fit into Ada's life after I left."

Victor was silent for a long moment. "If I recall correctly, your mother once told me that there was some family turmoil when Ada's husband died and left the property to her. It had been in the family for generations and traditionally, it should have gone to her husband's brother. That would have been Jeremy's father, Daniel. I think he had some trouble with alcoholism, and he went away for treatment not long after Annie went missing."

"So then Jeremy would have been the heir, instead of me," she replied.

The line crackled with the transcontinental connection, and she thought she had lost him. "Victor?"

"I'm here," he replied, the connection skipping in and out. "I am going to have an old friend contact you, my dear. He's an attorney in Burlington. This situation is making me a bit uneasy and I'd like for you to have some impartial advice. I'll email you his information."

She agreed to the assistance, feeling a bit of relief, but also, some new anxiety. It was a double-edge sword to have her unease be justified by someone with vastly more experience.

"And Christina, my dear, please be careful."

Her nerves tensed immediately at his words, and unease grew in her belly. She wondered to herself if he had a specific concern that he was not sharing.

They said their goodbyes. He had to run to his next meeting. It was likely he would be in England for the remainder of the summer, but she had planned to have everything taken care of by then. She knew she could handle things, but it relieved her to have some additional help and guidance. She hadn't planned for the mess regarding the financial files. That would make her business projections more challenging.

She began sorting through the files on the desk, making organized piles of years of statements and receipts. It was a dusty and arduous task. It was obvious that Ada had not been the best businessperson, but she had done what she could. Christina found that the files grew to be more disorganized in the most recent couple years. The focus stopped being on the business when Annie disappeared and was even more removed when she did not reappear.

She pushed the power button for the ancient desktop, and it reluctantly started to come to life. There had to be some useful files on this computer. As the desktop booted up, a password entry screen popped up. She groaned to herself. There had to be a way to get into it. She immediately thought of Shawn. If he couldn't get in himself, it was likely he may know someone who could get to the files. It was not illegal;

she owned the property and had the right to access the business information.

She shuffled more papers, looking for anything useful that would identify a bank or an accountant. She pulled open desk drawers, leafing through files of paperwork, and growing increasingly discouraged by the volume of disorganization. She found a file of bank records, which she pulled out and opened on the desk. A red envelope with the words "past due" stamped on its front fell out onto the desk. Her stomach dropped. The envelope was unopened, which struck her as odd. Opening the letter, she found it was from a mortgage company and dated late last year.

This made no sense. The inn would not have needed a mortgage, as it had been in the family for generations. She thought, *maybe a mortgage has been taken out for the funds used for renovations and the 'swanky' cabins.*

She pulled out her phone to write Victor an email regarding the bank details. She noted there was no cell service. She wondered if there was an internet connection, but at least the land line had been working. She had not looked for a signal since she arrived, unused to having any service at the inn as a rule. Hoping her aunt had upgraded from dial up, she used her cell phone to verify the presence of any Wi-Fi connections. There was one, labeled "Stone House," but it stated that there was no internet connection. It looked like it may have been a satellite link, given the name of the provider. She would need to see if Jim or Maude knew where the modem was, since there was nothing resembling a modem in the office.

A board squeaked in the hallway outside the door. The dog issued a low warning growl, rising to position himself between whomever was approaching and Christina. She shoved the folder into the desk drawer and turned to the door. Jeremy leaned on the doorframe.

"Looks like you found your way in all right," he said, his eyes darting around the small office. Finally, they rested downward, inspecting the office door lock for damage. "How did you manage to get in?" He reached in his pocket and tossed her a set of keys. "Never mind. I thought I saw the police cruiser when I pulled in."

"Just helping out a friend," Shawn interrupted from the hallway, joining Jeremy in the doorway.

Jeremy shifted subtly away from the Sheriff's proximity in the doorway.

"Actually, I could use a bit more assistance from either of you," Christina implored of the two men, "I wonder if you know the password to the computer? Or maybe you could help me figure out a way to get in?"

They both jostled past each other from the doorway to stand over her shoulders to view the computer screen.

"Hmm I am surprised it even turned on," Jeremy sniggered. "I can't recall Ada ever really using it for bookkeeping."

Shawn nudged Christina from the desk chair and sat in front of the computer. He typed a few keystrokes, which were not successful. He made a few more attempts and suddenly, the entire screen went completely blue. "Uh oh," Shawn muttered.

The room became silent.

"Sorry Crissy," Shawn said, rising from the office chair shrugging his shoulders.

"Like I said, I don't think she used that much, so I doubt you'd find anything you're looking for there." Jeremy spoke to the group with annoyance.

"And now you won't get anything from it," Shawn said. "Anyway, I should leave before I make anything worse. I'll let you know if I find anything out about the dog."

Once Shawn left the two of them in the small office, Christina felt vaguely uncomfortable to be in such close quarters with Jeremy. After their exchange last night, it felt awkward to be alone with him. She was glad the dog had positioned himself between them.

He gestured around the office, saying, "Not sure what you may find in here to help you out." His tone was a mix of impatience and annoyance.

She shifted her focus to the tasks at hand, asking, "What banks did Ada use for the business?"

"I have those files in my office. Sorry, I didn't think to bring them with me," Jeremy responded. "But her business checking account was set up through the local co-op. I am sure you'll want to continue there if you decide to operate."

"I'll drop off the checkbooks and such later. Or you can stop by the office if you are in town."

Jeremy's words irritated Christina. Of course, she would like to have the checkbooks and "such." That was the reason she had come all the way to the inn at his urging. She wanted to take care of matters, and now he was lukewarm about her getting the information she needed to do any kind of due diligence. The whole situation was beyond irritating for Christina, topped with the computer's 'blue screen of death' and the fact that she had had no breakfast and only a few sips of her coffee this morning. This project was not starting out well.

Just as she was opening her mouth to tell Jeremy what she really thought of his plans, Gina entered the tiny office a food tray in hand, stocked up with coffee and heavenly smelling muffins. "I thought you might like a little breakfast, because Maude said you hadn't eaten." She chuckled to herself and added, "and I thought preventing murder would be a clever idea."

Christina fell onto the coffee and sipped the hot liquid gratefully, digging into a warm pastry. She mumbled her thanks to her friend through hearty bites. Jeremy's expression morphed into one of disdain as he observed the woman gobbling down the food.

Gina piped in, noting his expression, "This one–she can eat like no woman I know, and yet she stays so thin. Unlike some of us rounder and shorter ones."

Jeremy looked from one woman to the other, obviously growing uncomfortable in the small space and with the topic of conversation. His discomfort increased twofold as Gina ran her free hand down her body from her breasts to her buttock as emphasis to her words.

Next, Gina spotted the computer. "Oh nice, is there internet here?" she asked hopefully.

"Yes, we upgraded a few years ago with a new satellite provider," Jeremy answered. "Likely it needs a reset since no one has been using it for a while. I'll go take care of it; the modem is by the front desk."

Jeremy exited and both women exchanged a humor-filled glance. "Thanks for the food –much appreciated." Christina smiled at her friend.

Jeremy's comment had not fallen unnoticed by Christina, and instead, was striking a chord. *'We' upgraded...* Victor's comments regarding Jeremy were fresh in her mind. She wondered how involved he had been in the day-to-day management of the inn. Had he gone too far in acquiring responsibilities?

"I heard the commotion with all the men's voices in the hallway, back when they were getting the office door open. That's when I went down to the kitchen. I'm not sure what I said, but it put Maude in a better mood today. Eager to get you to eat your breakfast, she said she didn't want any bloodshed. Guess she knows you just as well as I do. We've bonded over the need to feed you."

Christina laughed. It was true that low blood sugar and her temperament did not go well together. Both ladies would know this well, having both been subjected to it at one time. "Well, as Aunt Ada used to say, 'nothing to be ashamed of to have a healthy appetite.'"

Gina noted the ominous blue screen on the computer and suggested that they take it to a local business supply store to see if they could retrieve any of its documents. Christina recalled that there was one in town–if it was still in existence. There was also a chain store, a bit further away, which may have more options for retrieving the hard drive if the local option didn't pan out. Christina had her own laptop that she had planned to use to do business projections, so maybe the information could be transferred to an external memory drive.

The two women discussed the options and made plans to have lunch and visit a few local sites. Gina wanted to see a covered bridge and take in some other scenery, reminding her friend that she was on vacation after all. She also wanted to stop by the grocery store to pick up a few ingredients for a couple meals she wanted to experiment with. Now that she and Maude were no longer at each other's throats, she should get a good opportunity to do some cooking.

Christina secretly wondered if Gina's morning truce with Maude would last into the dinner hour, but she didn't put anything past her friend. She knew that Gina had a way of achieving miracles in the kitchen.

CHAPTER 11

The two women made their way down the mountain later in the morning, after all the male visitors had left to go to their own jobs. Kevin went into the woods; Shawn went off to patrol and Jeremy went back down the mountain to his offices. They had located the wi-fi router and had gotten the internet going. The email from Victor regarding the connection in Burlington arrived, conveying that Christina should hear from him directly.

"I know that I am not used to being outside of the city, but this road seems steep," Gina commented as Christina drove down the mountain. Gina was gripping the door handles and the center console so hard her knuckles were white.

Christina laughed at her friend. "Yeah sorry–I learned to drive on this road, so I am pretty confident. I'll slow down, no worries."

She slowed her speed and her companion relaxed.

"You know," she continued, "this road was not the original way to get up the mountain–the path we walked on yesterday was the original road to the inn. It's a lot longer, but it's also a lot less steep on the other side."

Gina nodded, glad for the diversion of the conversation. "Where does that old road go?"

"Well, it meets up with the Long Trail and the Bald Mountain trail. There also used to be a road that went over to

Woodford and Bennington that forked off of that road. And there is another intersection that used to take you to Glastonbury, but that's a ghost town now. Wilderness had completely taken over."

Gina stared at her friend with a horrified look on her face. "Where have you brought me? A ghost town in New England? I used to think that those were all out west, with tumble weeds and scorpions."Christina laughed at Gina's vibrant image.

"This is sure an interesting place," Gina continued, tut-tutting. "It's not at all what I expected, especially with the talk last night about the woods. What did Kevin mean when he mentioned the trouble that they were having in the woods now? I didn't quite get all that."

Christina noted her friend's clear avoidance of mentioning the missing persons topic that had also occurred as part of the conversation last evening. She knew Gina was curious and wanted to know more about the circumstance of Annie's disappearance, as well as the other stories of missing persons. Gina must have known that it struck an emotional chord with her friend and took pains to not mention it.

Christina nodded, concentrating on the road in front of her. She tried to choose her tone carefully as to not upset herself, and also, so she would answer Gina without further freaking her out. "There have been some stories about the area, through some documentaries and a few novels, about missing persons and weird occurrences. Most of them specifically take place over the mountain in the area of the Glastonbury wilderness."

Gina listened intently as she continued to grip the door handle.

"Over the past 70 years or something, there have been quite a few people that have gone missing. And as a result, some people try to promote the area and its stories by sensationalizing them. You know that movie about Shirley Jackson? She lived in North Bennington when a girl from the college went into those woods and was never found. I think with that film coming out, as well as the other obscure legends, there has been more activity on the trails. The locals–well some of them, anyway–try to capitalize on the increased traffic. Typically, it's mostly college kids hiking through and planning to be in the area for the summer solstice. There are always a bunch of parties and group camping events in the woods. Invariably someone gets lost or hurt.

"Practically speaking, it's a remote area and it's easy to get lost here, even if you know your way. If you aren't prepared for it, you can get lost easily and die in the elements."

"You sound like Kevin," Gina replied. "He said the same thing last night. And by the way, he is pretty hot. Any plans to tap that while on vacation? You know, for a little old time's sake...?"

Christina glanced at her friend and burst out laughing at the teasing look on her face. She knew she was making light of the situation and the conversation, so she smiled despite herself. Heat rose in her cheeks at her friend's comments.

"Oooo girl... you were thinking about it!" Gina teased at her friend's blushing, "He's a fine-looking man and so is his friend, the cop."

Christina picked up on her comment, taking the opportunity to turn the conversation away from herself. "Shawn is pretty nice. I still can't believe he's a cop though. He got in so much trouble when we were kids."

Gina nodded her head, notably relaxing her grip on the door handle as Christina guided the car onto more even road. "He is nice. He had all sorts of questions for me this morning. Honestly, it almost felt like I was getting interrogated."

"Really?" Christina asked, interested in this information. She wondered about his motive to question her friend. Perhaps there was a mutual attraction there as well?

"Yes ma'am. While you were in the office, he was looking over that camera box in the kitchen and talking to Jim. He asked a lot of questions about you and me, and I couldn't get away from him for a few minutes. It was all very intense."

"That's curious," Christina replied. "I've known Shawn for years. He knows everything about me."

"Well darling, now he knows everything he missed." Gina chuckled. "Where we work, where we live, and both our dating statuses. Hell, I think I told him our new favorite songs!"

She laughed out loud then. "I am sure he was not at all interested in me, sounds like he has taken a shine for you. You should check into that."

"Well to tell you the truth, I really didn't mind the questions," Gina stated. "I was trying to get to know him as well."

"Ahh, I thought you were watching him with *interest*," Christina replied. She smiled sideways at her friend. "Actually, your mouth was even hanging open.... but not judging here."

"No! Tell me I wasn't. Did he notice?" she asked. She slumped into the car's seat, mortified. "It's been a long dry spell, what can I say?"

The two women laughed together. "I was wondering about what they mentioned as his less than stellar past. Just being curious, as now he's a cop," Gina asked.

"Oh, I think he is well reformed now. He had a tough upbringing, spent a lot of time at the inn when he and Annie were dating. My aunt and a female State Trooper took interest and helped him to mend his ways. Nothing horrible, if that's what you are asking," replied Christina. "Are you interested in him?"

Gina grinned back at her friend. "We aren't going to be here that long, but I think I'll leave myself open to the possibilities." She raised her arms over her head and crossed her elbows, leaning her head on her hands. "How about you and Kevin? He couldn't take his eyes off you last night at dinner."

She was not surprised at this news, but it didn't match his response to her on the patio when they were alone. He could have leaned in, and she would have been willing, to have him kiss her.

But he didn't. And it made her, well, it made her want him to do it more.

After taking a brief detour to drive through one of the region's covered bridges, the ladies arrived in the small, picturesque town of Wilmington. Gina had been thrilled with the covered bridge and had taken several pictures when they stopped to have a closer look. It was fun to play tourist and see the area through Gina's eyes. It really was a beautiful and quaint location.

While they made their way into town, Christina noted that there were a few bed and breakfasts in the area, but hardly any other hotels or lodging with more than a couple rooms. There was a small, run-down motel chain with 10 rooms, but it was unappealing at best. She knew from experience, having stayed there for Ada's funeral. It was interesting that she had not noticed this before, but she imagined the observation was related to her current project, since she was evaluating the inn for viability as a business.

They lugged the large CPU of Ada's computer into the local computer repair shop. The young man who waited on them assured them he would have something for them in a few hours. If he could access the hard drive, he would download the files to an external drive. They opted to grab lunch at the local diner while they waited.

They took a booth once in the diner, which was housed in an old-fashioned, remodeled rail car. Gina was interested in the menu, which had everything from scrambled eggs to nut burgers and vegan meatloaf. They ordered and waited for their meal in the bustling restaurant.

The walls were covered with specials written in different vivid colors on the back of paper placemats. "I am always intrigued by how they run these small diners with the tiny kitchens and the huge variety of food on the menu," Gina said. "There has to be precooked portions of all these meals, right? How else could they possibly whip them up?"

This was as fascinating to her as shoe shopping was to Christina, who amiably nodded while her friend chatted on.

Their meal was delicious. While Christina had ordered eggs benedict, Gina ordered a more complex vegan meal. She was impressed with the quality of the food. The conversation then tilted to dinner and the other restaurants in town. This interested Christina, as she couldn't recall more than two or three restaurants in the area that had drawn the local crowds when she was growing up. She could really only remember the local pizza parlor.

"If you decide to keep the business," Gina started, "you would really need to consider expanding the food offerings at the inn. Even though it seems pretty far out of the way, having good food options for guests would be essential. I bet it would appeal to both locals and visitors."

Christina accepted this opinion while silently nodding, her mind working. "I've got to really get a business plan going and see what's possible for the place."

"From what I have seen in the past 24 hours, the location really speaks to me. It feels like there would be a lot of business in the fall. I wonder about the winter though, especially with that road. But I bet you can figure it out. It seems like a nice place for a family weekend or a romantic getaway. It would be a great place to stay with all that nature around."

"It really is far out there," Christina replied. "I think my aunt didn't do much advertising, though she had developed plans to expand the dining area. If I recall, there were a few guests throughout the time I spent there—though the inn was never full. I think she liked it that way. It was just enough to keep them going."

"I see potential," Gina stated. "I think you better get that business plan together. Do you think the computer is ready now?"

They paid their bill and walked back to the small business service shop. The lanky young man triumphantly handed Christina an external hard drive. "I was able to download the files on the drive—however, it died before I could wade around to see which programs she was using. Likely she used an older version of a common bookkeeping software; you should be able to open them in the current version. If you have any trouble, let me know."

"You'll have to take the CPU with you though. I can't keep it here. Garbage collectors will take them on the last Friday of the month, so just check the local paper for that information." He looked them over, his eyes resting on the shapely Gina, and he blushed.

She noted his reaction and decided to capitalize on it, placing a hand on her hip, "Do you mind taking the CPU out to the car, hun? It was pretty heavy."

Christina smiled quizzically at her friend, crossing her eyes. She was always fascinated by Gina's ability and willingness to use her feminine wares to her benefit. Her sexuality was something she was unable to conjure on her own. Blushing deeply, the young man took the CPU in his arms and followed the ladies out the door.

As they were pulling out to head back to the inn, Christina noted a sign for the local banking co-op. Gesturing in the direction, Christina asked if Gina would mind if she went in to make some inquiries about the business accounts.

"Not at all. I'll go in that bookstore right next door, so you can take your time. If they have a cookbook section, I may need a few hours."

Christina pulled in the alley lot between the two buildings and parked the car. They each went their own way, with Christina hoping she would find some answers about Ada's finances. She checked her phone before entering the bank in case she had any new messages from Victor. Instead, she noted an email addressed directly to her from the attorney Victor had referred. It was so like Victor to take immediate action and elicit a quick response. She was glad he was on her side.

She entered the bank and was whisked into the bank manager's office. "So very sorry about Ada," the young manager, Brian Martin, offered. "What can I do for you today?"

She smiled to herself. Brian was young and very formal for the rustic setting of the co-op with its old, planked boards and antiqued tin ceiling. Christina explained her situation to him.

He nodded his understanding, and she instantly knew he was listening intently. "Yes, I had heard that Ada had left the property to a relative instead of the members of the Stone family. It was kind of a surprise to some, especially since Jeremy had been the one helping her out all along."

Christina rocked on the balls of her feet. She felt a little uncomfortable to be reminded that she had not been assisting her aunt.

"Of course, the inn was hers to do what she pleased with it," he went on. "I suppose you are here to come on as a signer for the Inn's accounts?"

She paused. She had not considered this initially, but it would be a wise decision. "Yes, thank you," she answered. "I would also like to get copies of the statements for the accounts under both my aunt's name and the Stone Inn, if they're available."

Brian looked down at her as he stood behind his desk, getting up for a signature card. "Please sign this, but I will need to get some further documentation from you as well. I will need a certified copy of the death certificate and probate if there is one.

"I can add you as a signer on the business accounts for now. Once you have all of the required paperwork, we can get everything transferred to your name."

He left the office, and she contemplated what he needed. She would seek out help from Victor's contact to make sure things were being handled properly. She waited for several minutes for the branch manager to reappear. She could see Brian through the glass walls in the small bank, talking on a phone. It appeared that the conversation was not a pleasant one, as his face became redder and redder. After a few moments, he hung up the phone and disappeared from her sight.

She pulled out her phone and began to scroll through emails, noting a few from work and the new one from Victor's contact, asking for a suitable time to set up a call. Abruptly, Brian returned to the office. His face was less red, but he still appeared distracted.

"If you would please go ahead and sign here, we'll start to process your request to get you access to the business accounts. Once we have the death certificate, it will take some time to go through our main offices, but we can assure you that you will have access in about a month."

"A month?" she asked, perplexed. "I'm sorry, but in the meantime, who has access to these accounts. How are the expenses being paid?"

He looked down at her notably agitated, and his face grew red. "Mr. Stone has access to these accounts as he has been managing the estate for some time."

Christina stood, grasping her jacket closer around her. She felt a mixture of humiliation and anxiety rise in her belly. Jeremy had been dealing with the inn and its expenses since Ada was ill and apparently, hadn't been able to count on Christina. However, she was sure there were business expenses, electricity, gas, food, and caretaker wages that needed to be paid. Without access to those accounts, she would be obliged to pay out of her own pocket for the upkeep expenses. It wasn't the best of circumstances.

"Is there any way to obtain the account statements?" she asked. "I'm putting together a business plan and would like to capture the true history of the business...."

Brian Martin shook his head. "I'm sorry, but I can't share those with you without the required paperwork." He gestured toward the door of his office. "Is there anything else I can help you with today?"

She stood and exited the office. "No, thank you," she answered with her mind racing, as she tried to determine what her next steps should be. She had not foreseen these obstacles and required paperwork.

She also failed to see the man she ran directly into on the steps of the bank. "Whoa," he said, grabbing her arm and catching her before she fell hard on the pavement.

Embarrassed, she looked up into a friendly, familiar face. "Jeff!" she called out, surprised.

"Well, hello there," he responded with a huge grin. "Looks like someone in the bank has made you mad. What a scowl!"

Of all the people to run into after the interaction in the bank, she was glad to see Jeff. He had been part of the group of friends that she'd hung out with throughout the years with Annie. He was always a sweet guy and a huge animal lover–always rescuing dogs and cats and taking them home to his family's small farm. The last she knew of him, he had been working with racehorses in Saratoga.

They exchanged a brief conversation, detailing what they had been doing since they last saw each other. Jeff had heard that Ada left Christina the inn and was interested to hear about her plans. He joined her on her stroll to the bookstore, where she planned to reconnect with Gina.

"You know, I had been talking with Ada about offering horseback and wagon rides at the inn. I thought it would be a great mutual business opportunity since it'd expand the inn's amenities. I have my own stable down at my parents place, but could look at stabling horses on site as well."

Christina was impressed with his business growth. "That sounds lovely, but I haven't decided what I am going to do with the property. I'm not sure if I will run it or sell."

Jeff looked at her in surprise. "I never imagined it being sold," he replied. "I can't imagine anyone else running the place and living there except Ada or you. I hear there are lots of developers around looking for some property to plunk down some more ugly condos. It would be a shame for them to buy and destroy the old Stone house."

They entered the bookstore and Christina looked around for Gina. "Hey, look at this," Jeff said, pulling a book off of a large display. "It's one of those Shirley Jackson books. And look at all of these about the Bennington Triangle."

Christina took a moment and looked over the display, which advertised the movie release that was based on the local author's books. "All fiction," Christina responded dismissively.

"Well, I sure believe it!" Jeff replied. "I've seen some of these things. Plus, you know the story, right?"

It took her a moment to recall what he was referring to, but Christina responded, "The story about the skull?"

Jeff had been teased mercilessly for years by the other boys in their group of friends. When they were young teens, a group of boys had spent the night in the woods. Jeff had gotten separated from the group, but they were able to locate him due to his screams. He had fallen into a cave and swore that there was a human skull in there with him. The boys were able to pull him out with no harm done, but they were unable to ever locate that same cave again. Obviously, they had just gotten twisted around in the dark woods and their location had been misconstrued.

"Kevin says there is a lot of activity up in the trail lately. Both he and Shawn were worried about the summer solstice this year because lots of unprepared people have been heading up there. They all want to see this legendary place for themselves and are hoping to see something."

Gina appeared from behind a bookshelf, her arms cradling a few heavy cookbooks. "I'm about ready to go. Let me just check out."

Christina introduced the pair. Jeff was nonplussed and continued to chat with Christina. "Hopefully, the weather stays warm enough for those new hikers. I've seen it snow in June up there, so if they come unprepared, they will be cold. There's always the risk of hypothermia."

Gina checked out with her pile of books, and they headed for the door. Jeff leaned down and took the package from Gina without missing a syllable in his conversation. He escorted them to their car. "I'll stop by up at the inn tomorrow or the next day. Or maybe you come to me–we'll do a trail ride with the horses so you can see what an appeal it would be if you decided to stay open."

"Whoa, that your car?" He asked as they approached her vehicle.

The back window had been smashed out. The glass was all over the road between the two businesses. Christina leaned in and looked at the back seat.

The computer was missing. *Who would have wanted that ancient thing?* she thought. She dialed Shawn's cell that he had given her earlier that morning.

Just a few minutes later, Shawn arrived at the parking lot in his Sheriff's cruiser. Christina noted that he did not have his lights going as she would have expected. He arrived calmly and coolly, approaching the parked car with wary and observant eyes. She could tell that he was gathering minute details as he approached the trio around the vehicle.

"This your car or is it a rental?" he calmly asked Christina as he made his way around the vehicle, looking for any details of further damage.

She sighed. "It's mine."

Keeping a car in the city was costly and frivolous, but Victor had insisted on it. He said that she should have the freedom to leave the city whenever she wanted. At the time, his thoughts had centered around her visits to Ada.

Christina was mentally doing the math in her head about the cost of getting the window fixed. She stretched her mind to recall the glass coverage of her car insurance policy.

"What did they take?" Shawn asked, noting that both women had their purses over their shoulders and that Jeff was holding a large bag from the bookstore.

"I actually had that old CPU from Ada's desktop in there." Christina stopped herself from saying more. She didn't feel that it was pertinent to Shawn's review that the CPU had been deemed 'dead' and that she had an external drive of its files in her purse.

Shawn was busy inspecting the car door and the glass. "Looks like they smashed the window, opened the door, and took the CPU."

Nothing else in the car was disturbed. The glove box was untouched, and the fifty dollar-bill she had tucked in the center console remained.

"We've had a handful of break-ins here and there. Mostly people seeking to get items to sell in order to buy their heroin," Shawn said. "Though the break-ins don't usually happen out in broad daylight."

This surprised both Christina and Gina. They hadn't expected this challenge in an idyllic setting as Vermont. "I didn't realize that was a problem here."

"Lots of families have been impacted," Jeff replied, "mine included."

"How is your sister doing, anyway?" Shawn asked, while pulling out a note pad and making out a report.

"Better," Jeff replied. "She got into some trouble here and there with some bad folks, but she's better. Got her kids back last month."

Shawn nodded. "Good to hear. Not everyone has such a supportive family. That makes a lot of difference."

Shawn ripped a page from his pad and handed the paper to Christina. "Here you go. Your insurance company will want that."

Christina took the sheet from him and glanced through it. "Is that all?"

"Pretty much," he replied. "Jim can help you to put something over the hole to keep the rain out for now. There is a glass company a couple towns over that will come around to you to make the repair. I'm not sure if they will do it for car doors–it's mostly for windshields–but it's worth a try."

Christina purposely avoided saying anything about how the computer repair clerk had been able to access some of the files for her. Overall, the response to her car break-in was disappointing. As they stood near the car, Christina felt angrier and more violated with each passing minute. It wasn't the loss of the computer; it was the damage to her car and the unwelcome element of danger in this rural area. She had assumed such a thing was a rarity, or it at least, thought it was supposed to be rare. Now, not only would she have to deal with the emerging challenges of inheriting the inn, both on a personal and business perspective, but she also had to face the annoyance of organizing the repair and dealing with the insurance company.

This whole situation was becoming expensive. Not only the car repair, but now the likely expenses associated with managing the business that were clearly going to come out of her pocket for the time being. Jeremy had access to those accounts if there was anything in them. She had assumed there would be at least some starter funds to ride out a few months of operation before she made some decisions about what to do with the property.

With the events of the past 24 hours, she realized, this was not going the way that she had thought. She felt discouraged and angry. Angry at herself for believing naively that the business side of this endeavor would be smooth. She had assumed the more difficult part would be the emotional impact she would have to face by coming back to this place that she had long avoided. Now that these facts were remarkably reversed, she felt mostly at peace here, because it was not the jarring emotional experience she expected. Instead, she was at a loss to be dealing with the business side of the inn, which was something she was not used to. In business, she was always in control and in her element.

She sighed, kicking a rock across the parking lot, and interrupting the chatter between Shawn and Jeff. They were continuing to catch up on the local gossip. Her trio of companions looked at her. "I should be going," Shawn began. "Let me know if you need anything else, Crissy. I'll be out on patrol, and you have my number. If I find out anything, I'll be sure to let you know. Sorry that this happened. Apparently, there's enough metal in those old CPUs to appeal to someone for scrap value. Sorry you lost those records."

"Thanks Shawn," she replied, getting into the drivers' side of the car. She ignored Gina's questioning glance at her lack of full disclosure to the police.

CHAPTER 12

He watched them from his vantage point on the street. She deserved to have the computer stolen from her car and the window smashed out. She was butting in where she didn't need to be. They never intended for her to be able to stick her nose into their business.

It had been so easy with the old bat out of the way. He could do whatever he wanted. Now that she had come to stake her claim–one she should have never gotten–he needed to make sure she didn't want to stay.

It was perfect to see the look on their faces when they found the window broken and the computer gone. He had almost laughed out loud but stifled the outburst. He didn't want to give away his vantage point.

He had one of the druggies do the job. They were more than happy to do it for money that they would inevitably use to buy more drugs. It was remarkable what those people would do for some cash.

It was a win win for him.

She needed to be silenced if she stuck around. She had a chance at survival. It was up to her to take it.

If she stuck around, it would all be over. She would go the same way of her relatives. This break in should be enough to scare her away. That, and not having access to the cash in her aunt's account. He couldn't allow that.

He started his car and pulled out to drive around the block, gloating to himself at the success of the afternoon.

CHAPTER 13

Later, back at the inn, Christina had a phone call with the attorney from Burlington to review the circumstances of her inheritance. He was kind and thorough and would investigate any information that was available. He also said that he would handle the co-op's needs so she could access the bank accounts. He assured her that she was within her rights, based on the conditions in Ada's will, to access the business files. She shared her additional concerns that in this role as executor, Jeremy had contacted investors and real estate developers. She also gave him an overview of Jeremy's ideas for the future of the property. There was a notable silence on the line before he responded, piquing Christina's interest.

The attorney changed the topic and offered to have her connect with one of his other clients in the Stowe, Vermont area. They managed a similar hospitality business, so he thought they might be able to shed some light on the market and potential recreational offerings. He would need to obtain their permission before Christina reached out, but he was sure it wouldn't be an issue. He assured her that he would get back to her in 48 hours or less. He also would provide Victor with a recap.

Christina started to object to Victor's further involvement, concerned with the expenses it might create, but she stopped herself. With the uncertainty of the amount of operating money she had available, she was grateful to be able to rely on her stepfather's considerable and generous resources. Silently though, she vowed to pay him back.

Gina joined her in the small office shortly after she ended the call. Her friend handed her a very full glass of wine, settling onto the ancient, winged chair that was nestled in the corner of the small room. Gina studied her friend while they sipped their wine.

"You going to tell me why you lied to the Sheriff?" Gina asked.

Christina sat back in the office chair, making it creak loudly. She sipped her wine, appreciating the flavor. It was such a privilege to have connoisseurs for friends. "I didn't really lie; I just left out some details."

Gina sipped and waited, raising her eyebrows in a question. "I got the feeling there is something you aren't telling me."

Christina took a large sip and swallowed, setting her glass on the desk. She reached in her purse and located the memory stick. "Let's see what this has on it."

She proceeded to insert the memory stick into her laptop and opened the files. There were jpg files among others in the listing, but she avoided the picture files. Instead, she proceeded to work through the other files to see if she could open them with her software.

"You think something is up, don't you?" Gina asked.

Christina nodded, sipping her wine, and leafing through the files. "Just a hunch." She gave her friend a sidelong glance while continuing to open and close files from the memory stick.

Gina crossed her legs, yoga style, further settling in with her wineglass. "Well, so far, this trip is not what I expected. But you've got me interested–so dish."

Christina rose and closed the door to the tiny room, causing her companion to raise her eyebrows. The office chair creaked as she took her seat, facing her friend. She exhaled, reached for her wine and settled back in her chair.

"Something is off," she started. "Jeremy was so hot to get me here to 'take care of things.' And now that I'm here, it feels like I am walking through mud to get anything I need to make an informed decision about business operations."

"He has come up here twice, and each time, he has 'forgotten' to bring the checkbooks or any details about the business accounts. I think it's weird that he has been the only one with access to this office. His attention has been more on what the developers want than what I asked him for."

She took a sip of wine and continued, "I think he assumed that I'd want to get rid of this property as fast as I knew it was mine. He's making things easy when it concerns the option of selling to developers, and he's putting up roadblocks when I want other information."

She paused, leaning back in her chair, looking meaningfully at her friend. "I found some mortgage paperwork on the inn. She would not have needed to get a mortgage. This place was paid for nearly a century ago. So why was there a mortgage?"

"Maude mentioned some work they had done to the cabins," Gina said. "Do you think they could have taken out an equity loan or something to make renovations? The kitchen re-work and the plans for the dining area expansion may have been part of all that," Gina added.

Christina turned her creaky office chair back, so she was facing the laptop again, and resumed her methodical review of the files. She shook her head. "Anyway, that was just the hunch I was having. It feels like something isn't as it should be." She resumed clicking on her keyboard.

"Sometimes that's when you need to pay attention. Intuition can be pretty spot on," Gina replied, her tone serious.

Christina glanced back at her friend and smiled teasingly. "You watch too much of the *Dead Files*. The next thing you know, you'll be telling me that we are getting guidance from beyond the grave!"

Both women chuckled. Gina loved to imagine other-worldly influences; she would say sometimes it was the only logical explanation for certain occurrences. "Makes you wonder," she whispered with a low chuckle, sipping her wine in the armchair.

"Bingo!" Christina shouted, "there are some old QuickBooks files here."

She turned her attention to the to the electronic files and opened them with the version she had on her computer. She found older records with suppliers, plus some of Ada's invoices and payments. There were sporadic records of guests staying in the inn, and some restaurant records. It would at least get her started.

As she worked and studied the files, muttering to Gina and herself about her discoveries, fresh ideas came into her head. The operations for this inn had seemed like a background noise when she was growing up. Its activities and people moved through the atmosphere around her, paying no heed, as it was all part of the life. Seeing the records now from a different perspective, with experience in the industry, she felt like her eyes were opened and unclouded. The beverage supplier, who to her young self was a friendly man with a brown truck, was now a quality company with desirable wares.

Recalling her conversation with the attorney from Burlington, she mentioned his offer to Gina, about connecting her with their client from Stowe. "Stowe? Hmm, I've heard of that," Gina said, pulling out her phone to google the location while Christina continued working on the computer.

"Hey, wait a minute! Crissy, look at this place!" She jumped up from the armchair to show her what she was seeing on her phone. "Fine dining, antiques, a historical tavern.... And look at these outdoor activities. There are cross country, hiking, and horse trails.

"I wonder if this is the lawyer's client. This is really quite a place," Gina said showing her friend the screen on her phone.

Christina absorbed the photos of a beautiful location in a quaint town, and her mind began to hum. Her aunt's place was historic and had similar offerings, but none that had been promoted to the extent of The Inn in Stowe. Ada had obviously not marketed the inn and instead, was running the business as a small operation that made just enough to make a decent living. She wondered at her aunt's choice, but quickly arrived at the thought that this had been their home. Ada's attention had always been on her family while Annie was growing up. It certainly had given Christina the opportunity to have a close bond with her cousin and wonderful memories of living there.

Her mind began to race as she thought about amenities, activities, and the inn's potential for hosting events. She began to shift from looking at the inn as Ada's home with the occasional guest, to something more. But was it possible?

Gina stirred. Rising from the chair and stretching, she said, "I can feel your brain waves from over here. I think I'll go and find out what Maude has planned for dinner."

Christina nodded absently, clicking an occasional key. The files were older, but they gave some detail about the business. One file that caught her eye was labeled "roof repairs." Jim only took care of minor repairs and the grounds, so Ada usually had to have outside help for larger projects. Inside of the folder, there were bills from a roofing company and other miscellaneous bills for Stone Construction, which was Jeremy's father's company. From the records, it looked like Ada had outsourced several projects over the years to his company.

She searched for details about the cabin repairs, but the records were sporadic and looked incomplete. Likely, this is where Jeremy had stepped in because Christina was not around. The familiar guilt rose in her gut, and she wondered why Ada had not left the property to Jeremy or his father. Why had she chosen Christina after she had literally abandoned her?

Jeff's words from earlier circled in her head: "She wanted you to have it, to run it."

Frustrated, she slammed the cover of her laptop shut and stood. She'd better take a walk around the place, take a good hard look at the condition of the building, and see if her thoughts about the inn's potential were actually feasible. Maybe they had just been a fancy after looking at the pictures from Stowe.

She set out to the grounds and over the path to where the old cabins were located. They had been forbidden to play in them as children due to their lack of upkeep, so she wondered what they looked like now. She followed the path Kevin had come down that morning, noting that it too had been installed in her absence. Solar lights lined the sides of the gravel path, placed strategically in the landscape. She approved of this safety measure and made a mental note to check on it later, when the sun was down.

The path led to a ridge, carved into the mountain by the long-ago glaciers. It was now adorned with trees–pine and birch offered most of the species that surrounded the cabins dotting the landscape. The contrast in the tree bark assisted to disguise the grey sided cabins as they blended into the craggy hillside. The cabin closest to the path was evidently Maude and Jim's, as the latter sat in an Adirondack chair. He was clearly sound asleep with his audible snores mixing in with the birdsong in the trees.

With the gravel crunching under her feet, she moved past quietly as she could, as to not awaken the older man. In a short while, she approached the neighboring cabin. It appeared to be unoccupied, but the door was locked. It was apparent that the structure had had significant remodeling. The new siding, roof and windows were sparkling in the light through the trees. She tried to peer through one of the windows to see the inside, but it was difficult to make out anything. Flustered, but not deterred from her curiosity, she looked around to the other cabins. From the records, she knew there were seven, but she was only counting six in view.

Her eyes followed the path she had taken. It forked through the trees, with one branch heading up the ridge, clearly connecting the cabins in view. The other continued over the hill rise and through the trees. Curious as to where it led, she opted to follow it over the hill.

The path meandered through the tree line before turning sharply downhill, connecting to another dirt trail that led further down the mountain. After a few steps, she realized where she was. In front of her was the old fishing cabin footpath where she and Kevin had spent much of their time alone, all those years ago.

Even more curious, she continued walking, knowing what she would see ahead. The pond sparkled in the sunlight as Christina emerged from the forest with her shoes crunching on the gravel. The small beach area had a fresh section of sand with two benches and pairs of Adirondack chairs placed along the shoreline. It was visually appealing; she marveled at the transformation of the area. Across the water was the old fishing cabin, fully renovated. Its windows reflected the water in the sunlight.

Her stomach fluttered at the sight of it, bringing back memories of Kevin naked on the makeshift bed. She swallowed hard, pushing down the recollections of their young physical love.

She couldn't get distracted by him; she had far too much to consider and do in the next few days. She needed to make important decisions and shouldn't get clouded by a rekindling of young romance. So much had happened since they were together that it was as if several lifetimes had passed—Annie's disappearance, the never-ending searching and waiting, Ada's illness and death. But they were adults now with adult problems.

He had made clear last night that his feelings for her had not changed.

Her feet propelled her forward, curious about the cabin's rebirth into a usable structure. It really was quite nice; Ada must have really thought ahead and was planning for the future. The timing was curious, however. If Christina had the facts straight, this work had been completed as Ada's health was declining.

Approaching the cabin, she tried the door, and surprisingly found it unlocked. She looked around and saw no indication that anyone was around, but she knocked anyway to be sure. "Hello?" she called, opening the door and entered a small galley kitchen.

The room was adorable and modern, with a completely outfitted kitchen and a small sized stainless-steel refrigerator, stove, and dishwasher. The miniature area had light grey wood cabinetry and shining metal handles. The counter was a gleaming granite top, and Christina ran her hand over the cool smooth surface as she looked around.

The amount of work that had gone into the cabin was amazing. It was a different place with the same layout. There was a small sitting area off the kitchen that led through to a bedroom where a large, king-sized bed was visible. The windows all looked out onto the pond, shining in the sunlight. Although small, the cabin's layout was well designed and made good use of the space.

She continued her self-guided tour by going through the bedroom door, stepping into the cozy space as she slowly pushed the door fully open. Immediately, the small door to her left abruptly opened, engulfing her in the warm steam of a recent hot shower. Kevin appeared before her, dripping wet with a small towel wrapped loosely around his hips.

She gasped, startled. He glared at her, black eyes burning with wariness at her intrusion. Recognizing her immediately, his demeanor changed from murderous to a surprised welcome. "Well, hello," he said, a crooked smile growing on his lips.

Her body immediately responded to him. After all, she had been recently thinking of their past in this cabin. She awakened at his nearness, his nakedness, and his dangerously distracting presence. "Oh, so sorry to bother you... I was looking around and saw this cabin.... where we–" She stopped herself, stumbling over her words and using lame hand gestures to fill in what her brain could not.

He stepped closer. She could smell the scent of fresh soap off his warm, damp skin. His tangled black hair dripped onto her toes as he leaned over her. His brown eyes were dark and treacherous. Her body tingled with his nearness, and she found herself unable to speak. She licked her lips.

"I remember," he said, his voice a low murmur.

Not believing the instant effect he was having on her after only minutes of stepping into his bedroom, she stepped closer to him. She was close enough to feel the heat from his skin, which brushed her bare arms, making her nipples hard. They pushed up against the thin fabric of her t-shirt. She could feel his breath on her face and in her hair.

He reached out a large, calloused hand and placed it on her hip. His fingers pressed into her buttock, pulling her close. "Tell me you remember."

He ground his nearly naked body into hers, pulling her even more closely with one steely, muscled arm. His breath covered her face, his lips inches from her own. "I... I remember." She whispered as he took her mouth with his demanding lips.

The world swayed. She reached her arms up to place her hands on his muscular biceps, sliding them upward to clasp his broad shoulders. She leaned into the kiss as her mutinous body responded to him. He rumbled against her lips, as one hand released the towel it held, wrapping her in his arms.

She melded into his body, which was now naked and hard against her shorts.

Ending the kiss, he ran his mouth over her ear and down her neck, biting and tasting as he went. The heat between them rose in a turbulent wave, undulating rapidly between them as they kissed again. He clasped her in his arms as his lips traced her neck down to the rise of her breasts. Her blood coursed through her veins, waking rapidly to his touch. A wanting rose inside of her with a terrifying need.

She pulled away from him as he grasped her behind. She ripped her t-shirt over her head and threw it on the floor, quickly disposing of her shorts in the same manner. She reached for her bra, and his hands stopped her.

"Let me," he said. Again, his head dove for her breasts as he gathered her up in his arms. His teeth grazed the delicate skin of her breasts as he slipped the straps from her shoulders. He unhooked her bra and let it fall to the floor. As his hands caressed and cupped her breasts, he kissed and sucked her nipples. She arched her back, thrusting them further into his grasp.

She was on fire. Her skin burned at his touch, and she felt herself become drenched and ready for him. She shook with the immediacy of need.

He took her again in his arms, moving her back to the large inviting bed. He pushed her down on the edge as he pulled her panties off, and covered her with his mouth, incinerating her as she came hard and fast. He continued to tug and lick as she moaned and lurched on the bed, mindless in the intense pleasure he brought her.

She reached for him, pulling him to her as he reached to the bedside table to retrieve a foil packet. He was then on top of her, his hands everywhere as she moaned and responded to his touch, her skin burning and electrified. He kissed her deeply as he entered her, hot and boiling. Unable to hold himself back from her matching demand, he thrust into her as she cried out and orgasmed again. And then he followed her into the oblivion.

They lay joined together for several moments as their heartbeats slowed and they caught their breath. He gathered her in his arms, wrapping himself around her as they settled into the soft bed.

"What just happened?" she whispered.

He chuckled low in his throat, shaking his head. "I think you may have missed me."

She smiled and smacked him weakly with her open hand, surprising herself as she snuggled into his arms, settling in. She closed her eyes, trying to get her bearings. What just happened was indescribable and so very out of character for her. She was not accustomed to taking to bed immediately with any man, much less someone who she had not seen or spoken to in years.

*He **was** an ex.*, she thought as she tried to rationalize her behavior to herself. It was not like he was a complete stranger and she just ripped off her clothes and had sex with within minutes of being alone and in a bedroom together. She kept her eyes closed as she tried to determine her next steps. Should she leave? Stay? It was later in the afternoon by now, and she had wanted to discover what had been done with the cabins. She needed to piece together what the status of the inn was in order to develop her plans.

There wasn't time for this–whatever this was. She wasn't that kind of girl, whatever that meant.

"Just relax," he whispered, laying his hand over her shoulders. "I can feel the tension rising up in you, while you try to figure out your next steps."

She opened her eyes and looked up at him, lifting her head from his chest. God, he was gorgeous. She had forgotten how handsome he was. She had pushed his memory away, just like she'd pushed all the memories of Vermont away when she left. It had been suffocating to stay and wait for Annie to return. She had left to survive and move on. She had left him behind–simply walked away from this man that loved her.

They gazed into each other's eyes. Emotions began to rise in her for this man as he held her in his arms. Her eyes began to well with unshed tears as the beginning edge of her feelings rose up from the depths of her soul, where she had kept them under lock and key.

Abruptly, he kissed her lightly, and turned over in the bed. His back was to her as he pulled the covers around him, leaving her unceremoniously uncovered in the middle of the bed. "I'm going to nap before I head back out on the trail. I have to be out there for a few days."

He snuggled into the pillows, getting comfortable and settling down. Then he immediately addressed her. "See you around. Shut the door tight when you leave." He settled in and closed his eyes while she sat stunned on the side of the bed.

Dumbfounded by his lack of overture and sudden indifference to their afternoon tryst, she quietly located her clothing. She grew more insulted and disgusted with herself as she pulled on each article, yanking up her shorts and shoving her feet into her sandals. Kevin began to snore, further pushing her over the edge.

Heading out the door, she shoved it closed, making a loud bang as it closed against her efforts. She was mad now. She had not wanted him to pursue her, and yet she had thrown herself at him the minute they were alone. As she was thinking of a way to gracefully leave and act as though the afternoon hadn't happened, he had just pushed her aside and asked her to close the door on her way out!

She stalked back to the inn, covering the path at double the speed she had coming over, her feet crunching loudly in the gravel. Jim had moved from his afternoon siesta, but she failed to notice.

She yanked open the back door to the inn and let it close behind her with a bang. "Hey!" yelled a chorus from the kitchen as she stomped her way up the back stairs to the third floor. She charged into her room, where she slammed the door closed behind her.

She ripped off her clothes, throwing them where they fell and stepped into a scalding shower. She immediately poured bodywash all over her skin to remove the scent of him.

Then the sobs came, silent and wracking at first. They grew into hearty cries as she wept, releasing the feelings that had been kept under her strong façade for so long. Long moments passed as she sobbed and sobbed. Her tears streamed down, washing away in the stream from the shower. Over and over, she gasped and moaned, letting the grief and sorrow leave her.

After a long time, with her fingers wrinkled and her gut sore from her sobs, she turned off the water. She wrapped herself in a soft bath towel and flopped down on the bed exhausted and strangely relieved.

She wrapped herself, still damp, in her bedclothes and closed her eyes. She was drained.

Because maybe, just maybe, she had wanted Kevin to want her.

CHAPTER 14

The past few days had been quiet after the break-in with her car and her encounter with Kevin. His absence had given her the space she needed to think things through and explore her feelings toward him more. It was clear that she still had a strong attraction to the man—the sexual connection to him was visceral. He had been her first love after all, and much of their relationship had revolved around getting away to be alone together.

The potential of their relationship had been stymied by Annie's sudden disappearance. Her feelings of guilt and worry about Annie had clouded the last year of their time together. Kevin had been supportive, since he had similar feelings about Annie, but he couldn't fully understand the depth and misgivings that she had felt. She had pushed him away, and eventually left him and her aunt behind. Their relationship did not survive the distance, and admittedly, she didn't even try to make it work. At the time, she had needed to put space between herself and this place. The distance had lessened the heartache over her missing cousin.

Now, she felt grateful for this time, where she could sort out her feelings without Kevin around. She knew, based on his nonchalant response to her, that he did not harbor any depth of emotion for her. She had just been a convenient option presented in his bedroom the other day when he was naked. She had clearly only been affected by the environment and her memories of him.

Today, she dove into the inn's business records and had made significant headway in creating a business plan as she reacquainted herself with the overall operations of the inn. Gina had offered further insight and guidance into the potential for the restaurant. She was grateful to have included her on this trip–not only was she an easy guest and travel companion, but she also offered endless depths of information on restaurant management. She truly brought enthusiasm and vision for expanding the dining area.

At the advice of Victor's attorney, she had opened a new business account, and was forming a new corporation to manage the inn, instead of using what had been established and long used by Ada. This move untangled her from any dubious transactions that could have occurred when her aunt was ill. Apparently, the attorney had uncovered irregularities regarding the inn operations and was digging into it more deeply under Victor's direction. They had both advised her to not worry about it and told her she should start fresh with a new account and funding.

She planned to follow their direction, but instinctually, felt that something was amiss, simply due to the diversion from Victor. Telling her 'not to worry' was an invitation to be concerned from her perspective. He knew she would inquire about the irregularities, but she also knew her stepfather kept information close to his chest before he would divulge his conclusions. She respected that about him. He was not one for gossip or rumors, particularly in business, where there were reputations at stake.

Victor had transferred a substantial sum to the new business accounts, and Christina had been mortified at her inexperience in terms of what was needed for start-up funds. She quickly realized that her expertise was in the overall operations, not in the start-up activities. Victor had assured her that he was considering it an investment, and that he knew she would pay him back eventually, regardless of whether she sold the inn or if she continued to run the business. Her drive for independence was ingrained, and she fervently wished that she didn't need to be subsidized by family. She was Victor's only child–even though he was only her stepfather–and she knew he supported her out of love, but she did not want to rely on his money. She needed to continue to establish herself as a strong, independent woman.

Victor's money would support operations for several months as she made decisions, and either got the inn running or sold. This infusion of cash really helped her to focus on making a good business decision, instead of being influenced by the need to make immediate money. She was unsure about the need for renovations, and should she decide to keep the inn, wondered how that work would be funded. She would like to avoid debt if possible, and since the profit margins would be narrow for the first years, seeking alternatives would be the best strategy to consider.

Last night, she and Gina had a call with the operators of The Inn at Stowe that had been referred by the attorney. It had been enlightening conversation in that there were many opportunities to have the inn run in a similar fashion with seasonal outdoor activities and special events such as weddings and formal parties. The owner of The Inn at Stowe happened to be on her way back from a long weekend on Cape Cod and promised to stop by that afternoon on her way home. She had been excited that Christina had contacted her, as she had not ever been inside the Stone House Inn and was eager to see the historic building.

Christina was inspired by the possibilities she had seen offered at The Inn at Stowe. Even if she opted to sell the property, there were other potential opportunities for the property that would make it appealing to anyone that was interested in running it as an inn.

This morning, Jeremy was going to bring by the developer who was interested in buying the land surrounding the inn. Back in her youth, Christina had not visualized the full expanse of the property that her aunt owned. The overall acreage was surrounded by national forest, except for the few farms along the road into town. The expanse of land was impressive to someone that was used to living in the close quarters of New York City.

As she knew from all her years with Kevin, land took attention and maintenance with trees and hazard avoidance. Not to mention, expansive property came with high taxes and liability, which concerned Christina. Right now, the land around the inn was not posted, and was open for hunting and other outdoor activities. She needed to have a conversation with the attorney and insurance company to determine if there needed to be any action taken, or if there were any risks if she decided to expand amenities and offer outdoor activities. When she opened her mind to the possibilities of risk with the land ownership, the prospect of selling became more enticing.

A low growl from the dog under her feet indicated Jeremy was approaching the office as footsteps sounded in the hallway. The recently named Chipper had become her constant companion since he had found the two women on the trail in the woods. So far, no one had claimed him as their missing dog, although his picture was all over Facebook and the Sheriff's website. She had grown fond of the animal who was determined to not leave her side. Maude and Jim had adopted him as well. She caught Maude in the act of feeding him some choice table scraps last night, so she wasn't alone in liking the mangy mutt.

Jeremy knocked on the open door. "Hi there. Aren't we looking productive?" he commented, his eyes taking in the newly neat and orderly office. "The developers are just behind me and should be arriving shortly. Do you want to meet in the front room? It's more private."

"Let's go into the dining room," she offered. "There is a bit more space to spread out."

A shadow passed over Jeremy's face and was gone as quickly as it had arrived. He placed an overly cheery smile on his lips, but the fake smile did not reach his eyes. "It's a bit open, don't you think?" he asked.

"Its fine. I've nothing to hide," she added, gathering a notepad and pen, and heading out of the tiny office toward the dining area.

The small office seemed to be made more confining with Jeremy's arrival. She found herself uncomfortable when she was close to him, and the confines of her Aunt's old office exacerbated the feeling.

Maude was in the dining room, brushing a feather duster over the windowsills that looked out onto the patio and stone walls just beyond. The morning sun shone brightly through the gleaming windows. "We're going to have a meeting in here shortly," Christina advised Maude, "Is there any coffee left or maybe muffins? Really anything of the sort would be great."

Maude turned and smiled at Christina, ignoring Jeremy completely. "Sure thing, Hon. I'll bring some in."

Jeremy's face changed to a snide expression, but he failed to make further comment. It was clear from the set of his shoulders and his stiff expression that he was displeased with Christina's setup for the meeting. He refrained from commenting, and Christina chose to ignore the derisive look he gave her.

He was getting more difficult to be around, and her patience with him rapidly degenerated at every turn. Clearly, he was dismayed at the loss of control he was experiencing as Christina took over the inn and sifted through the business records to make an informed decision to keep or sell the inn. As they settled into their seats at the large dining table, Jeremy looked at her as if he wanted to say something, but then quickly looked away, all while rubbing his hands on his thighs.

Christina noted a sheen of perspiration on his forehead and the dark circles under his eyes. He kept quiet while they waited, for which she was thankful. She was not feeling generous to share her business plans with him or to ask further questions of him. It was apparent that he was aware of her change in demeanor toward him. Undoubtedly, he still held out hope that she would still engage him in the overall business and there would be a role for him in the plans.

They both heard the heavy front door of the inn closing and Jeremy leapt to his feet to quickly attend to the expected visitors. Christina pledged to herself to keep an open mind to the discussion they were about to have, as she followed Jeremy to greet the team from the development group.

Much later, after several cups of coffee and a few freshly baked cookies conjured by Maude; Christina's mind hummed as she studied the large map of the property that the group had left behind with her. They presented a professionally put together presentation, along with prototype sketches of the proposed buildings, which would house the condos they were planning to build if she accepted the deal. It was all a bit mind-boggling to absorb, especially with the enormous offer they had provided to buy the property from her.

She was dumfounded at the amount they were willing to pay for something that she did nothing to own. From her own assessment, she knew that sum would be more than substantial to support the inn into the future and provide a nice living for her. The developers were not interested in the inn itself or the immediately surrounding property. The tract of land that they were interested in would set them close to the ski area toward the east, therefore attracting more buyers and renters for their condos than the property immediately alongside the inn. Therefore, the overall tranquility of the inn would not be impacted directly, per their explanation.

From their perspective, it was worth a strong consideration. If she decided to run the inn, then according to them, it would not impact the overall activity of her business. But at the same time, if she decided to sell the property, she would be breaking her land into two separate parcels, with a smaller one remaining for the inn. She would need to consider the impact of that transaction. Either way, she stood to have a substantial financial gain from her inheritance.

Sitting back in the dining chair and running her hands over the property map, she considered her options. There were a couple of wild spring fed ponds on the land parcel that the developers were interested in. As she ran her fingers over the pages, memories of watching a family of deer drink from one of those ponds with Annie arose in her mind. She had been fascinated to see the wildlife so close. Then another memory took its place–it was of Kevin, jumping naked into one of the ponds many years ago. Her mind drifted to the keen recent memory of his warm flesh beneath her palms.

"Hello," Kevin said softly while clearing his throat. He stood in the doorway from the kitchen. "You are a million miles away."

Startled, her hand flew to her chest, and her belly flipped, surprised with his unexpected appearance. It had been particularly shocking, as she was just fantasizing about him. "I... I didn't know you were back," she said, rising to her feet.

He held her gaze and approached her slowly. Her heart began to race in her chest. The last time she had seen him was their encounter in his cabin that had left her humiliated. She could not believe that her body was responding to him again. Anger and desire rose conflicted in her belly; her heart pounded in her chest.

He reached the table and smiled, as a smoldering flame rose in his eyes. "Did you miss me?" he asked huskily, with his eyes on her lips.

She stepped back from his approach, and an unexpected warmth grew on her face. In her awkwardness, she let go of the map and it floated to the floor, along with the developer's proposal. The falling paper distracted both of them, and they knelt to retrieve the documents.

The map caught Kevin's eye as he replaced the paper back on the table. "Building something?" he asked, his eyes taking in the content of the documents as his brows furrowed deeper the more he absorbed.

He was about to ask further questions when Gina and an elegant woman, attired in white pants and white flowing blouse, entered the room. "Look who I found wandering about the parking lot!" Gina exclaimed over Kevin.

The woman had an easy grace with her hair pulled back in a classy French twist. She revealed her brilliant blue eyes as she removed her Jackie O sunglasses. "Hello, so nice to meet you all. I am Claire Stone Devine from The Inn at Stowe." She put her perfectly manicured hand out to Christina.

Christina took her hand and introduced herself, subtly wiping cookie crumbs on her pant leg. "Stone? Are you related to my aunt?" This was an interesting development, although Stone was a common name.

"Yes, but only distantly. Her husband was a cousin. My condolences on the loss of your aunt, my dear," said Claire. "Oh, but I'm so happy to be stopping by. I have always wanted to see the inside of this inn." She paused a moment, taking in the room before her eyes went to Kevin.

It was then that Christina realized that Kevin was filthy, since he was freshly back from a few days and nights on the trail. His grime was in direct contrast to the white attire of their guest.

Surprising them all, Claire gasped, clutching her chest. "Kevin?" She laughed; her voice melodious as she beckoned him to her. "I didn't recognize you."

He took her offered hand tentatively, cautiously avoiding soiling her gleaming outfit.

"Let me look at you. I haven't seen you in years." She took him in as her gaze traveled thoroughly over the tall man.

Christina felt an unexpected pang of jealousy and tried to tamp it down. She interrupted the inspection. "It's so nice of you to stop by, on such a short notice...."

Claire waved her off with her free hand, not taking her eyes away from her assessment of Kevin. "Not at all dear, not a bother. If I had known you were harboring the only child of my dearest departed friend, I would have come by sooner."

She touched Kevin's arm gently. "Anyway, give us a kiss, young man, and go get cleaned up. We can catch up when you are scrubbed and shaved. You clearly need both," she directed authoritatively.

Kevin obeyed and wordlessly leaned in to kiss the older woman's cheek. She waved him away, saying, "Now go. I'll wait for you, and we'll have a chat after I am done talking to these lovely ladies."

Kevin exited, summarily dismissed. Claire turned her superior gaze to the two women, saying, "All right then, let's have us a tour. Then we can chat over a nice glass of wine."

The three women chatted amiably on the patio after the tour of the inn. Christina's initial impression of Claire dissolved as she recognized the astute business sense the older woman possessed. Claire and her husband had bought The Inn at Stowe immediately after they had married, and at the time, it was a run-down local bar. Together, they had transformed the property into a charming estate that benefitted all the businesses in the town by bringing in weddings and business retreats. Their location turned out to be a solid centerpiece for increasing tourist activity to the area.

"In my opinion, my dear," Claire offered, "you are not starting from nothing as we had been. This inn is fully operational. And highly desirable should you decide to sell. If you decided to run it, though, I would gradually expand the overall offerings and amenities. You have two major things we didn't have, and that's property to expand to and a true history. You can expand to four-season outdoor activities. Your stables are in decent shape, so you could consider expanding to horseback riding, mountain biking, cross country skiing, or even snowmobiling."

Both Christina and Gina sat open mouthed as Claire shared her knowledge of all the business opportunities they might consider. It was overwhelming and exciting at the same time.

"Engage with your local businesses and establish relationships as you can benefit each other as you expand. And work with the town to do something about that road up here. It needs to be better maintained and widened to support the additional traffic your inn will create."

She took a moment to sip the Sauvignon Blanc Gina had procured that morning. Claire smacked her lips. "Exquisite. What wine is this?"

Christina glanced at Gina to answer. Smiling, she handed over the bottle, saying, "I got it just this morning at a local wine shop."

"Now that's what I am talking about, working with the local vendors and suppliers, creating a symbiotic relationship," Claire said, studying the bottle.

"What about food?" Gina asked.

"Getting to that, my dear. I take it it's an interest of yours?"

Gina nodded attentively, perching herself on the edge of her seat as she eagerly took in the advice.

"Food is of utmost importance. Your guests will expect to have fine dining options as well as a tavern fare. Your bar area seems sufficient to accommodate the tavern options. Of course, you will not want to become the local bar, so I wouldn't recommend too much expansion in that area. But it's always good to have a few interesting local ales on tap."

She peered into the windows of the dining area and then looked around herself at the patio section. Her keen eye also took in the view of the gardens and the valley below. "You have some real potential here to capitalize on this space. Frankly, my dears, I am jealous of this outside area.

"Honestly, should you decide to sell, I'd like to consider the option of buying. My husband and I would kill for an opportunity for a place like this," she said laughing gracefully.

The three women took in their surroundings as Claire continued, "I see weddings, receptions, family events, corporate events…. It would be easy to pitch a tent in this area."

"My vote would be to expand the dining room to include the overall patio," Gina offered.

Claire nodded. "A larger dining area would be nice. I am sure there are ways to work around the historic preservation needs in order to enlarge the overall space. A good architect can help you with that. It will be important to the overall financial success of the inn if you are able to accommodate larger groups by expanding this area while preserving its beauty."

Just then, they were interrupted by Kevin's appearance on the patio. He was freshly showered, and his hair combed neatly back. "I agree on the preservation of beauty and nature," he said.

Keeping Christina in his sights, he continued, "Preserving the natural beauty of the area, you will also help the overall business of the inn. That's the much better option over parceling up, selling off the land, and digging it up to build ugly ski condos."

Claire nodded her head in agreement. "Developers are the scourge of good land. They come in and build acres of ugly condos, trying to sell clients on the beauty of the place, but they are the ones who are ruining it by building there. Vermonters want to keep Vermont, Vermont. It's such a waste. You aren't considering selling to those people, are you?"

Christina inwardly shrank at the condescension in Claire's tone. All eyes were on her as she opened her mouth to speak, but then Claire interrupted. "No matter, my dear. It's none of my business. But before you make any decisions, please do your due diligence by looking at their other properties in person and not by examining the builder's 8 x10 glossies. I am sure there are other ways to raise cash if you need that. There are lots of conservation funds available in the state. Now, if you ladies will excuse me, I'd like a few moments to catch up with this young man." She waved the two women away and beckoned Kevin to sit beside her in the chair vacated by Christina.

Christina and Gina entered the dining room and closed the French doors behind them. Gina was excited, exclaiming, "I see such potential here! It's so enticing. Imagine if we both were to quit our jobs to stay here and make a go of the place?"

Christina smiled. "Sounds nice after everything Claire was saying. You would come with me if I decided to run the place?"

Gina smiled and nodded. "You tell me if its pure fantasy or not, but it sure is appealing."

Christina stood and looked around the dining area. It really was exciting and scary at the same time to have the option to run her own business. The thought of no longer working for a large corporate empire appealed to her. She wanted to be her own boss and build her own brand of hospitality. But it was also terrifying. She would no longer be protected by being an employer, and she would have employees and be responsible for the ebb and flow of the business. A business partner–someone she trusted, knew well and was a crackerjack chef –would be appealing.

Gina gestured to the documents left on the table from the developers. "You want to talk about it?"

Christina was again grateful for Gina's company and presence on this trip. Together, they reviewed the offer from the developers and discussed the potentials for the property. It was becoming clear to both of them that the inn had a great business potential that they could tap into and develop. Unspoken between them was what this opportunity would mean to both of them, if they were mutually included in the plans. It was wild to think that they might leave the lives they knew in the city–including their jobs, apartments and social circles–to take a chance on a new venture. It would be a big step, and a potentially life changing move.

CHAPTER 15

Christina entered her small office. She stood at the desk, sliding the note pad pensively across its surface with her back to the door. She was lost in her thoughts. All the potential aspects for the property were whirling in her mind, and she didn't sense a presence behind her until she heard the click of the office door closing. A flash of apprehension shot through her veins when she heard the sound. Suddenly, an iron grip clasped her wrist as Jeremy yanked her around to face him.

His face was contorted by rage and his eyes burned with fury. "I don't know what you are up to," he said with a voice shaky with rage, "but the bank accounts have been frozen."

She shook her head and tried to pull her hand out of his grasp. Her mind immediately inventoried whatever was in her reach to defend herself. Her years of living as a single woman in the city, complete with several self-defense classes, benefited her response to this outrage. Her free hand fell on a heavy, old-model stapler. She grasped it tightly, as her self-defense strategy fell into play.

"Let go of my hand," she demanded evenly, controlling the fear that rose in her.

They stood for a moment eye to eye. His rage was seething. Help was not far away, as Gina and Maude were in the house.

Kevin was just on the patio. Distantly, she heard the dog barking, likely outside.

"I said, let go of my hand," she repeated, raising her voice authoritatively.

He removed his grip on her hand and stepped back, releasing his breath, and looking at her with a disgusted sneer. She continued to clasp the heavy stapler in her other hand, stepping back as far as she could from him in the small office. He continued to stand between her and the closed door.

"There are bills to be paid and expenses to cover," he sneered at her. "I need access to the accounts to pay them."

"Then let me know what the bills are. They are my responsibility now, so you can forward them to me. If you have any expenses, submit an invoice and I will see that it is paid," she replied as she tried to keep her tone civil.

"I've been taking care of the place for years; a little notice would have been nice. I have payments set up in the accounts."

"I am the new owner, and I wasn't able to access the accounts. My attorney has formed a new corporation to manage the business and the property, so I will be managing everything from here on out," she said in a dismissive tone.

He took a menacing step toward her again. The look in his eye caused fear to rise further in her chest. Her heart pounded.

"Your lawyer?" he asked. The words dropping like acid from his lips.

His forward movement was interrupted by a frenzied barking at the office door as the dog pawed the wood of the heavy panels. Jeremy hesitated, and a shadow seemed to pass over him as he contemplated his next move.

The office door burst open as Jim let the dog into the office. "Here Boy," he said, "What's all the racket about?"

Jeremy stepped back, fear flashing across his face as the dog hurtled into the tiny room, growling. Christina bent down to welcome the dog as he burst in the room. She was grateful for his protective interruption. "Here boy!"

He immediately went into her arms, placing his body between the two adults. A low growl emanated from his throat as he fixed his eyes on Jeremy and bared his teeth. Jeremy stood stock still as the dog settled himself between them with his watchful eyes never leaving the tall figure.

"I think we are done here," Christina stated, attempting to end the conversation between them.

Jeremy glared at her, unmoving. "What about the land offer?"

"Like I said before, there is a lot to consider. I head back to the city in a few days, so I will need that time to think about all the options. They didn't give me a deadline to consider the offer, and I won't be pushed into a decision," she stated, becoming bolder now that there was space and a protective animal between them.

Although she had known the dog for less than two weeks, she had spent nearly every hour with the animal at her side. She had no doubt that he would likely attack Jeremy if he approached her again.

Jeremy raked his hand through his hair, leaving it disheveled. The dog growled quietly at the movement. He looked down at the animal with contempt written all over his face. Clearly, his plans were unraveling. The depth of the reaction puzzled Christina. She was the new owner, and it was in her rights to do everything that she had done so far for the inn. She had made it clear that she was capable of making decisions and would fully consider all options before taking any steps for the future of the inn.

Perhaps he had expected her to simply sell and walk away, just as she had done all the past years. Maybe he thought she'd want to maintain the distance between herself and the painful past. She was further puzzled by his reaction to the bank accounts. Did he really think she would have been fine to let him continue to handle things? And since she was not able to access the accounts, did he originally plan on locking her out? Clearly, there was more to this story. She also thought Victor had more information than what he was sharing. It was unnecessary for her to continue to work with Jeremy, since she was totally competent to move forward on her own.

"I can take over this project from here. Please send me the bill for your time. If I decide to sell, I'll connect with the developers. I have their information," she said authoritatively.

The venom in his look was disconcerting. "Fine. I'll send you my bill."

He yanked the office door open and it swung against the wall in a loud bang, rattling the old window in the office. Loud footsteps marched down the hall and the heavy front door slammed behind him, reverberating through the lobby.

The dog looked up at Christina, wagging his tail. His tongue lagged from his mouth in a half dog smile. She reached down and scratched his ears. "Well, that was interesting," she murmured to the animal.

Clearly, things were not going as Jeremy had planned. She knew she should be disconcerted by his angry reaction, but she was distracted by the conversations of the day. It wasn't the first time she had encountered an angry male when she showed her authority and independent thinking. He had had no right to question her, and she felt comfortable in her decision to let him go. Now, she wouldn't have to deal with him again directly.

After a brief time passed, she had moved onto other tasks and plans. She reviewed the options discussed earlier and her mind drifted away from Jeremy's behavior and their unpleasant interaction.

CHAPTER 16

Much later, after they had said their goodbyes and thanks for Claire's helpful visit and connection, Kevin found Christina in the office. The dog gave absolutely no warning of his approach; and instead, lazily wagged his tail when Kevin appeared in the doorway.

Kevin took her in for a moment, taking advantage of the time before she noticed his presence. It seemed so natural to have her sitting at the small desk as her eyes took in the information on her computer screen. He smiled at the furrow in her brow as she seriously studied what appeared to be a spreadsheet on her computer. She had always been a studious and contemplative individual when she was young, so it was nice to see that hadn't changed.

He was concerned about the sketches he had seen earlier in the dining room. They depicted the creations of the development in the pristine woods that he worked so hard to protect and preserve.

He had such an aversion to the development of wild land that it made his stomach roil. The ski condos at Haystack Mountain and further north exemplified his hatred. They housed a few hundred luxury seasonal residents. And therewithin was the issue; they were largely unoccupied. Their development had razed several acres of natural forest and disrupted the ecological landscape, and yet they didn't even fulfill their purpose. Instead, they'd only created an ugly scar of building along what used to be a scenic ridge.

Kevin wasn't opposed to the overall concepts of development and housing but felt that corporations should do so responsibly and where there was need. Destroying the overall nature as past developers had done was a major mistake. Selling a bill of goods and building expensive subpar buildings that created vacancies–and eventually rundown buildings–marred the landscape.

Honestly, this kind of development hadn't happened that much in the state, due to the regulations that took developers through their environmental and economic impact. A most recent memory was the debacle with the ski resort developer up north, who defrauded his partners and the investors with poorly constructed real estate that was nothing like the buildings he'd promised. He'd left the state and the courts to settle things while the buildings lay empty and decaying in what was pristine wilderness.

Kevin also knew that even though the landscape would be marred, there was something of an economic boom to the local area if more people would be brought into town. Restaurants and shops did well during the season, which then carried them through from foliage to springtime. Some of the region's ski resort developers had also built resort restaurants and shops, creating no need for the visitors to go into town for their dining or shopping needs. The interdependencies of business for the well-being of the local economy were vital to the survival of the small town. He saw the impact of tourism firsthand. He loved the local area and intended to remain there, making it his lifelong home, so its survival was important to him.

The hope was that the development and the economy could be in balance, so one did not damage the other. Kevin fostered the hope that Christina would see this issue from his perspective. The inn had a chance to be successful by capitalizing on the natural environment it sat in the middle of, as Claire had suggested. It would take a lot of work and some investment, but it was possible and likely to be a success. It would be easy, he knew, to sell the land she had no connection for development, but he hoped she wouldn't do it.

Claire had mentioned to him that she was extremely interested in the property, should Christina decide to sell. That had surprised him a little. He had forgotten that Claire was related to the Stone family. He wondered what that relationship had been like, as she seemed overtly intent on the overall plans.

He glanced at the proposal sum when the papers fell on the floor in the dining room. It was a tantalizing figure. Christina could cash it in and leave, never looking back.

Kevin realized that the decision was not his. He hoped that Christina would make the right choice, not only for what would be right for her and the business of the inn, but for the town and for conservation. His stomach roiled as he realized he couldn't push her in either direction. If he pushed, or encouraged her at all, it would drive her away. It was the last thing he wanted.

She was so close. She had come to him the other day, and he had been ecstatic to have found her in his bedroom. He was overjoyed when they made love, and he knew as soon as she came to her senses, she would overthink the situation and pull away. So he had withdrawn instead, and it had nearly killed him to do so. In that moment, he had what he wanted most, but he had let it go. He had spent the last few days on the trail, doing the hard labor of repairs just to give her space. He hoped he could prevent himself from screwing things up between them by showing her his true feelings.

But now he realized that the situation was changing. He felt that she was about to make a serious mistake. He would need to balance the need to protect the pristine forest and the driving need to have her back. He would have to convince her to see it his way.

His heart thudded in his chest as she noticed him at the door. She glanced up at him with a friendly smile on her face. All he ever wanted was feet away. He wasn't sure he could live through losing her again, even if it meant marring the wilderness he loved. He swallowed, his voice catching in his dry throat, and said, "Do you have time to go for a walk or a ride?"

She continued smiling at him, from the distracted look on her face he imagined her mind whirling with ideas and thoughts on the discussions from the morning. "Actually, I think that would be nice. I'd like to get a fresh perspective on the layout of the land."

An idea occurred to him. It was a glimmer at first, and then it became a full-fledged solid idea. It may just be what he needed to show her his perspective. And there was still enough daylight left for his plan.

"I have just the thing, if you can spare me the rest of the afternoon."

Speculatively, she nodded. "I hope you aren't suggesting a hard press hike through the woods."

He reached out and took her hand. "Come on, let's go. I actually have a plane–but don't get too excited, because I'm only a science teacher, not Christian Grey. It's a communal plane, so I own it with a couple of college friends. It's a four passenger Cessna."

She hesitated. "You fly it?"

He smiled, tugging on her hand. "You've missed a lot since you've been gone. I have my pilot's license now, so it's perfectly safe."

He noticed her hesitation and smiled. "Really, it's the quickest and clearest view you can get to see your whole property. Bring a camera, or your phone if it takes good pictures. You can refer to them later."

He smiled his most dazzling smile and said, "you know you want to."

CHAPTER 17

As they arrived in his restored '72 pickup to the tiny airstrip, Kevin appeared to be excited to demonstrate a side of himself that she had never seen. "Are you nervous?" he asked, noting she was rubbing her palms on her thighs.

"A little. I've never been in a small plane before," she replied. "Kind of both nervous and excited all at once."

She had gaped when she saw the tiny plane in the hanger, but then quickly hid her surprised expression from him as he proudly showed her around the plane. He seemed giddy to have her to himself and to be showing her the view from a few thousand feet in the air. "It's a crystal-clear day, there's only a little wind, so the flight should be generally smooth. We might run into some turbulence once we're over the mountains."

He went through his pre-flight inspection of the small engine, and all along the perimeter of the aircraft. She didn't understand what he was doing. He saw the puzzled expression on her face. "Routine safety inspection. It's normal procedure for any flight. Not just in this tin can."

Kevin helped her to get into the small plane and took a seat in the cramped cockpit. Christina took in a deep breath. "Oh boy! I guess we are really doing this…." She wiped her sweaty palms on her thighs.

Kevin started the engine and taxied them to the small runway. They both donned their headsets, as Kevin connected with the air tower and completed his pre-flight check list. Then they took off down the runway, rapidly gaining speed as they felt the nose of the plane lift. She took in a rapid breath. As the ground disappeared beneath their feet, her stomach fell and her brain tried to keep up with the sensations and the absolutely stunning view. "Holy cow! OMG!" she exclaimed. "It's so beautiful!"

It was a gorgeous late spring day with all the fresh green leaves showing in contrast with the deep colors of the pines and granite of the mountain rocks as they soared overhead. Beneath them, a river sparkled in the sunlight as it meandered into the distance. Homes with mowed yards and farms with plowed fields dotted the landscape. "Can you make out where we are?" he shouted over the noise of the engine.

She studied the earth beneath them. Her nervousness seemingly taken over by the awe-inspiring beauty below. "There's town, and the highway," she replied, pointing below.

He banked and climbed the plane higher, causing her to grip onto the seat. He shouted again, "There, just coming into view. Got your camera ready?"

She could make out the road to the inn as it appeared through the trees, and then the building came into view. It looked stately sitting on the mountain high above the town. Kevin gestured, saying, "All this land around the building is the inn's... so, it's yours."

She took in the immense space of green that surrounded the old building. It was overwhelming to realize the vastness of what she now owned and was responsible for. The plane bounced in a sudden burst of turbulence from the mountain air as Kevin again banked the plane so she could have a better view. She took advantage of their stalled position and snapped a few pictures as they coasted over the countryside.

Kevin pointed again. "Going further west and north is national forest land. That all continues through to East Arlington and to the north is the Glastonbury wilderness."

Christina snapped more pictures. It was likely she didn't know exactly where one ended and one began, as she was absorbing the overall expanse of her property. Kevin banked the plane again, turning back to fly over the inn and toward the east. "I think I see Gina down there!" Christina exclaimed. "It looks like she's in the garden, could I see her from up here?"

Kevin laughed. "It could be her. You have good eyesight to make out that it was her. You can see people pretty well from up here.

Now we can see the east and north end of the property. There is a strip of national forest between your land and the mountain ski area to the north." Kevin had apparently intended to show her the land from the sky, but his brow furrowed as they flew. She knew he really wanted her to see what he saw as they approached the developed land.

Shortly, a huge open ski area came into view. The open land was like a treeless gash on the mountain and had lifts and buildings dotting the landscape. Beyond the ski area was a large development of buildings, likely condos and a larger building that looked like a hotel. Parking lots dotted the surface beneath them.

Kevin again banked to the left, taking them closer to the mountain peak. The tiny aircraft shuddered in the winds. He glanced her way and smiled, saying, "Turbulence. It's the mountains, so you will always get it when you get this close. But I want to show you something."

They flew past the ski area and over a vast space of green. "See below?" he said. "That's all national forest. It's all protected into perpetuity. People still use the land for hiking, snowmobiling, hunting, fishing, and even some camping. But it will stay as it is now and remain a resource for everyone–undeveloped."

"I'm really not against overall progress," he added. "These forests help the fight against climate change. They absorb the carbon from pollution and keep the air and water clean, now and into the future."

He watched her face as she took in the vast greenness beneath them, and her expression became solemn. "I know you are trying to get me to see what you do," she said looking at him as he flew the plane. "It's really reassuring to see you're still passionate about conservation. It's nice to see that part of you hasn't changed." She smiled at him. It was reassuring and comforting.

They flew, not speaking for several minutes while taking in the incredible view beneath them. A large mountain loomed in front of them with its bare granite peak clearly visible. Kevin guided the plane higher, saying, "Let's see if anyone made it up to the top this afternoon."

Shortly, they passed the peak to the right, as a small group waved at them from the summit. Christina waved back, thrilled at the experience of being at eye level with people on top of a mountain.

"You don't see that every day!" Kevin exclaimed, laughing loudly, and smiling at Christina's ear to ear grin. Then he continued, "All right. time to get some work done. Keep an eye out for smoke or fire below. We can do a sweep to make sure all is well."

"Looking for forest fires, you mean?" she asked incredulously.

He nodded. "It hasn't been a big issue here, like in California. But there is always a chance that someone has lit a fire that got out of control. It's happened before."

They spent the next several minutes scanning the landscape beneath them, while Christina continued to appreciate the view. "I never expected to do this in a million years," she said. "I'm so glad and grateful that you brought me up here. It's thrilling!"

He smiled widely at her. She could tell that he was happy to offer her this experience. She knew that he had his own reasons to bring her to see the beauty of the land she now owned. Lands he apparently hoped that she wouldn't choose to develop.

After a time, Kevin turned the plane, so they were heading back to the airport. "Want me to pass over your land one last time?"

She smiled at him and nodded. He held her gaze for a moment, a grin growing on his face. He reached out and squeezed her hand. "I am so glad you came."

He quickly returned to the activity of flying the plane, concentrating on the numerous dials and buttons in front of him. She continued gazing at him after he turned away and she felt herself drawing closer to him emotionally.

She was not blind to his attraction since she had known him through his teens. This adult version of him was a captivating mix of rough outdoors and fine wine. His chiseled chin was freshly shaven after the dress-down by Claire. She detected a small nick just under the ridge of his jawbone and she resisted the urge to reach out and touch his face. His long fingers were wrapped around the yoke of the plane, and his wide shoulders brushed hers as it jostled through the air. She recalled how those muscles felt under her palms. She felt herself drawing toward him, recalling their passionate interlude a few days ago. A yearning began to grow in her belly.

He turned his head back toward her, and their eyes connected. She was watching him intently. The look in his eyes changed rapidly from surprise to sensuous intent and the air crackled in the small cabin.

A sudden jolt of turbulence dropped Christina's stomach and Kevin turned his attention back to flying the plane. "Distracting the pilot may be a federal offence," he joked. Then he pointed to the inn on his left. "Look there, beautiful view!"

Christina nodded and snapped some more photos with her phone, hoping they would do the spectacular view justice. The plane banked and they were again rocked with the air currents from the mountains, so she gripped the handle over her head. He turned and smiled at her; the earlier passion kindled in his eyes. She returned the smile, a promise passing between them, and she wiped her hands on her thighs as her stomach flipped. She felt her heart turn ever so slightly, creating a new tenderness toward him.

She enjoyed the feeling for a moment before pulling herself back to reality. She could not let 'whatever this was' with Kevin cloud her decisions or make her come back to stay. She had been given this once in a lifetime chance and she needed to make the right decision. There were a lot of opportunities for her to consider, as well as some big mine fields for her to avoid. She needed to be clear and pay attention to what was happening in front of her.

He again banked the plane to head back to the airport. His smile wide as he turned to her, seemingly unaffected by her self-inflicted coolness. "Time to come home," he said, prepping for a landing.

She had never realized how simple and complex flying a plane could be. The checklists and the procedures that Kevin followed to ensure their safety as the tiny tin can flew in the sky were necessary. After all, there was just a thin metallic sheet between them and the earth that was thousands of feet below. It was simultaneously terrifying and thrilling. She had never expected nor thought of taking a ride in a small plane–certainly never with Kevin piloting it. He was full of surprises.

He landed the plane efficiently at the tiny airport, pulling back into the hangar they left from earlier. He secured the plane as she waited for him, thumbing through the photos she had taken from their flight. Most were good and gave her an excellent perspective of the land surrounding the inn. This would make her decision-making so much easier as she considered all the options laid before her over the past few days.

"Hungry?" he asked as he pulled the hangar door shut and secured it. "Never mind, I forgot who I was talking to. Of course you're hungry!"

They laughed together, the light mood surrounding them. He took her hand, saying, "there is a new restaurant near here. I think we should stop by and give them a try."

She was hungry, but that seemed to be her permanent state of being. He opened the truck door for her as she slipped inside. She liked that about him–that he had impeccable manners for someone that spent most of his time alone in the woods. You would not have known that by looking at him, especially as he steered the antique truck out of the airfield lot. He was self-assured and at ease in his own skin.

She imagined he would be as much at ease in a boardroom as he would be deep in the forest, but he wouldn't be as happy. He had always been committed to staying in the rural town, or similar place, and she recognized that he had achieved his goal. His career as a biology teacher combined with his summers on the trail gave him what he was looking for. He had built a life and had not pined away in her absence. Life had moved on.

They arrived at a quaint restaurant built in what was an old home from the early days of the town. Several of these stately residences still existed in this neighborhood, although most had been converted into apartments, and others had been repurposed for business use. Along the same street there were signs for attorneys, dentists, and real estate agents in similar old buildings.

A young woman with long, straight dark hair met them at the door of the restaurant. She was shapely and attractive with a long dark dress that swept the tops of her high heeled sandals. Her eyes lit up seeing Kevin, and it was obvious she was attracted to him as she greeted them both, because her eyes never wavered from his face. Christina felt an unwelcome twinge of jealousy for the second time in the past several hours, but she tamped it down. She had no claim on him.

The young hostess showed them to a small table situated in a large bay window looking out onto the street of the small town. "Here you go, Mr. McKinley. Your waiter will be right with you," she said, smiling at Kevin seductively.

She left them at the table and Christina raised an eyebrow at him. "Mr. McKinley?"

He smiled. "One of my ex-students. She graduated a few years ago."

"Seems interested in biology," Christina commented.

Her meaning passed over him, as if he were unaware of his impact on the hostess. He nodded absently, moving his attention to his menu.

They settled in with their menus for a few moments in silence. She noted that although the menu was small it offered fish, meat, and vegetarian options. They all looked appetizing, and Christina's stomach growled. A waiter appeared in a starched white shirt, black tie, and black apron, and inquired about their drinks.

"What do you recommend?" Christina asked while searching the short wine list.

"There is a nice Oregon Pinot if you like reds, or a sauvignon Blanc from California. Nice and crisp. Perfect for a day like today."

Christina agreed and accepted the latter. Kevin ordered a stout ale.

"Nice place," Kevin remarked, looking around the dining room. "It's small, but classy. Good to see that they are busy on a weeknight, and so early in the evening too."

Christina nodded, looking around and noting the fine points of preservation in the house from the marble fireplace to the soaring ceilings and ornate moldings. It appeared that they had taken the time and consideration to restore the building back to its heyday in the early 20th century.

Kevin noticed her scrutiny, "So what are your plans for the inn? Are you thinking of remodeling?"

She noticed his hesitation in the conversation; this was a touchy subject between them. She really wanted to avoid getting into a conversation about her overall plans for keeping or selling the property fed right into whether she was planning on staying or leaving. She vowed to be careful where their conversation went. She really wanted to have a pleasant meal, hoping it would give them a chance to reconnect.

She nodded, returning her attention back to her dinner companion. "Yes, I am thinking that we would need to expand the dining area to help establish the restaurant. It would also be nice if we were able to offer space for events."

Kevin nodded. "Events? Like weddings?"

She smiled at him. Clearly, this was not a topic in his sphere of comfort, but it was nice that he was attempting to make conversation with her. It felt good to be with a man who did not constantly turn the subject to himself, as most of her dates in the past years often did. "Yes, weddings and corporate events. We would be able to put up tents if we expanded the dining room and the patios to accommodate for that."

"Sounds like you know what you are doing. Did you do this sort of thing in New York?

The waiter quietly placed their drinks on the table, promising to be right back to take their orders.

She sipped her wine before answering. It was delightfully crisp, as the waiter had promised, and tingled her tongue. "At the hotel, I manage the overall operations and have been involved in some of the expansion and construction of new or remodeled properties. So, to answer your question, yes and no. I've been part of the team, but I haven't been the front-line person and decision-maker. Yet."

He nodded and sipped his beer. She knew he was curious about her life in the city. "Sounds interesting," he offered, staying neutral.

She smiled, sensing his caution. She appreciated that he was interested in her life, and also wondered about him and the turns his life had taken. But she decided to pick a safe topic, saying, "I was so sorry to hear about your dad. You said he is doing better?"

He visibly relaxed as she switched the conversation back to a subject he was fully comfortable with. "Thanks for asking; he's really doing well. He had a rough patch, but came out of it. He is a tough guy."

"I'm glad to hear it. I hope you relayed that I was asking for him?"

"Sure, or you could tell him yourself," he started to say something and caught himself. "I meant, he stops by the inn on occasion. You might have the chance to run into him."

She nodded, catching on to his attempt to be neutral in their topic of conversation. "That would be nice to see him."

The waiter reappeared, distracting them both from the awkwardness of the conversation. Christina decided to try the fish and Kevin ordered the beef. The waiter took their orders and disappeared again, leaving them sipping their drinks.

She took out her phone to glance at the pictures taken during the short flight. "Kevin, I really can't thank you enough. These pictures are great. It really gives me a perspective I could not have gotten any other way." She handed him her phone with the photos displayed.

"Oh yeah, these came out really well. Nice camera you have there!" he exclaimed, thumbing excitedly through the pictures.

She pulled her chair closer, allowing both of them to see the photographs. Her leg brushed against his, and she didn't pull away. She felt as though it was natural to be so close to him. Their confines inside the cockpit of the plane and his truck had her feeling relaxed with his proximity.

He set her phone on the table in front of them, reaching under the table to grasp her hand in his. Her heart leapt in her chest as her small hand disappeared in his. His gaze smoldered. "I was glad to be able to take you up."

"I was certainly surprised that you fly," she replied, not removing her hand from his. She sipped her wine to distract herself from his intense gaze.

She fumbled, her hand shaking slightly and causing the wine to miss her lip. He reached out a long finger, capturing the dribble and smoothing the liquid over her lower lip. Heat rose in her immediately at his touch. Her face blushed as he stared at her mouth.

"I like surprises," he whispered huskily.

The waiter reappeared with their salads and bread, interrupting the moment.

She was glad for the distraction. He had such a profound impact on her. It was immediate and strong, so unlike when they were younger. It was as though their attraction was enhanced over their absence from each other. She had not ever felt anything like it.

They ate their salads in silence. Her chair remained close to him and their thighs touched under the small table. The entrees arrived quickly, leaving no time for further conversation.

The meals were excellent and artfully plated. Simple fresh ingredients, she noted, always made the food taste better. They knew that in the kitchen of this restaurant. They made small talk as they ate their meals. Both enjoyed their selections as they cleaned their plates.

"Is Gina your partner at work?" he asked as they ate.

She thought about how to answer him. "She is one of my best friends and we work together. She is also one of the best chefs I have ever worked with. There is nothing that she can't cook or create."

"She made breakfast the other day–it was fabulous. I can't believe that Maude has been letting her in the kitchen. They must have really bonded."

Christina nodded enthusiastically with her mouth full of food. "I know! And Shawn has been hanging around quite a bit."

"Might be some interest there," Kevin smiled knowingly.

"He says he is just checking in on the dog," she said as they both laughed together.

It was obvious to them that Shawn was interested in Gina, and not just for her knack in the kitchen. "I hope he makes a move," Kevin started. "But he may be hesitant, not knowing how long she'll be around, I'm sure."

"Well, I hope he makes a move. If not, she will," Christina laughed. "But we both have to be back to work on Monday."

There it was; the timeline. The expression on his face abruptly changed as she answered his question, searing his heart at the same time. Monday was only four days away, if they stayed through the weekend.

She felt his hand reach under the table to find her hand again, but his hand found her thigh instead. Her skin felt as though it caught on fire as he touched her soft flesh. He swallowed deeply, gazing intently into her eyes. Her heart flipped in her chest at his touch. Her eyes fell to his lips. He was so close she could feel his breath on her face, warm and enticing.

His hand shifted up her thigh, and her eyes flew open. "Don't worry, no one can see," he whispered, leaning in to delicately take her lips in his.

She couldn't believe this was happening. The effect he had on her was mesmerizing. She wanted him.

Their delicate kiss ended, and Kevin signaled to the waiter for the check. He completed the transaction wordlessly, keeping one hand on her thigh under the table. They exited the restaurant, thanking the waiter and hostess while moving efficiently to Kevin's truck parked on a dark side street.

He mutely assisted her into the cab of his truck and slid into the driver's seat next to her. In a flash, he took her in his arms. His mouth covered hers as his strong arms clasped her against his hard chest. She was instantly on fire, kissing him back passionately and pressing herself against the hardness in his jeans. He groaned loudly at her movement, gaining control, and holding her still in his arms. "I want to take you right here. God, Crissy, you are so beautiful."

She wantonly pressed herself against him, kissing his neck.

He groaned. "God, I want to, but I can't. I'm a teacher and this is a public place—not a good idea."

She stopped on his words, trailing kisses up his cheek. "Let's go home," she whispered sexily against his chest as she pulled back.

He nodded, starting the engine, and roaring the old vehicle to life. They headed back up the mountain. She remained next to him in the middle seat as he drove down the highway, before the turn off on the bumpy dirt road to the inn. He reached over, wrapping an arm around her, pulling her as close as the seat restraints would allow.

Old memories surfaced for both of them, of the many nights like this where they drove around the rural roads, thigh to thigh in his old truck. This vehicle was similar, but a slightly newer model. They turned onto the dirt road to the inn, and Kevin laughed out loud. "This is just like old times, with you and me riding down the road."

She smiled, as she was thinking the same thing. Back in the day, they'd ride down the road looking for a place to park–someplace private where they could be alone together. Her mind drifted further the closer they came to the inn.

Bad memories began to rise in her mind. They had been alone together before, and something horrible had happened while they were consumed with each other. She had been selfishly distracted by their own sexual desires, while Annie was experiencing something that made her go missing. Annie was likely dead, and she had not been around to help her when she needed her most.

A chill rose in her chest, consuming her, and tamping down her desires for the man beside her. Immediately he sensed the change in her, he asked, "Crissy?"

He slowed the speed of the truck, as he tried to see her face in the dim light of the dashboard. Tears glimmered on her face. "Babe, oh baby."

He pulled over to the side of the road, taking her in his arms the minute they stopped. "Oh Crissy, Oh Crissy..." he whispered to her, kissing her face, and wiping her tears.

He held her against his chest while she attempted to compose herself. It was suddenly overwhelming as she experienced a flashback to a happy time with him where their whole lives were ahead of them, until they suddenly weren't. Annie's disappearance had changed everything.

Emotions that she had controlled for so long welled up in her. Feelings of guilt and longing for her missing best friend rose to the surface like a rising storm. It was uncontrollable, as wave after wave of sobs rose and fell as she wept.

He held her as her body rocked with the unshed tears from years of suppression. It was shocking that she had held in this depth of feeling and sadness. She had pulled away from him all those years ago. He had likely felt the sting of her withdrawal. She blamed herself, blamed them both, for not being there when Annie needed her the most. Inheriting the inn in Annie's place had given her a jolt. It was like a switch had flipped inside her.

"Shh," he said, "It's all right." He continued to hold her while she shook with sobs.

Years of tears rose from her depths, released by the trigger of being with Kevin. She cried until her sobs were reduced to minor tears and her throat was sore. Her chest ached and her breath burned in her lungs. Kevin's shirt was soaked from her tears. She quieted; sobs still wracked her breaths as he continued to hold her close.

"I'm so sorry, baby," he said, wiping the tears from her face. He pulled her close again, kissing her hair as he did so. "It must be so hard for you, coming back and reliving this all again."

She nodded with her face against his chest. She felt embarrassed to have let loose like this with him. Her outburst had been uncontrollable, and she was mortified. She was in conflict. She wanted to be with him, but when they were together, it brought back all the turmoil she had left here to forget.

"It's not your fault," he said in a whisper.

She stilled in his arms; he could feel her body stiffen as he said the words. He tightened his hold on her ever so slightly. "It's not your fault," he repeated firmly.

Her sobs lessened after a time, and she lifted her head to look into his face. It was shadowed in the light from the dashboard. "I should have been there for her," she whispered up to his face.

He pulled her tight against him again. "There was nothing you could have done," he stated solidly. "Whatever or whomever made her leave was not any of your doing."

Her darkest thoughts often went to what would have happened if she had been with Annie the night she disappeared. Would they both be gone? Would whatever force that caused Annie to go missing have swept Christina up in its clutches? They had discussed this many times in the past. The realization had stunned Kevin. His desire to keep Christina safe thwarted his feelings of guilt. They had been together the night Annie went missing. He had always said he was thankful for that. He had always said he did not regret the sin of feeling grateful that she had not been in danger.

The police had theorized that Annie may have been a victim of a random abduction and was likely dead. She was supposed to have left the inn to drive to a party with their small group of friends. Her car was found parked along the side of the road to the party – a long dark stretch of country road with which they were all familiar. There was no signs of struggle or foul play.

She was just gone. Not a sign, not a trace, and not a speck of evidence. It was like she had vanished into thin air.

They sat in the truck at the side of the road, holding each other, as the storm of her emotions passed over. She felt comforted by his words. She knew in her own sensibilities that she was not at fault for Annie's disappearance. The guilt she bore, simply because she hadn't been there, was overwhelming.

"I think we all felt the same," Kevin said. "If there was something we could have done differently, something we could have picked up on, that would have made a difference for her.

"We have all had this trauma squarely in our rearview mirrors for such a long time. I have worked through it, Shawn has made peace with it, and Ada... well, she lost her only daughter." He continued, holding her in his arms. "I know it's why you left and why you never really came back."

He held her away from him to gaze into her face. "My feelings have not changed, Christina," he proclaimed, his voice hoarse with emotion.

Her heart flipped in her chest, and a combination of hope and dread filled her. It was what she had hoped for and what she feared. Deep in her soul, she knew she still loved him, and it tore at her. It was a deep and unending ache.

"I don't know if I can do this..." she whispered.

At her words, an insidious chill slowly rose and passed between them. They both felt it. Her skin prickled with the coolness that grew between them.

Quietly, he reached around her and buckled her seatbelt. He slid over and refastened his seatbelt in the drivers' seat. The engine roared to life, and he gunned the truck forward, spraying rocks behind them. They jostled over the dirt road and arrived in silence to the inn, pulling up to the front portico.

He leapt out of the truck and opened her door as soon as he cut the engine, his feet crunching on the gravel drive. It was still early evening and the inn's lights were lit. Christina was unsure of what to do. His reaction to her words chilled her, and more than that, she was emotionally spent.

He took her hand and led her to the front steps, pausing to face her. She looked up into his face, shocked by his tortured expression. Was she the cause of this pain?

He looked into her eyes, pausing before speaking, as if he was searching for the right words. Her heart thudded against her ribs as she tried to gather herself. Dread and fear began to grow in her belly. It was a long moment before he spoke, his voice raspy and low.

"I can't live with wanting you more. You say you can't do this. But do what, Christina? Can't be here? Can't live with living while Annie is gone?"

His hands grasped her upper arms as he spoke into her upturned face. "Can't be with me?"

His words stung, searing her heart. It was true, he was here where all those memories resided. The guilt she felt for loving him had driven her away. She bit her lip and fought back tears.

He leaned in further. "You threw us away to lessen the guilt. You chose to not live because your cousin was gone. It won't bring her back." Then he relaxed his grip on her arms and pulled her to him, cradling her face in his muscular chest. "I am right here. I am alive." He whispered in her ear, "It's up to you."

At those words, he released her, leaving her unsteadily on the steps as he got into his truck and pulled away. Tears streamed down her cheeks as sobs wracked her breaths.

Everything she could ever want was in her reach, yet she was unable to allow herself to claim it.

CHAPTER 18

Christina felt herself relax in the saddle, giving way to the symbiosis of rider and mount. The horse knew this trail, she realized, relaxing a bit more. She barely had to guide the horse's chestnut head down the path. The leaves of the trees overhead created a green canopy with small openings for the light of the day to reach them. Christina smiled contentedly in the saddle, remembering other rides like this years ago. Jeff had carefully chosen their mounts and guided them through the woods.

Today the group was considerably smaller than it had been in those other outings in years past. She realized she was very happy that Jeff had suggested they take a ride today, even though it had been a last-minute decision. The weather was perfect for it, and it was soothing to have something else to think of. She and Gina needed to leave by early afternoon to get back in the city for work first thing Monday morning.

Christina knew that this outing was more than a joy ride on horseback from Jeff's perspective. He was very interested in working with the inn to provide trail rides in the warm weather, hayrides in the fall and sleigh rides in the winter months. Even as she was enjoying the day, and the lulling movement of the animal, her mind was considering the business opportunity – if she decided to run the inn, that is. She knew next to nothing about horses; her only experience had been with Jeff. With his livelihood now linked to horses and their services, he spoke about them endlessly and with apparent passion. The idea intrigued her.

The horses nickered to each other. She wondered what they were saying as they both slowed, and Jeff pulled his horse next to her on the trail. "You should be aware of the hiking trail ahead," Jeff said, taking the bridle of Christina's horse in his gloved hand. "I don't see anyone, but they are both acting like someone else is around."

Jeff lifted the horses head to face him. "You do as you are told, lassie," he said, scolding the animal.

He turned back to Christina. "I take these two on this trail a lot with the tourist groups," Jeff said. "You could just sit in the saddle, and they would bring you back to the stables. However, you still need to pay attention. Sometimes we run into hikers crossing the trail, but most of the time we don't. People get surprised meeting horses in the woods, so their reaction can make them uneasy. Mind yourself."

He nudged his mount. "Let me go ahead of you on the trail. Just in case we meet some pot head hikers who want to pet a horse..."

Jeff moved ahead of her on the trail and her horse followed without any urging forward from Christina. She laughed out loud. "She sure knows the way!"

Several yards up the trail, Christina could make out the place where the hiking trail intersected the path they were on. Surprised, she thought she saw some movement ahead. She could barely make out the figures through the trees, but it looked like a man was standing while another was lying on the ground. Jeff had noticed them as well and urged his horse forward.

Christina's horse abruptly stopped and snorted the air. She suddenly leapt forward in a fast trot to follow her master and her mate. Christina startled but held on, her legs gripping the horse's sides. "Whoa, girl..." she called, bouncing in the saddle.

They quickly caught up to the pair, and saw that Jeff was now dismounted. He and the other man now crouched over the person laying on the ground. It was a woman, and her leg was wrapped in what looked like a makeshift bandage of a red t-shirt and other clothing.

Kevin's voice was immediately recognizable as the men who were leaning over the woman on the ground spoke to each other. His tone was urgent as he spoke. "I stopped the bleeding with this pressure bandage. I'm not sure how long she's been here. She's lost a good amount of blood."

Christina startled, what she had originally observed as a red shirt on the woman's leg, was not naturally that color at all. It was soaked with blood. The woman's face was pale and gray, but her youth and striking beauty remained apparent.

"I radioed for help. Mountain rescue is on their way," Kevin said. He stood up and looked her way, nodding a bare acknowledgement. His eyes moved from her horse to Jeff's, and his expression shifted from a frown to hope.

"Hey Jeff," he said. "Do you think we could take her out on the horse? It would save some time if Rescue didn't have to come up here on the four wheelers."

Jeff stood and considered. "We can, but it looks like she may experience some shock. It'll be a slow go, walking her down on the horse."

Kevin looked at Jeff. "I wasn't thinking of walking her – that'd take too long. Could one of us take her on horseback down to trail base?"

Jeff contemplated the idea briefly, then nodded. "We could, but I'd better be the one to do it – I can keep her steady as I ride... she looks to be pretty light."

"Of course you could! You are the best horseman I know. Want me to hand her up to you?"

"She needs to keep that leg up," Christina chimed in. Both men looked at her as though they had forgotten she was there. She slid off her mount. "Let's get her up. I can help."

Although injured and clearly woozy, the hiker smiled through grimaces of pain as they gently lifted her onto Jeff's horse. They laid her awkwardly astride his saddle while he supported her in his arms. They bound her leg in a makeshift splint and positioned her so her leg wouldn't dangle.

Seconds after settling her into Jeff's arms, she smiled up at him. "Ready?" Jeff asked of his wounded passenger. With a nod from her tousled blonde head, Jeff nudged the horse forward urgently. "Go!" he cried.

They watched the trio bolt through the trees. Christina placed a hand over her heart as the urgency of the situation became real. She turned to Kevin, who was keying his portable radio. "Mountain Rescue... victim on her way with Jeff on horseback. Should meet at trail head. Copy?"

He spoke into the radio while gazing at her intently. The penetrating eye contact caused a fluttering in her stomach. She pushed the feeling aside. She was angry her body was still responding to him, even after the mess of their last encounter. Guilt and a tumble of confused thoughts and feelings filled her.

Unsure of what to do under his scrutiny, she reached out to steady her horse, grabbing onto the bridle. "I suppose we should follow. Do you have to go to the hospital with her?"

she asked uncertainly. She prepared to mount the horse, but then realized that Jeff or someone usually helped her up.

Kevin watched her, which made her sincerely hope she wasn't about to fall on her backside instead of into the saddle. Then he moved toward her. "Here, let me give you a leg up," he said, grabbing hold of her leg as she hopped onto the horse. With the movement, their bodies brushed closely.

Christine inhaled sharply, responding to his proximity. "I'm not as fast as Jeff, or as sure on horseback, but we can get going...." She trailed off at the questioning look on Kevin's face.

The portable radio crackled in Kevin's hand and the horse nickered in reply. "McKinley... you copy?"

Kevin put the radio to his lips. "10-4," he responded.

"You have an ID on the girl?" the staticky voice queried.

"Negative, but her first name is Layla – that's all I could get from her," he replied, shaking his head.

"10-4," the voice in the radio responded.

"Let me know when they get there," Kevin asked.

She looked down from her mount at him, knowing the look on her face had question-marks all over it. He smiled up at her and effortlessly mounted the horse, landing gently and snugly on the saddle behind her. It surprised her, as she was not expecting him to join her in the saddle. Her body immediately came alive at the contact.

"Relax, relax," he said softly in her ear. He reached forward for the reins, pulling her more closely to him. His breath was hot on her neck. He clucked his tongue and urged the horse forward.

"I'll drive," he said as the horse trotted down the wooded trail. "We should get moving in case they have trouble before they reach rescue. Luckily, Jeff is the best horseman I know, so he'll get there as fast as he can."

They were silent for a while, as the horse hooves made rhythmic thumping sounds on the forest floor. The movement of the horse forced their bodies to move together rhythmically. She could feel the heat rise in her face and knew she was blushing deeply. All the while, though, he remained focused on the trail.

"What happened back there? How did she get injured?" she asked, attempting to take her mind off their proximity and the arousing motion of the horse.

She felt him shake his head behind her. "She was really lucky I found her. I almost didn't see her since she was laying off the trail. I could have easily missed her."

The radio crackled again, and he waited several moments before answering as the trail had become steep and the horse had slowed. Kevin guided her expertly down the mountainside. She felt his body tense behind her as he held the reins loosely, letting the horse have her head.

The radio crackled again. "We've got 'em. Heading to hospital."

"10-4," Kevin responded.

"Taking Jeff with us," the radio continued. "Could you make sure the horse gets home?"

"He all right?" Kevin questioned, pulling the horse to a stop. His body tensed again.

"He's fine – coming along for the ride. Girl won't let go of him."

"10-4," he replied.

"Sounds like she latched onto him." Christina smiled.

Kevin stored the radio on his belt. "She was pretty scared. There was no telling how long she had been by the side of the trail. It's not a well-traveled spot so there aren't a lot of people out here like the other trails. Weird she was all alone though."

"I take it this is an unusual occurrence?" she asked.

He shuffled in the saddle behind her. "Very," he answered, again wrapping his arms around her waist. He pulled her even closer to him, while nudging the horse gently forward. "Take it easy, nice and slow," he murmured to the horse.

Christina's blush deepened. This physical closeness made her body act of its own volition. Whether her heart wanted to be close to this man or respond to his hard, strong body was completely out of her control. The cadence of the horse was mesmerizing as she gradually began to relax against Kevin's chest. She was moving back to the bucolic state of mind that she had been experiencing before coming upon the injured hiker. She sighed heartily, thinking that if this had been another time without so much pain between them, this horseback ride would be romantic and ideal.

"I was surprised to see you today," he said. "I thought you were heading back."

"We go later this afternoon," she replied, leaning back, and tilting her face up to his.

He stared at her, openmouthed as if someone struck him. The sun lit her eyes and danced in her hair. He pulled up on the reins and the horse came to a halt. His expression changed and she knew he was thinking of kissing her. A fire erupted in her chest. She wanted him; she wanted his lips on hers. It was wrong. She knew she should not open herself to him like that if she wasn't sure of her intentions

She abruptly turned away and faced forward, out of the way of immediate temptation. He exhaled slowly, she felt him deflate behind her – if it was possible with their proximity. But still, she felt him pull his body away from hers. Her reaction to him was laid clear. After several uneasy moments, he gently pushed the horse forward and they continued the trek down the mountain in silence.

After what seemed like forever, they reached the trailhead. There were wheel tracks in the grass, indicating that vehicles had recently been there. No one remained and there was no sign of Jeff's horse.

"Oh no, the horse!" Christina exclaimed, looking around for the animal. "He must have gotten away in all the commotion."

"I'm sure that both these horses can find their way back home with no issue. Maybe they'll take a side trip to check in on the new filly on the way, but I can assure you, the horse will be back in the barn and eating his oats by the time we arrive."

"It's another mile or so from here, right?" she asked.

"We'll be fine," he answered, clucking to the horse to move on. "Riding like this is much more enjoyable," he said, chuckling. He wrapped one arm around her body and readjusted himself in the saddle.

"I need to check in at the hospital and do some paperwork. Damn inexperienced people on the trails, making more work for me."

"I hope she'll be all right."

"Me too. She seemed like a nice kid," he said, shaking his head. "It's very lucky you guys came along. I'm not sure how well she would have fared if you hadn't. Sorry to have ruined your outing."

Christina realized how difficult the whole ordeal must have been for Kevin as well. It must have been scary, finding someone who was severely injured and so far out of reach of immediate help. Kevin became her only source of support at the time. It was a great responsibility.

The old logging road was level and the horse had picked up its speed, trotting rhythmically through the woods. They were quiet for several minutes, each in their own thoughts as the mood lifted between them. Their bodies moved in sync again with the movement of the horse. He reached out to pull her closer and his hands lingered on her thighs.

Soon, they arrived at the barn. The horse whinnied as they approached the stables. The call was answered by several responses from within the barn. "Sounds like Jeff's horse has made it as well," Kevin said, swinging his legs down from the horse. Once dismounted, he led the other animal into the barn and closed the paddock behind them to contain both horses. He served out some oats and removed the saddle from Jeff's mount before turning to Christina's horse. He reached up and helped Christina dismount the horse, landing her body close to his own, between him and the horse.

He stood for a moment, looking into her eyes with his hands on her shoulders. She thought he was going to kiss her as he leaned toward her. Then he stopped, staring at her lips. "I want to kiss you," he said softly.

His statement shook her. She swallowed hard, looking at his mouth. He was so close she could feel his breath. Instinctively, she licked her lips. The slow burn that had risen in her belly grew to bursting as she looked at him.

His head moved downward, catching her mouth in his. The horse behind her moved away suddenly, startled by their movements and eager for oats. She stumbled forward and he caught her, pulling her in close in his arms as the kiss deepened. Her body responded to his, and she quietly moaned as he pulled her against his hardness. Stars burst behind her eyelids as all the cells in her body rang out for more of this man.

Abruptly, he pulled away, pushing her away and holding her shoulders. His breathing was fast as if he was trying to calm himself. They stood like this for seconds, at arm's length, breathing deeply.

"My car is here," she said after several minutes. "I can take you to the hospital."

He nodded his reply. "Let's see to the horses. Then you can drive me."

"I need to head back soon," she said. Her eyes were downcast as guilt began to rise in her chest again.

"I know," he replied huskily, making himself busy tending to the horses' needs.

He vowed to himself silently that he would do whatever was in his power to convince her to return to him.

CHAPTER 19

Christina shoved the last of her belongings into her bag. They hadn't been shopping, but it seemed like she had more to bring back with her than what she had brought in the first place. She contemplated leaving some belongings – how bad would it be to stow a pair of jeans and a sweater or so? It would be just in case. Even though she realized that she hadn't made any decisions yet as to what she was going to do with the inn, she was clearly going to have to come back here to settle things. What harm would it do?

She removed a few items from her bag and hung them in the closet, knowing this meant she intended to be back. She heard Gina making her way down the stairs. Her foot falls were heavy with the burden of her bags. They needed to get on the road, but Christina was finding it hard to get herself going and together. The activities of the morning and the injured woman were on her mind, but mostly her hesitation was coming from her lingering feelings toward Kevin. She could still feel him against her body and his scent lingered in her nose. She pulled the collar of the shirt she wore toward her face and inhaled deeply. His scent was still there. She smiled inwardly.

Heavy, tired steps sounded on the stairs. Maude knocked on her open bedroom door. Her face was flushed, and she seemed sweaty and out of breath. "Pull those sheets off that bed for me, will you, Crissy? I'll wash them with Gina's." She turned and walked down the hall.

Christina was thankful for the elder couple and their presence at the inn. They did a respectable job keeping things in hand. She knew they both were interested in her decision, as the property was home to them. Their well-being was a top consideration; Christina wanted to make certain they were well taken care of if she did decide to sell.

She zipped up her suitcase and lugged it to the car, down the two flights of stairs and through the quiet lobby. Jeremy had not been back, and she had not heard from him since their last conversation. Victor had not been in touch to provide any further detail on the old accounts, and she made a note to follow-up with him. She wanted him to disclose what was behind the frozen accounts and was certain there was more to that story than what Victor was letting on.

She put her bag in the trunk of her car. The broken window had been repaired by a local car dealer. The missing computer had not been returned nor were there any leads for the Sheriff to follow. It was an odd occurrence, but they had attributed the break-in to the recent rash of petty crimes likely driven by the need for drugs. Not unlike many parts of the country.

Gina was leaning into the passenger side of the car, riffling through her handbag. "Dammit Christina, I can't find my phone. I had it earlier, but I can't find it now. You didn't happen to see it, did you?"

Christina shook her head. "No, the last time I saw you with it was this morning, when you were taking pictures. Did you leave it in the kitchen?"

Both women entered through the main door into the lobby. Jim was at the desk, looking over what appeared to be a broken box. Gina went into the kitchen to search for her phone. Upon further examination, Christina realized the broken box was actually one of the game cameras Jim continued to have issues with. With this one, it appeared that the outside casing was smashed. "What happened there?" she asked.

"I don't know. Seems like I just can't keep these things workin' where I put 'em," Jim replied, flipping the broken box over on the desk. He seemed pitifully sad about the broken camera. "This is the last one of the bunch. Now, all of them are broken. Useless."

Christina felt bad for him. She had always been fond of Jim. These broken cameras were really disturbing him. There was something mysterious about what had been happening to his game cameras, because each one had been dislodged, or fallen from the trees, and broken beyond repair. It was a puzzle. He liked to use them to capture pictures of animals that were in the area. That way, he could locate any that were causing disturbances in his gardens.

Gina walked past them and up the stairs on her way from the kitchen. They could hear voices upstairs as she encountered Maude making the beds in the rooms in which they had stayed. She was likely searching upstairs for her phone.

Christina sat with Jim for a bit, discussing the game cameras and whether he would replace them. They were a gift from their son, who lived somewhere out in Arizona. She realized it was unlikely that he would replace them, and she felt bad for him that his gift had been ruined. He evidently enjoyed looking at the animals he photographed.

They conversed further as they heard Gina's footsteps overhead, moving to the second floor in her search for the phone. "You know how to reach me?" Christina asked Jim.

"You can go ahead and use that credit card I gave you for expenses, but make sure that you save your receipts. I think I've got everything covered."

"Still not sure what you are doing with the place?" Jim asked.

Christina shook her head.

Jim reached out and patted her hand. "You'll be back."

The dog sauntered into the lobby, perfectly at home. He approached the desk and flopped himself on the floor at their feet, dropping his toy on the floor with a clunk.

Puzzled, Christina looked down at the dog. She had not bought him any toys, but had snuck him a few dog bones, which he seemed very satisfied with. What Christina had thought was a toy was actually Gina's phone. The dog had retrieved it from somewhere.

"Gina," she called, "I found your phone."

She and Jim laughed together.

"Are you sure you are all right to keep this monster?" she asked him. "We still haven't heard that the owner has been located."

Jim nodded his head. "He's no trouble at all. Reminds me of the dog that Annie had when she was a little girl."

Christina nodded. She wondered to herself if she should warn them off Jeremy. She didn't trust that he wouldn't be around in her absence. Then again, the older couple had been around him forever, so forbidding their interaction just seemed like it would cause more problems.

Footsteps came down the stairs and Gina appeared. "I looked everywhere! Where did you find it?"

Christina handed her friend her cell phone. "You may want to wipe it off really well," she said, nodding her head toward the dog laying at her feet.

"Oh, you animal!" Gina exclaimed. She reached down to scratch his ears and she pressed a few buttons on her phone. "Still works fine."

The three of them laughed lightheartedly. "Guess it's time for us to hit the road," said Christina.

They heard heavy footsteps coming down the stairs. Maude reached the lobby; she was sweating profusely even though the day was not overly warm. Big damp circles of perspiration darkened her dress under her arms and in the middle of her back. Jim's smile slowly faded to concern as he observed his wife's approach. "Ya all right? You're lookin' winded."

Maude approached the group. She went to say something, but her speech was all garbled. She clutched her chest with both hands, dropping the bundle of sheets in her arms. She collapsed onto the floor as the three all grabbed for her to stop her fall.

"Maude, Maude!" Jim cried. "What's going on?"

She clearly lost consciousness as she lay on the floor with the three of them gathered around her, shocked at what was happening. Christina immediately thought she was having a stroke or a heart attack. "Call 911," she directed Gina. She felt for a pulse. It was there and she was breathing. Christina desperately tried to recall her training in first aide.

"Oh no, no..." Jim cried holding her hand. "Don't leave me, Maudie..."

Christina realized that the paramedics would be far away, as they would have to come from town. They needed to do whatever they could to help Maude. "Jim, is there anything we should know. Does Maude have a heart condition or high blood pressure? Has she started any new medicine?"

He looked as if he was struggling to remember. "No.... nothing new really. Recently, her sugar's been really high and really low, on and off. She has to take shots now and then when its high."

She and Gina exchanged a look. She was on the phone with 911. Gina repeated what Jim had just said. She listened, and then looked up at Jim. "They are asking if she had to take any insulin today?"

"I .... I think she did." Jim stuttered, trying to calm himself. Maude seemed to be getting worse. Her breaths were coming faster, and she seemed to be uncomfortable.

Gina relayed this information. "What? A blood sugar level? Glucagon? But how..."

Christina immediately knew what that was. A school mate had had a testing kit and glucagon injections in case of emergency. "Jim," she said, "does Maude have any test strips or shots for emergencies?"

His face went blank for a minute as her stomach fell, they needed to do something quickly if Maude's blood sugar wasn't controlled. "Oh, yes, yes. She has a kit in the medicine chest."

"I'll get it!" Christina bolted from the floor and ran out the back to the caretaker cabin. She would retrieve it faster than Jim could. She bolted into their cabin and into the bathroom. On the small counter she observed finger sticks for blood sugar monitoring and a machine as well as a vial of insulin. She grabbed the insulin bottle, the monitor and the red emergency shot of glucagon.

She ran back to the lobby as fast as she could move. Gina told the 911 operator that they had the monitor and the injection. She placed the operator on speakerphone, and they walked through a few steps to get a blood sugar reading and then gave Christina instructions how to give the injection to Maude quickly. Jim jumped in to take the reading, as he had been taught recently as well. It read "low". The operator instructed them to give the emergency injection. Christina's hands were shaking as she tried to hurry. She injected the medicine into Maude's thigh.

After a beat, she noticed that Maude had bright pink icing on her lips. She looked questioningly at Gina. "That's icing from the cupcakes we made yesterday," Gina explained. "They thought it would help."

Maude seemed to be calming down, her breathing seemed easier. Outside they heard sirens as the ambulance made its way up the mountain. Christina exhaled; help was here! She was hopeful that they acted fast enough for Maude to be all right.

She went to hold the door for them and direct the paramedics to Maude. The squad was just pulling in the driveway followed closely by the Sheriff's vehicle. Shawn barreled out of his cruiser and joined Christina. "What's happened?"

"It's Maude. She passed right out. She's in the lobby on the floor. Jim and Gina are with her."

The paramedics entered the lobby and quickly began working on Maude, taking her vitals, and examining her. One took a fingerstick blood sample. They were on their radios to the local hospital, relaying information and reporting their findings. One of the paramedics started an IV and waved Christina over.

"When did you give her the glucagon?"

Christina relayed the information and showed him the insulin vial from Maude's bathroom. The paramedic took it from her and examined the vial. "Why does this have Ada Stone's name on it?" he asked, puzzled.

"Oh, that's nothing. Maude was just using it after she passed away since they have the same prescription. I thought it was okay."

The paramedic frowned and looked more closely at the vial. He peeled up the prescription label and examined the label underneath. Christina observed as he carefully peeled a second label back on the vial. A stunned expression crossed over his face as he double checked what he was looking at. "Shit," he stated quietly heading back on the radio.

He turned away from the rest of the group and spoke urgently to the hospital. He had a brief and serious exchange with his colleague. Apparently, the hospital was giving them further orders, as they both rapidly responded and injected medication into the IV they had started. They worked quickly and moved Maude onto the stretcher and into the ambulance. "Her blood sugar is dangerously low. We have given her medicine to bring it up, she is stabilizing, but we need to get her to the hospital. He put the insulin vial back in Christina's hands. "Bring this with you to the hospital. The ER doctor wants to see it."

Christina stuck the vial in her pocket, realizing it could have been so much worse. Maude could have been home alone when this happened. She could have had the same fate as Ada. Her hand touched the vial in her pocket that was originally Ada's medicine. Something reared up in her mind, but she couldn't get her brain to focus on it due to the current emergency situation.

Something wasn't right.

CHAPTER 20

The small group sat closely together in the fluorescent lights of the hospital waiting room. Their posture was tight as they sat in the uncomfortable chairs. Anxiety filled the air as they waited. Christina tried to nonchalantly check the time on her watch.

Gina caught her eye, and they exchanged a worried gaze. Jim had remained latched to her side throughout the ride to the hospital and throughout the lengthy period that they'd been waiting to hear word on Maude.

Kevin joined them after running into Shawn and hearing what had happened. Kevin had been in and out of the group, taking some time to talk at length with Shawn, who had arrived after them and was elsewhere in the building. Shawn had attempted to have a conversation with Gina alone, but Jim would have none of it. Christina was apparently a poor substitute for the kindness of her friend, who had been a stranger only a few days ago. She tried to not take it personally.

There was another small family that had been waiting in the lounge prior to them, but they recently left after hearing the good news for their loved one. Anxiety flared in Christina's chest as she thought of the ramifications of what could have happened. The insulin vial rattled against the keys in her pocket, reminding her of what the paramedic had said about the labels.

She pulled it out of her pocket to have a look. The bottle was small and more than half full. The label on top was a normal prescription label, beneath that was a label that said *regular insulin U 100*. Underneath that label, that the paramedic had peeled off, it read *regular insulin U-500*. She didn't fully understand what she was looking at and pulled out her phone to Google it.

She did some quick research, and her stomach dropped. The original label on the vial had a higher concentration of insulin than the second that had covered it. The prescription matched the lower concentration.

The doctor came out to speak to Jim and did so quietly. Jim responded with smiles and was eager to go and see Maude. The doctor guided him back and Gina went with him. After they had disappeared through the double doors, the doctor turned back to address her. At that moment, Kevin joined by her side. "Christina?" the doctor asked.

"Yes," Christina nodded. "Do you have something the paramedic asked you to bring?" he asked. She showed him the vial. He took it from her and closely examined it. "The paramedics reported that Maude was using your aunt's insulin. Typical frugal Vermonters," he said, shaking his head and handing her back the vial. "This is mislabeled, as I am sure you have seen. The vial is a high concentration insulin. I believe that is what caused the low blood sugar reaction. It was a good thing that she was not alone."

The realization of what might have happened to Ada started to form in Christina's mind. "If Maude had been alone, and no one was there to help, what could have happened?" Christina asked the doctor.

"She would have died."

The doctor took in her shocked expression. "Look, I am not telling you what to do, but this is clearly mislabeled. The fact that Maude was taking someone else's medication may be a factor here, but I was working the morning that your aunt was brought in. Now, I have a very strong suspicion about what happened to her."

He hesitated. "I really can't say more except that the mislabeling of that vial means that the patient will get five times the dose of insulin they are expecting. You have just seen what it can do to a person."

"Is Maude going to be okay?" Christina asked.

"We're going to keep her to be sure. But she was lucky you were all there and knew what to do." He pushed the vial back into her hands and walked away.

Christina sat down heavily in the waiting room chair and looked closely at the vial. Kevin sat next to her and studied her. "Can I see that?" he asked. He carefully reviewed what she had already seen. "It was filled at the local pharmacy. I have heard of pharmacies making mistakes before, but that doesn't seem to be the case here. Here, the drug is clearly mislabeled, like the lower concentration label is covering the higher concentration label."

They sat side by side, staring at the vial, each trying to piece together the scenario. A deep foreboding came over Christina. It could have been an error, but it also could have been intentional. It appeared to her that someone could have popped off a label from a lower concentration insulin and placed it over the higher one. An unsuspecting person could use it, thinking it was the lower concentration, and their blood sugar would decline much lower than intended – just as Maude's had done. If they were alone, that person would be dangerously low, just like Ada had been – except she did not recover.

A chill climbed up her spine. Did someone do this intentionally? Was Ada murdered? What would have been the reasons for it? Who would want her dead?

Christina deftly slid the vial into her purse. Later, she would take the time to figure out what to do next. Her gut was guiding her to say nothing more. Everyone except Gina and herself had been involved with Ada closely over the past years. Christina would figure out a way to dig deeper and find out what happened. She and Gina would need to call work, because there was no way that either of them would be there in the morning. They were needed here in Vermont.

Kevin took her hand easily in his, seemingly oblivious of what she was thinking. It was as though they had not been apart for years, she reflected. She appreciated the ease with which he offered his comfort to her. He was so solid and comforting. She took reassurance in his presence and was wordlessly grateful for his attention as her mind turned over all her worries.

Two additional figures appeared in the doorway to the waiting area: Shawn and Jeff. Christina looked questioningly at the latter. "Jeff?"

"Just wanted to check in to see how things were going," he said, acknowledging her question. "I was up here, checking in on Layla."

It took her a moment to recall who he was referring to, as she had momentarily forgotten that their trail ride from that morning. It felt like a week had passed, not less than six hours.

"How is Layla doing?" she asked.

"Going to be okay," he replied. "She was incredibly lucky that Kevin came along when he did."

The doors opened to the ER and Jim and Gina reappeared. Both were smiling. "She's gonna be okay. They'll keep her tonight anyway, and maybe a couple days." Jim took a seat next to Kevin and Jeff sat next to him, engaging him in conversation about the events of the afternoon.

Gina grabbed her arm and led her down the hallway to the ladies room, leaving Shawn in their dust. "We need to call in. We *can't* possibly make it to work tomorrow," Gina said in a rush to get into a stall. "They are all going to freak since we've already been away for two weeks. The place has got to be a mess."

Both women finished up quickly, washing their hands and exchanging mutual anxieties about Maude. "Shawn's still out there," Gina said, opening the door to leave the restroom. "I think he wants to talk to both of us."

Gina hesitated, looking at her friend. "He is so hot in that uniform. I swear I am going straight to hell. Not the time or the place for dirty thoughts like mine."

They made their way back to the waiting room where the men waited, and Shawn approached the pair.

"What happened exactly?" Shawn asked as the women took their seats again, waiting for Jim, who had gone to talk to the hospital admission clerk about insurance.

Gina proceeded to tell Shawn what she had observed. They became immersed in their conversation, shutting out the rest of the group.

"You're not heading back tonight, right?" Kevin asked Christina.

She shook her head. She was so relieved that Maude was going to recover that she hadn't realized that she had been holding herself so stiffly. As the tension left her body, she found herself exhausted. A long night drive back to the city was totally out of the question.

The priority would be to get Jim calmed and taken care of now that they knew Maude was going to be all right.

Kevin reached out and gently squeezed her hand. "Let me know what I can do for you."

For yet another time that day, she was thankful that he was there for her. His solid presence was reassuring and comforting, and she knew she could rely on him.

Jeff slid easily into the chair beside Christina. "Busy day for us both. I haven't been back home since I left you on the trail. Thanks for seeing to the horses."

"Glad to hear she's doing okay; whatever happened to her?"

"No idea. She apparently was on the trail with a group, but she got separated and was off on her own. She's a little spotty with her memory apparently. They think she has a concussion in addition to her leg injury."

"Nice of you to stay for her."

"Had to. She wouldn't let go of me."

The door to the ER swung open and Jim rejoined the group with a relieved expression. The tension was reduced in his shoulders. He looked years older but bore a smile. "She's a little groggy but she's telling them what to do."

Gina reached out to hug him and he held onto her shoulders with one arm.

"My cousin's girl works upstairs and will be her nurse all night," he told her. "She told me to go home. She said she'll call the house if anything changes."

"That's wonderful, Jim," said Gina.

"I know. She's going to be all right," Jim said, tears pouring down his face again.

Both women hugged the sobbing man, adding tears of happiness of their own.

"Let's get you something to eat," Gina said, leading him out of the hospital waiting room with the rest of the group trailing behind.

CHAPTER 21

"You're firing me?" she said, her voice rising an octave as she tried to respond to her employer's idiocy.

She watched the color in the younger man's face grow redder as he struggled with how to handle her explosive reaction. She realized it was likely that his uncle had left him with the dirty task of terminating her, so he could take her place. It was common knowledge that he likely really needed the job now that he was going to be married and had finished college.

"Not exactly firing you," he explained. He spoke slowly, as though he was making his voice as calm as he could. She knew she looked out of control and would like nothing more than to reach across the desk and throttle him.

She rocked back on her heels, venom rising in her throat as she looked at this kid with no experience in the business world. With just a few words, he'd capsized her world. "What the hell would you call it then? You just told me my job was being eliminated."

The whole thing was stunning. She worked all hours, and on holidays and weekends, to bring this resort to the level of financial success it was now experiencing. Without her work, her sweat and worry, as well as those she inspired to work hard with her, the resort would have not survived in the competitive marketplace of New York City. It was a family-owned business and when the current owner – the uncle of the brat that stood before her – hired her, they were headed to financial ruin. She saved this damn company, and this is how they repaid her? Promoting someone over her last year, and now sending in this spoiled kid to fire her? She knew that he would be taking her place, and she also knew that they would be right back where they were when she started, as they would have no experience and little business sense.

Good riddance.

As she stood looking at the privileged face of the young man that was desperately trying to fire her, she felt all the emotions from the past few weeks rise to the surface – the looming decision of what to do with the inn, Maude's close call, Jeremy's persistence, and the emotional turmoil with Kevin. Now this issue piled on top of everything she was feeling. All her hard work and drive, but for what? To be pushed aside by someone that was merely related to the owner? She was sick of being passed over and taken for granted.

As she stood there, she felt a sensation of calm wash over her. Her perspective subtly shifted as she realized in that moment that there was another clearly obvious option. She had her own inn that she could run. She had the talent, and the work ethic to make it successful. It was there in the palm of her hand. She did not need to try to play nicely in the sandbox with these juveniles that did not appreciate her any longer. From now on any hard work she did, would be for her own and her family's benefit.

"I quit." She said quietly. And then more loudly as she affirmed her choice, it was so obvious what she should be doing. "I'm done."

Then she walked out of the offices her head held high. She just left – they could send her personal things, although really, there was not much she wanted. There were no photos or personal mementos on her desk or on the walls of her office.

She waited until she reached the street before laughing out loud. A huge weight just lifted off of her shoulders. This was the push that she needed. She had a whole inn of her own to run, and she could be her own boss!

Hours later, she was wrapped in her quilt and laying still on her couch, in shock from the immediate change in her circumstances and contemplating her next steps. Gina called before she let herself in.

"Oh honey, you're going to be all right," she said hugging her friend cocooned on the couch. "I brought the necessities."

She unloaded her shopping bag of wine, ice cream and cookies while she consoled her friend. "Those bastards. I heard that they also demoted John from housekeeping, and they are announcing some further changes when the dinner shifts arrive. I am on my way in, but wanted to stop in to see my girl."

Christina appreciated her. Gina knew when to reach out and when to leave her alone. She also brought the right treats without being asked. Gina sat on the couch next to her, covering herself with another quilt and wrapping her arms comfortably around the other woman.

"I think that this was the universe giving you a sign – pushing you in the direction of your destiny. This was meant to happen."

They sat quietly together for a long moment, each in their own thoughts.

"I've been thinking," Gina started hesitantly, "I am not sure how you would take it, and if I could really pull it off...but after what happened today, I finally have the push to say it."

She inhaled deeply, fortifying herself. "Now that you are going to keep the inn and run it, I know I could make a go of it there too. I'd like to be your business partner, and I'd like to run the restaurant portion of the business."

Gina's words made perfect sense. There was no one that she would rather work with, or whom she trusted more than Gina. Her natural talent for food was unsurpassed. Christina believed that Gina would 'go places' she just hadn't gotten the chance to be fully in charge of her own place, yet.

A smile grew on her face as she considered it. "I wouldn't have it any other way."

Gina leapt from the couch, her small frame bouncing around the living room as she spoke. "Imagine the two of us, in charge of our own place. Doing the things that we know work well and not having to report up to the corporate boys."

"In charge of our own destiny," Christina replied.

She felt her energy changing, as if a weight were lifting. It was becoming abundantly clear that having the inn was a blessing, especially with the turn of events that morning.

"Are you ready to do that? To leave everything behind here to work and live in Vermont? There is not much happening there – socially, I mean. But running the inn would certainly keep us busy."

Gina appeared to be buoyed by her comments. "It's a wild leap for me, but I really feel right about it. I have been pondering the idea since the first day I walked into the dining room at the inn."

Christina knew she would likely need to sell her apartment to be able to buy into the business, and that would leave her with no home base in Manhattan. But with an ex-husband potentially moving back into the area, Christina knew that the idea of leaving Manhattan was even more appealing for Gina.

Christina's mind was whirling with ideas for the inn. It made her feel alive with potential concepts. It was appealing to consider being her own boss and making the inn a successful tourist destination and a local treasure for special occasions. It was a direct contrast to her bitter feelings of her job at the resort.

"What about your job here?" she asked Gina.

"With you leaving, I don't think I could stomach staying on. Those bastards have no appreciation for what they lost, or what they have."

"Don't throw it away just yet. I need to figure out financing for any kind of renovations," she replied. "I'm really hesitant to sell any of the land to the developers to raise cash."

Gina smiled to herself. She was sure that it was in both of their best interests to take the opportunity that was in front of them and make the best of it. The unexpected inheritance of a country inn with such potential would bring them both a decent living and give them control over their lives. The trade-offs between living in the city and all it offered to living in the quiet country seemed to be worth it. They could always visit the city again; this was a chance of a lifetime.

They sat together and chatted about their future, both deeply excited for the potential that it held for each of them.

CHAPTER 22

He knew this was a risky move. She could tell him to get lost. He could not risk it though. It was the thing that he didn't do the last time she left – go after her. Youth, inexperience, and his own heartache had kept him from acting when she left and did not return. The hope that she would come back had died over time, but his love did not.

It wasn't the actual city that he disliked, but he did not fit in here. The idea of all those people, living on top of one another on the 13-mile island, was disturbing. He was used to being one of the only humans in that size space, open and free. It was a nice place to visit, he chuckled to himself as he approached her address. It took him a bit of effort to get his bearings after getting off the train earlier and checking into the hotel. He was thankful for the common sense of the numbered streets and avenues because it made it easier for him to find his way around.

The day had passed achingly slow as he waited until early evening to go to her building, assuming she would not be home until later in the day. Likely she had a lot to catch up on after being away for two weeks. Doubt entered his thoughts as he considered that she may not be home yet. Perhaps she was out meeting friends for dinner or with someone else. He brushed the uncertainty aside; he was doing the right thing.

He was in love with her and wanted her in his life. He hoped she felt the same way – she had too.

She had to stop blaming herself for Annie's disappearance. It was not her fault; she had no blame in the matter at all. The lack of an answer for what had happened to Annie haunted them all of course. Maybe someday they would find out what had happened. Life had moved on in time, and they had learned to live with the absence. Most of them had moved on, and even Christina had learned to exist and focus on her work and career. She had shuttered herself emotionally, blaming herself for Annie and separating herself from the place where it had occurred. But that place that was a home for her; it was where she had family, friends, and love. Not able to face it, she had not dealt with the emotional impact. By going back this time, Kevin was really putting it out there for her. He wanted to place his feelings in the forefront, forcing her to face what she had avoided for so long.

He hoped that she had realized everything that she had missed by leaving. Her home was still there and he was still there. He stopped in the middle of the sidewalk; this was a big step forward for him. Her rejection was a possibility. His heart thudded loudly in his chest.

No, I'm doing the right thing, he thought to himself. There was a solid chance for them to be together and for her to grow whole and purge the guilt she felt. She had a chance to build a wonderful and prosperous life. It had been literally handed to her. They had a chance at love again, and a lifetime to be together. He had to convince her of that.

He approached the entry of her building. It was an unassuming building with a serviceable impression. A uniformed guard manned a desk in the small, subtly decorated lobby. As Kevin let himself into the lobby, uncertainty rose in his chest as a last-minute chill entered his thoughts. But he was here to see her. He had come all this way.

Yes, he was sure. The guard called up to Christina's apartment to announce him and get her approval to let him up. Based on the conversation, Kevin could tell that she was home and also, surprised by his visit. He had envisioned her opening the door to her apartment to find him there and was a little disappointed for the lack of surprise. Yet he was glad she was well-protected.

The guard guided him to a set of elevators and gave him directions. "Ms. Wade said that you should go right up."

Moments later, he was at the door of her apartment. The door flew open, and she was there. For a moment they stood just looking at each other, then Christina flew into his arms. His heart soared. She pulled him into her apartment and closing the door behind them. "What are you doing here?" she asked. "Is everything all right? ...Maude?"

He held her face in his hands. "I came after you. I did what I didn't do the last time. I love you and I want you in my life."

Tears clouded her eyes as sobs issued from her throat. She was unexpectedly overwhelmed with emotion.

"I have always loved you, I never stopped..." He kissed her then, a gentle touch on her lips.

Immediately she responded, kissing him back. He was bolstered and relieved as his heart soared with her response. They held each other, both heartened with the other. Love filled his heart as he held her. She was all he ever wanted.

After a moment, she took his hand and led him to the couch in her sparsely furnished living room, sitting closely together. She looked up into his eyes, hers were sparkling and shiny with unshed tears. "I can't believe this is happening, that you are here!" she exclaimed, kissing him again.

"I quit my job today. They said they were eliminating my position, but in truth, they were just bringing in a family member that needed a job.

"All that time, all those hours... all the late nights, weekends... it feels like I just wasted my life on a place that did not care about me."

He pulled her into his chest, where she rested her head, still in disbelief that he had appeared on her doorstep. He looked around the room, taking in her home. There was not much to look at since she only had the essential pieces of furniture and no personal touches. There were no individual pictures on the walls or bookshelves. There was little evidence of the woman who occupied these walls as her home. This relieved and worried him. Had she isolated herself in order to be away from loss and guilt? She'd tried to build a life but hadn't quite succeeded. She had wrapped herself in work and building her career, yet she had neglected to build a life.

He felt relieved that there were no pictures of other men in her home. It didn't seem as though she'd had relationships while he was out of her life. He had had a few, short-lived and half-hearted attempts to find a relationship. No one had come close to his feelings for Christina. Deep down, he had not wanted to even try to replace her.

It was clear that she had worked hard, putting in the time and energy to make it work and they had not been grateful for the results that she had achieved for them. They'd taken her for granted for years and never reciprocated the investment she'd put into the place.

He could not believe he was here in the city and with her in her apartment. As his fingers brushed strands of her hair away from her face, he brushed gentle kisses on her brow.

All he had ever wanted was here in his arms. His love for her grew at every moment.

She curled into his arms, resting her head against his broad chest. "I can't believe you are here, and that you came."

He shifted his position so he could look directly into her eyes. "I wanted you to know..."

His words faded as she pulled his mouth to hers, giving him a gentle kiss full of love and passion. After a moment, she pulled away from him and looked into his face. "Wow, today has been a day. My life has shifted in an instant, it seems."

He realized that with his appearance on her doorstep and the loss of her job, life must be sending her into an emotional tailspin. Everything was moving her back to the place she had run from, and her life was unfolding before her, pointing her in a direction in which she had not expected. He understood his appearance was surprising, especially after the way they had left things between them. He had clearly put the ball in her court. He had made his position clear.

But by coming to New York, he demonstrated that he would meet her halfway. He would be willing to come to her to have a relationship with her.

He would not press her.

"I'm so sorry about work. It's going to be all right," he said adamantly. "There is no need for you to waste your time on anything or anyone that does not appreciate all that you have to give."

She chuckled into his chest. "Especially you?"

He laughed. "Babe, I am ready to be with you wherever and whenever you are. Just as long as I have you in my life, all will be well."

"Even if we are starving and homeless somewhere?" she laughed. "Speaking of which, I'm starving. Let me get cleaned up from my jobless meltdown so we can celebrate."

She gave him a few take out menus to order from and went to the master bedroom.

After ordering food and finding it would be delivered in about 45 minutes, he realized how hungry he was. Finding his way through the bedroom to the master bath, he took in his surroundings. The lack of decoration and personal touches in the apartment continued into her bedroom. There was one picture on the nightstand. He noted quickly that it was likely a photo of her mother. Nothing else indicated any personal mementos. It was like a hotel room, except for the full closet of clothes.

He noted the scattered clothing on the floor and imagined she had rapidly shed her work clothes after the day she had had. She was now naked in the bath, just steps beyond him.

He knocked lightly, in order to not startle her, and entered the bath. It was an expansive room with marble fixtures and a gleaming marble tile floor. The whole vibe was very feminine. She had her hair tucked up into a loose bun and was relaxing in the tub with her eyes half closed. She looked beautiful – like a mermaid resting in the surf.

He knelt at her side and gently reached out to massage her shoulders. Using a washcloth, he moved the hot water over her neck and back. She kept her eyes closed while murmuring her pleasure. His body responded.

"Food is on its way," he whispered to distract himself.

"Mmm," was her response, making his self-control a shade more difficult.

"Feeling any better?" he asked, taking a seat on the edge of the tub.

She reached a wet arm out to touch his leg. "I still can't believe that you are here or that you came."

She had gone from feeling horrible to joyous, and was now wallowing in the middle, not able to experience either fully. It was clear that she was weighed with worry.

"I want us to have a wonderful life," she started, taking his hand. "I am so happy that you came."

Tears coursed down her face as she looked up at him. He reached out and gently wiped them from her face. "We will have a magnificent life," he said. "Wherever you want that to be."

She pulled away from him and looked down into her bath, moving the bubbles around absently. "The inn is the only opportunity for me now. Gina really feels strongly that it would work, and she is willing to become a partner with me."

"That's great news!" Kevin bolstered the conversation. "Do you have enough funding to make the changes you were thinking of?"

"I don't fully know. The money those developers were throwing around was pretty nice." She joked, splashing him teasingly with the bathwater.

He laughed, boosted that they were falling back into their easy camaraderie, it was nice to see her to kid with him. "That so?" he said as they laughed together.

"I guess I can ask Victor to invest as well," she started, "but honestly I would rather not. I want this to be my own project. I want to do it independent of Daddy's money."

"I am sure he doesn't see it that way," he answered.

Kevin always liked Victor. He was a reserved Brit, but it had been apparent that he loved Christina immensely. He had a lot of class and style as well. All things that endeared him to

Kevin. "I can check into the conservatory. That was an option Claire had mentioned."

She slid back down under the water. The bubbles barely covered her skin. He noticed.

"What was that?" she asked.

"I've known them to buy big tracts of land. They keep it undeveloped, and you can still use the property for recreation and such. I actually sort of know... someone that used to work for them. I think she may be in their New York offices actually. I can look her up if you want to go that route, or you can contact them directly."

She looked at him with interest. He could tell she wasn't just focused on the fact that the conservancy would be an option for land purchase, but that he was referring to a "she" that he used to know.

"She?"

He cleared his throat. "Just an old friend from college. It's just a thought. It may be a quicker introduction that way," he explained.

At his words, she rose from the bath, naked in front of him. His mouth went dry, taking in her form.

"Can you hand me that towel over there?" she asked sweetly.

Speechless, he retrieved the towel and gently wrapped her in its softness, helping her out of the tub as if she were a child. Clearly, she was not – he was all too aroused by her nakedness. She stepped away from him.

"Actually, if you don't mind, that may be a great idea," she replied to him, walking into the bedroom, and pulling the bath towel around her figure. "We may as well seek out other alternatives to raising some cash for the renovations. It can't hurt to have a backup plan."

At her words, he knew she was finding her footing. Her tone was business-like and strong; she sounded more like herself when she was thinking about business. He made a mental note to make that call in the morning. He was sure he had his friend's contact information in his phone.

All thought melted away as she dropped the towel to the floor, facing him. "How much time did you say we have before the food arrives?"

His heart leapt as he embraced her damp, dewy skin. "Plenty of time," he growled, passionately kissing her neck.

CHAPTER 23

She woke to the sounds of the birds outside rejoicing in the new day. The birdsong danced in her heart, reflecting her emotions. She lay with Kevin's arms around her, as he gently snored behind her in the king bed that barely fit in the bedroom of his cabin. The early morning sun shone off the pond just outside, creating a dappled pattern reflected on the walls.

It was heaven to lay here in the morning, snuggled with her love. Life had certainly taken a turn in the past weeks with the full-fledged blossoming of their relationship amidst the loss of her job. It still hurt after all that work and dedication. She had a feeling she would be bitter about it for a long time to come.

It was a turning point, however, and the push that had moved her in this direction. She knew she could use her business acumen for her own benefit. Kevin pulled his arms more tightly around her. She knew now that he would follow her wherever their lives ended up, and she rejoiced that they had found each other again. Or rather, that she had found him, as he had patiently waited for her return.

Gina would be arriving later today. She had quit her job at the hotel in the city on the same day that Christina resigned. They were taking a few days together to seriously discuss Gina's proposal for the inn and the dining options. Christina was still developing the full plan and they were moving forward. The old guilt remained, however. Granted, it was diminishing as time went on, but Annie's disappearance was present in every corner for her.

Kevin had contacted his old friend at the Nature Conservancy. It turned out that they had repeatedly approached Ada and later Jeremy with an offer to purchase land around the inn, but neither had ever shown an interest. They had been thrilled at renewing the prospect with Christina and the financial terms were solid. There would be enough money and more to complete the renovations they had planned, in addition to some start-up funds. Gina's partnership would add to the already stable potential of the property. Christina would not have to depend on Victor for financial support.

All she needed to do was to say yes and to get over the hump of guilt that still assuaged her by being back in Vermont.

Maude had been recovering well and was going to spend a few weeks at rehab to get back on her feet. Her hospitalization had left her weak. Jim was spending a lot of time there with her. The matter of the insulin vial weighed on Christina. She had not taken any further steps to investigate the matter further, with the exception of a few Google searches. If it had been a medication error, they would have legal recourse for Ada's death, something she was unsure of pursuing. Maude's rights were less clear, as the medicine was not prescribed to her.

It could have been something more sinister, like an intentional mix up of insulin that killed Ada. Who would have done it and what would have been their motive? Christina and Kevin were the only people that were aware of the mis-labeled vial. Kevin had not mentioned it again. Christina pushed the idea from her mind. There were so many other things to be concerned with, so she was likely reading into the situation. She would mention it to her attorney when she next spoke to him. He was a trustworthy individual and she felt confident he would offer sage advice.

She and Jeff were continuing to discuss options for having horses on site, and the amenities they offered. He had convinced her to let him use the barn and stables for a bit, just while he looked for land of his own. Right now, he had moved a few animals into the barns. It was nice to hear them moving about in the daytime. It felt like old times when Ada had kept chickens and a few other animals.

Jeff was thankful, as he had horses stabled in various barns across the area, and it was a challenge for him to manage all of them. He would be able to keep most of his horses in the stables at the inn, but he had wanted to house more so he could get into breeding racehorses. That was the reason why he was looking for a place of his own.

Jeff had also talked Christina into hiring Layla to work in Maude's place for the housekeeping and minor cooking – just while they got themselves through this period. She had recovered from her injury for the most part and was quiet and efficient in her duties. Layla was perhaps too quiet, Christina thought. She tended to look just beyond her when she addressed her. It was a little disconcerting.

Christina had spoken to Victor a few times in the past weeks. He was happy that she was business planning for the inn seriously. He had been pleased for her to learn that she and Kevin had rekindled their relationship; he would often tell her how he had found love and happiness later in life. He had lost her mother after just a few years of marriage, so he was always one to encourage her to take the reins to be happy.

Victor had remained closemouthed about what they had found earlier with the accounts and reassured her that she did not have to worry about them as the attorney had everything in hand. It was still a mystery, and she had had a call with her attorney and a bank examiner about it. Of course, it had revealed nothing to her about what they were looking for. She put it largely out of mind.

Jeremy had not been around lately, or if he had been, she hadn't run into him. He had been a fixture for so long with her aunt that she had decided to not press the issue. She was no longer working with him and had effectively cut ties. She knew that he was not happy with her decision to go with the Nature Conservancy offer to purchase acreage, and she wondered what kind of business relationship he had had with the developers. He had been so eager for her to move forward with that deal.

Kevin moved behind her. His skin was warm against hers, and any further worries or concerns of the day were pushed aside as she turned in his arms to kiss him.

CHAPTER 24

"Hey…. What were you doing way up here?" Christina asked as Gina came down the path into the upper lawns. "I thought you were still locked in the office."

Gina sat down in the deep wooden Adirondack chair. Christina observed her friend's red stained fingers and the dirt on her knees. "Where in the world have you been?" she asked again.

Gina grinned. "I have found a patch of strawberries!" she exclaimed. "Jim had said I could have free reign if I found them. The patch is a little hard to get to. It's through the woods, off the trail, and kind of angled on the hillside."

Christina nodded. "Oh right," she remembered. "We used to call it the secret garden. But we never really spent a lot of time in there. It used to be that bears spent more time there than people."

She laughed out loud as the look on her friend's face changed from delight to horror. "You're kidding!" Gina said, smacking her friend in the arm. "Just for that, there will be no strawberry shortcake for you!" She uncovered the bundle she had been carrying, revealing a full basket of glistening red berries. "Aren't they beautiful?"

"Wow, they look great! Nice and juicy," Christina replied, reaching into the basket for a berry. She managed to grab a few before Gina rose from her chair, pulling the basket with her.

"Enough!" she shouted, pulling the basket out of Christina's reach. "I want to use them for dessert tonight."

Observing the size of the basket her friend was carrying, Christina said, "That looks like enough to feed the French Army. Are we having company?"

Her friend laughed out loud. "Just the usual suspects are coming, including Shawn. We saw him this morning when we went into town."

Christina shook her head, guessing she needed to pay more attention to Gina's interest in Shawn. She was spending most of her time worrying about how she would keep all the people who worked and lived at the inn employed. She was growing weary of her own drama.

She watched her friend walk down the gently sloping lawn to the big house. "Wait," she asked, "who did you go to town with?"

"Never you mind!" Gina replied, as she opened the door to the kitchen and disappeared.

Christina chuckled to herself. Gina seemed in a light mood, and she deserved it. She settled back into her chair and resumed her contemplation.

Set deep in everyone's soul is the compass of home. Home is not always the place where you think you will end up nor is it always the home where you started out as someone's child. Home is sometimes where you end up when you were waiting for the place you thought you'd live.

In the times when she had distanced herself from the memories and guilt of this place, Christina had dared to dream of a home where there was love and laughter with friends, a soul mate, and children playing. When she was young, that was everything that she longed for, ever since she had tasted it with Annie's family. All she had wanted was house full of noise and people, a great expanse of lawn, fields, and woods to run and explore. There were animals to play with, and flowers and vegetables to tend and pick. Hours of chores, cyclical with the seasons and with rewards of beauty and harvested crops to eat and sell.

Christina looked out over the big house, through the gorgeous beds of flowers in bloom, and over the expanse of lawn reaching the fields and woods beyond. She looked at the roof of the barn and imagined the orchards beyond that were just out of sight. Her mind reached further than her eyes to the expanse of acres spread over the side of the mountain with their beautiful views, dark thick forests, open fields, rocks, streams, and ponds. Its expansive size no longer felt like a burden, but rather, was starting to feel like an asset. It was starting to feel like her own.

Christina's thoughts lightened as the clouds that had covered most of the sky today parted to show the late afternoon sun. She turned her face upward to capture the rays on her skin. Its warmth spread throughout her body and gave her relief from the coolness of the late spring day. She smiled to herself. In her mind's eye, she could see herself living here, having a family here and living out her days. Deeply she realized, it was what she had wanted all along. The ghosts were still around, the guilt faded but over time she knew the good memories would take their place.

It was her home after all.

CHAPTER 25

"I really want to thank you for gettin' new game cameras," Jim said, approaching the porch where Christina was enjoying her morning coffee – or rather, her late morning coffee. Last night ended early this morning, with misty recollections of beard stubble rubbing roughly on her cheeks, chafing her skin, her breasts, and her thighs. In just a few minutes, she was lost in thoughts from the previous night.

Jim's cough startled her, and she reclaimed her awareness of the conversation as she sloshed her coffee on the newly painted boards. Jim was reporting some trouble with the new cameras. "You see," he said, leaning intently toward her from his stance on the porch steps, "every time that I think they have captured something, there is nothing in the picture. The camera just took a picture of the leaves or the ground."

He settled himself on the steps, notably wincing as he leaned back onto the porch column. His arthritis made him slower, certainly, but his blue eyes were bright with the topic of the conversation. "I really hoped we would catch a glimpse of some kind of creature," he said, shaking his head, "at least a tail. Or a back. Or a blurry photo to show us our beast that keeps messing with my gardens."

Christina settled back in her chair, sipping on the cooling coffee. "Gosh Jim," she said, "I am so sorry. I was sure we would capture something by now."

"Did the Sheriff tell you to get these contraptions?" he asked.

Christina nodded; Shawn had mentioned this type of camera to her when the others were damaged. Chagrinned, she recalled ordering them. Her lack of knowledge of the technology of game cameras was not offset by her purchase of the camera with the most elite features. Admittedly, the decision had been fueled by a bit of guilt from Maude's incident. What she bought was over the top with capabilities and included the full ability to reset and reposition the field of view remotely from a computer. The camera would also automatically text or email any motion detected photos, so there was no need to go out and retrieve them from the woods. Everything could be handled from the comforts of home. Much of the technological aspects were lost on Jim as he had limited access to email and therefore, some of the features were beyond his technological talents. Christina had figured that her technological ability combined with his skills in identifying the animals would get them far in locating this 'creature' as Jim referred to it.

Setting her coffee down, she rose from her seat. "You know, Jim," she said as she headed indoors, holding the door open, "we could look online and see what we can do to correct the situation ourselves. Come with me."

He chuckled, spitting into the day lilies by the porch steps and following her through the doorway and into her office. Together, they sat at the computer console and reviewed the camera specifications and locations. There were four cameras. The first was positioned at the base of the mountain, not far off from the trail leading over the ridge. Originally, they had thought that this camera would take most of the pictures that would capture the animal activity in the area. It was located at a known deer run, and people from town often walked their dogs on this portion of the trail leading away from the inn. Any animal moving in the direction of the inn would likely be captured here.

Really, any animal in that general vicinity of the inn would likely be photographed by the first camera. Jim had disagreed with its placement, under the assumption that it would catch anything – even something that wasn't really headed in the direction of his gardens.

Christina had insisted on placing the camera there, because in her mind, this was a natural path she'd taken to the inn many times. It was a good place to leave a car and walk through the woods to the inn. She and Annie had done it so many times to meet up with their friends – either by having them sneak up to them through the woods, or by sneaking out themselves to meet them. Christina felt that any animal would find that a natural path as well. It was a less obstructed way, although not truly a trail. It was perfect for illicit teenage activities.

Camera two was positioned on the outskirts of a meadow further up the mountain. This camera was what Jim referred to as the 'money maker.' His previous camera was in the same position and had captured photos of many animals over time. Deer were the main celebrities, but he'd also seen foxes, bobcats, and an infrequent bear. Once he caught a photo of a moose standing close to the camera. It was quite a shot, and a print still hung in the caretaker's cabin.

The remaining two cameras were closer to the inn. Each was positioned nearby 'scenes of the crime,' where Jim had claimed 'the beast' had done material damage to the plantings and stone walls in the inn's extensive gardens.

Christina logged into the camera's remote connections and attempted to trouble shoot and reconnect the cameras. Each of the devices came back online easily. The challenge was to reposition the sites for the cameras. As they came back online, they found that each of the cameras had been turned upward or directly downward, resulting in views of tree bark or leaf covered ground. With Christina guiding the technical aspects, Jim gave her feedback to correctly position the view finders remotely in order to engage the picture he was looking for. His expertise guided her to the best possible viewpoint for each camera to capture any activity.

The process was drawn out, as they had to wait for the camera to reboot and reconnect to the cellular network. Then they remotely repositioned the camera into a good viewing position. As they worked through the repositioning, Jim created a hand drawn map of the cameras and the positions that the cameras were facing. The lulls while the cameras reconnected allowed for discussion.

"Boy, these gizmos really are buggy!" Jim exclaimed. "They all slipped from their mounts around the same time. Must be loose set ups or something. That boy set these up with you?" he asked, referring to Kevin.

Jim had known them both since they were young, but he liked to tease Christina. She smiled and nodded as Jim commented, "Huh... not sure that boy knows much about these things..."

At the mention of Kevin, Christina's mind once again returned to the activities of the previous night. She was certain she was blushing as she tried to pay attention to what Jim was saying.

"Just seems off to me," he stated, shaking his head with evident disdain for the technology. "More features seem to always mean more trouble."

She had missed what Jim had been saying because she was thinking about Kevin. But his comments were ringing a distant bell for her, though she was not in the frame of mind to identify what it was. "Sorry, not sure what you mean..." she said.

Undeterred by her distraction, Jim continued, "I don't know. It just seems like these things should work without all this trouble."

She brushed away his concerns. "Oh, maybe it was a strong breeze or a loose screw... they probably just needed some adjustments..."

Jim shook his head. "Not on all of them at once!" he exclaimed.

The door from the kitchen banged open, interrupting their conversation before Christina could identify what was disturbing her about his comments. "Hi Jim!" Gina exclaimed, carrying plates of sandwiches. "Are you hungry?"

Jim's attention shifted to Gina and her plates of delicious food. Not to mention, the beautiful woman bearing the offerings.

Christina finished the final adjustments for the last camera setting, directed by Jim in between bites of his sandwich. Everyone always seemed to drop everything for Gina's meals and snacks. It was if she put a magic potion in the food.

Before diving into her own sandwich, Christina noticed that the website for the game cameras indicated that there was an app available for download that offered to automatically send captured images via text. On impulse, she downloaded the app to her smart phone and closed her computer before diving into her own sandwich.

Gina took a seat on the corner of Christina's desk. "So, what have you been up to lately?" she asked, her question pointed directly at Christina with insinuation that she already had an idea of what Christina had been doing last night. "You look a little tired," she continued, smiling slyly at the other woman.

"Oh, I'm all right," answered Jim, causing both women to giggle together in surprise that he'd answered the question pointed at Christina. "You got any of that pie left?"

Christina laughed with her two friends, feeling happiness in her heart, and in this house, that had not been felt for a long time. An awfully long time.

CHAPTER 26

He stubbed his toe on the tree root, cursing to himself. The damn woods really bothered him, and he hated sneaking around in the dark like a common criminal.

This is what she had reduced him to. Lurking in the woods at night, trying to find what he was looking for. There was a treasure in the walls. If he could just find it, then all his problems would be solved.

It was his, all his. What a genius, to have kept it in his family home.

He'd find it again, eventually. Things had been moved around, he had forgotten the exact location.

They were all distracted anyway, except for that damn dog. He knew he would not get close to her if that mangy mutt was around.

He'd make plans for him.

No. Murdering animals wasn't his thing. He just wanted the money.

But so did the boss. He shuddered. He knew what he was in for. That bitch had locked him out and now someone was watching him. All his contacts had been silenced.

He needed the money, and he'd find it.

CHAPTER 27

He knew he was early, likely too early to be wandering around inside the quiet building. Kevin wasn't surprised to find Shawn already in the kitchen. Since Shawn had been welcome here for so long – his presence was never questioned, day after day. It was his absence that drew attention. "Good morning," Kevin said. "Looks like Layla has kept up with Maude's tradition." Maude had grown to expect Shawn, brewing extra coffee, and setting a plate for him with baked goods or other breakfast item day after day.

Shawn nodded to him as he helped himself to a large cup of coffee. He looked a little bleary eyed this morning. "Late night?" Kevin asked.

Shawn scratched his beard and shook his head in a disgusted manner. "Oh yeah."

At first, when Annie had gone missing, it was natural for them all to convene and support Ada in her time of dire need. As time wore on and the waiting extended, everyone had moved on to their own lives, but Shawn had kept this one connection. Kevin was sure Ada had appreciated his dependable visits and the security that Shawn had brought once he began wearing the uniform of his chosen career. He was grateful that he had continued his visits through the years, especially after finding Ada that early morning laying at the base of the stairs. Maude and Jim had been away visiting family; if Shawn hadn't come in when he did, no one would have found her for days. It didn't change the outcome, but at least Ada didn't die alone, laying on the floor of her home.

It puzzled him sometimes, the draw that the inn had for Shawn. He was compelled to visit here nearly daily for the past seven years. They had all learned to not expect Annie, to know that likely, they would never see her again as the weeks, months and years passed. It was a challenging thing to get used to. In the early days, there was the constant hope of a phone call. The sound of a car pulling in the drive or a footfall on the steps elicited optimism, but they had to learn not to expect her.

She had been Shawn's first love. Their relationship embodied the powerful love of teenage years with raging hormones and labile emotions. Kevin knew from confidences with Shawn that he felt Annie had made him be a better man. He was a mess growing up. He'd always been the one getting in trouble and the one that got caught. Shawn was the daredevil and the bad boy of the group. Kevin knew from their long friendship that Shawn had always felt he needed to prove himself as tough and strong. Through all those times, she had loved him and made him want to be a better person. Their relationship had made Shawn want a better life than the destiny he was designing for himself.

They had just broken up when she went missing. Kevin had been unsure of the details at the time, but their relationship had been tumultuous all along, with many break-ups and reconciliations happening because of something stupid Shawn had done. But the last time it had been Shawn that called it off.

Through all of the police interviews Shawn had revealed that Annie had wanted to get serious and plan for their future. He had shared that he was not ready to move forward in that way. Kevin knew at that time, although Shawn had been somewhat reformed, he still had no plan for his own life. He was unlike others in the group that were graduating from college and starting out their careers. Shawn had felt that he needed to figure things out before he could include a partner. Everyone had assumed that they would eventually make up and get back together as they always had. But then she was gone.

Shawn had been the prime suspect for her disappearance since he was the recent ex-boyfriend. His involvement in the case ended up nurturing his interest in law enforcement. Even though Shawn had been initially suspected to have a role, it had not deterred his curiosity in the law. Additionally, an interested state trooper took him under her wing and led him to his career today.

"Boy, I just couldn't sleep last night," Shawn said, continuing to rub his beard. "I just kept thinking about the construction workers up here. No idea why." He took a deep sip of coffee.

"Yeah, they are here already. Seemed like they started really early." Kevin chuckled. "Bet the ladies sure don't like that."

They could hear the backhoe in the side yard with its loud motor and the sound of grinding rocks and dirt as the articulating arm dug in the dirt and rock. The construction equipment filled the driveway. Kevin had noted the name on the equipment, he was not surprised to see Jeremy's car parked alongside it. Likely, Jeremy felt the need to supervise his father periodically on jobs. It especially made sense that he'd monitor this one, given his involvement with the inn.

The forecast was for a sweltering day as the last few had been, so he didn't blame them for starting so early. Both men entered the dining area through the swinging kitchen door to check out the construction area. It would give them an unobstructed view of the action on the patio. Kevin was surprised to see a quiet figure gazing out the window.

Layla, the woman who'd been injured on the hiking trail, stood silently at the large windows, overseeing the work. Her slight figure stood still, and she did not acknowledge their presence. After a beat, Kevin cleared his throat gently, so he wouldn't startle her from her thoughts. She didn't move and continued her straightforward gaze. Her inattention to him gave him pause. The two men exchanged a puzzled look.

He wondered about her; this woman had been a stranger just a few weeks ago. She had been lucky that he had come along when she was injured on the trail, and it'd been an added bonus that Jeff and Christina stumbled upon them on horseback. She was one lucky girl; she could have bled to death, but her recovery had been quick.

Christina generously offered her a job at the inn, helping Maude with housekeeping duties, which was needed now that Maude was out recovering. But Kevin had his doubts about Layla. There was something about her that was a little off. He had questions about her. Why was she alone on the trail? Something wasn't right about it. Jeff sure liked her, that was clear. He would ask Shawn to look Layla up with his expansive resources to ensure she was who she said she was. Kevin wanted to make sure she would not bring trouble to his friends.

Layla's voice startled him when she finally spoke over the drone of the digger outside. "Do you know who that is?" she asked, pointing outside to the construction area where the backhoe was attempting to remove the section of rock wall.

Curious, both men moved to gain her perspective out the window and looked in the direction of her pointed finger. They saw the operator of the machinery and no one else. "That looks to be Jeremy's father, Daniel. Is that who you mean?" Kevin asked.

"No, no. Not him. The woman standing there," she continued, her voice a monotone.

Kevin and Shawn both looked harder into the bright light of the morning over the patio, scanning his eyes over the scene in front of him. Silently confirming with each other that neither was seeing what Layla was pointing too. It unnerved Kevin.

Layla continued pointing, her arm unmoving. "She's calling you. She's calling to you Shawn."

They both looked dumbfounded at Layla as she pointed outside. The immediate thought that passed in Kevin's thoughts was that she had lost her marbles. Shawn stepped closer to the patio doors as if something drew him to look closer.

Shawn opened the French door to the patio and both men stepped outside, scanning the bank where the machinery was digging through the rock. The morning light struck him in the eyes, momentarily blinding him. Kevin ducked his head and closed his eyes against the bright light.

As his vision cleared, he heard her voice, and his blood ran cold. He looked sideways at Shawn, who's face had gone ashen.

"I'm here," she spoke. "Right here."

Annie's voice roiled in his ears, or maybe it was his mind. He couldn't tell. Kevin struggled to see with the sun blocking his sight. The operator ground the gears of the machinery as it struggled and lurched with its load of rock and dirt. Then a cloud momentarily passed overhead, and he was able to see clearly. Annie stood feet from Shawn. Her long, flowing, blond hair glowing in the light. She smiled lovingly at Shawn as they watched openmouthed. She seemed happy to see him as she reached her hand out beckoning to Shawn. The charm bracelet Shawn had given her for graduation all those years ago sparkled in the morning sun.

His breath stopped; the world stopped. *How could this be happening?*

He watched as Shawn dropped to his knees, his coffee cup scattering across the stones of the patio. In the background, the machine shuddered and stalled, lurching as its load fell from the shovel scattering on the lawn and patio where Shawn knelt, debris knocking into his leg. Deafening silence ensued.

She was gone. The apparition of Annie had come and gone.

Kevin stood stock still on the patio watching his friend, he was speechless. Shawn reached down to steady himself as he struggled to his feet. In the background, they could hear swearing coming from the backhoe operator, likely upset with the mechanical malfunction. Shawn's hand rested on the debris on the ground. In a daze, Shawn picked up the object at his feet.

He gasped as his brain registered what Shawn held in his hand.

It was a human bone adorned with a rusted, dirt-caked charm bracelet.

CHAPTER 28

The room was uncomfortably quiet as every person in the inn and outlying cabins sat stunned around the living room. Christina sat in the center of the sofa, wrapped in a blanket. She was shivering, and completely unaffected by the warm July morning. Gina sat on one side of her, coaxing her to take sips of hot coffee. Kevin sat on the opposite side with his arm curled protectively around her shoulders.

She had awakened from her dozing a brief time ago by the sound of pandemonium.

She had been lying in bed, trying to block out the sound of the machinery in the yard and catch some more sleep. As she dozed, her dreams intertwined with the worries of the day; the construction of the addition was underway, which was exciting and terrifying at the same time. The expansion of the dining room into the terrace gardens would bring the additional space they would need to host an expanded restaurant and event space. This new dining area would have an extended view of the valley below and would open onto the enlarged patio and terraced gardens.

Anxiety crept into her thoughts as she considered the construction expense and the ROI of the overall plans. She had the business plan memorized as she ran through the assumptions in her dozing state. Victor had reviewed it and had given her his advice on the work. It should have offered her solace, but the anxiety remained. The events of the past few weeks were a whirlwind, and she questioned her decisions constantly, waiting for the other shoe to drop and a mistake to materialize, putting all the plans into an unrealistic reality.

The engine noise groaned on outside, and she could envision the equipment digging at the rock walls and scraping through rock and dirt.

Abruptly, the engine noise had stopped, leaving a sudden void and deafening silence. After a beat, the shouts of a man yelling madly outside and then from downstairs had rousted her from her cozy bed. She ran down the two flights of stairs with the dog on her heel to find out what in the world was going on.

Shawn had been in a state. His eyes were bulging as he bellowed for everyone in the house to come to the living room. His face was pale as his voice boomed through the rooms. He escorted Jeremy's father, Daniel, by his arm and roughly propelled him to a chair. The older man perched on the edge of the chair as if he wanted to bolt. He glanced at Christina, frowning as he looked at her, and he pulled a dirty rag from his back pocket to wipe the sweat that was running down from his brow.

"Where's Jeremy?" Shawn had commanded of the group.

"He's here?" Christina asked, puzzled at his presence in the early hour. She shuffled onto the couch next to Gina, whose her hair was as wild as her eyes as she took in the activity.

"Take a seat," Shawn commanded, "I need everyone to remain here in this room. The state police and the coroner are on their way. They will want to speak to all of us."

All eyes went to Shawn. There were exclamations of puzzlement and disbelief projected from everyone in the room.

He looked cautiously at Christina, as if trying to formulate his words. "The construction workers just dug up human remains in the side garden. The coroner and the state police will need to review the scene."

Christina immediately felt a chill envelope her entire body. Her skin tingled as goosebumps erupted on her bare arms and her mouth gaped open. Shock shrouded her as her mind slowly began to piece together the information.

Shawn watched her face as she felt the blood leave her cheeks. "I don't know anything," he began. He stopped talking immediately as Layla quietly entered the room and took a seat in an armchair on the far wall. She made no eye contact and sat with her gaze downcast. Shawn stared at her as if he wanted to say something. He opened his mouth as if to speak, but then hesitated. His eyes took in all the people around the room.

The back door of the inn banged loudly, and two sets of footfalls came into the living room. Kevin guided Jeremy by his arm into the area. He pushed him down into one of the free chairs. The tension between the two men had been palpable. Kevin then sat down next to Christina, grasping her hand, and anxiously watching her face.

Jeremy was sporting a bruise above his eye, and there was dried blood caked the corner of his mouth. His eyes were bloodshot with deep circles beneath them. Shawn raised an eyebrow at Kevin in a silent question. Kevin surreptitiously looked from Jeremy to Shawn and shrugged, indicating that he hadn't done the damage to Jeremy's face. Both men knew Kevin wanted to hit Jeremy, after learning about the exchange between Christina and Jeremy that had occurred when she fired him.

After what had seemed like eons, the State Police arrived with two cruisers and the coroner. Shawn had known each officer and introduced them to the solemn group in the living room. The officer in charge addressed the somber faces, "While the coroner analyzes the remains, my team and I will be asking you all some questions. We'd like to do this individually in a separate room. Can we set up in a few private rooms?"

The tall officer, Agnes, was familiar to Christina. Her stature and impressively strong physique was memorable. She had been one of the investigating officers when Annie had disappeared. She stood as tall and straight, but now, her dark hair was interwoven with silver strands and tiny lines rimmed her eyes. She felt a bit of déjà vu and was oddly comforted by the officer's presence.

"Christina, do you feel up to talking?" she asked firmly but gently.

Eager to gain more information herself about the situation, Christina nodded. She rose, leading the officer into the bar for the inn, and took a seat in the window. "Is it her?" she asked, wiping a tear from her cheek. "Do you think she was there the whole time?"

"We won't know anything for certain until the coroner does his review and examination. It will take some time to do a positive identification. They will have to review dental records and see if they can identify the cause of death."

Christina winced at her words. The officer's tone was empathetic but clear. "I realize that this is unpleasant and comes as an unwelcomed surprise. It would help us in this investigation to understand the current situation and activity that led to this discovery."

Agnes opened her notepad and waited for her response. After a pause, she nodded her understanding. The trooper pulled a chair closer to Christina and sat with her pen in hand. "All right then, tell me about the construction plans. Can you also tell me what you remember about the work being done on the patios when your cousin went missing?"

Christina took a sharp intake of breath. There was no mistaking what the officer was getting at, since her line of questioning focused on the construction work, the patio, and stone walls. A shiver went up her spine as she recalled the information in her mind. Annie had gone missing when the stone walls were being repaired. They were the same stone walls that Christina was removing to accommodate the new addition for the dining room.

The officer gazed at Christina patiently. "Well, my aunt left me the inn when she died. We have made plans to re-open the business and expand the amenities. We planned to build an addition for the dining area and expand out onto where the patio and terrace gardens are now. It would make space for larger parties and events and would create a place to put up a tent if needed."

Agnes nodded. "Nice view from there."

Shifting in her seat, she questioned more deeply, "Do you remember anything about the summer Annie went missing? Anything that would give us more information than what we discussed then?"

Christina stirred in her chair, pulling the blanket tighter around herself, trying to reach back in her memory to that dark time. "I am not sure I remember exactly what I said, it was such a tough time." She swallowed, her throat dry. "I do remember that my aunt was having the rock walls repaired.

Annie and I were both complaining about the noise in the early mornings – very much like this morning."

Agnes looked at her intently and nodded. "I see that Shawn Johnston, Kevin McKinley and Jeremy Stone are here. They all had connections to your cousin. What can you tell me about their presence here today? I understand that you were in bed when Sheriff Johnston woke you and brought everyone downstairs."

Christina took a few breaths formulating her response. "Kevin rents a cabin from the inn. It's the one that's furthest from the main building. Shawn usually stops by in the morning or evening…" At this she hesitated.

Agnes watched her face, and her response. "The Sheriff stops by every day?"

She waited for Christina's response as she studied her. Christina took a deep breath and swallowed the lump that had appeared in her throat. "Yeah, Shawn used to come by all the time when he and Annie were together. Ada was appreciative to see him… after Annie went missing. He was the one to find her when she…. fell." She hesitated. If there was a good time to mention the insulin vial, this may be it. Her addled mind considered how to bring it up.

"I see." Agnes nodded, her eyes piercing into Christina.

"I wasn't around then. I was living in New York at the time." Christina hung her head, the old guilt seeping in.

"What about Jeremy?" the trooper asked after a moment.

Christina hesitated. Honestly, she didn't know why Jeremy was there this morning and had thought it odd that he had been on site. They had closed their business relationship quite clearly at their last exchange.

Christina sensed Agnes noting her pause. Agnes patiently waited for her response. She was unsure how to answer the question.

"Jeremy had been Ada's attorney and executor. He kept things running for her after Annie left and she...well, it looks like she sort of lost interest in the business.

I am not sure why he is here this morning. I assume it was because his father's workers were on site." Christina paused and then continued speaking rapidly. "Honestly, I don't have a lot of details about the actual construction out there. I just know that they planned to get it completed and will review the overall results when they are done... I know the cost, but I don't know how many people they will be using in the crew, so maybe Jeremy had a role in that.... I... I don't know what he was doing here this morning."

The trooper stopped taking notes in her pad and looked directly and empathetically at Christina. "Is there anything else that you want to tell me?"

A vague memory rose in Christina's mind, unclear and just out of reach. She had a sense that she had had this same conversation with this same policewoman years ago. Her mind was not connecting the thread that felt so close, but was inaccessible. "I'm sorry." She shook her head woodenly. "I don't remember anything else."

She hesitated, knowing Agnes was watching her carefully. She knew it was evident that the shock of the morning's discovery was having an impact on her. "There's something else. I really don't know what to do with it." Christina hesitated, her speech stuttering. "Maude, our housekeeper, had a bad insulin reaction recently. It happened after she had borrowed my aunt's leftover insulin."

Agnes leaned in just slightly closer. "After your aunt died?"

"Yes." Christina hesitated, feeling as though maybe she was reading into the situation. "I mean, she asked my permission and all. We didn't see anything wrong with it as they take the same medicine." She swallowed. "It may be nothing. But Maude had a very low blood sugar episode after taking that insulin. I brought the vial to the hospital; the paramedics had suggested it. The doctor there told me it was mislabeled. She would have gotten five times what she should have received for a dose."

Agnes set her pad on her lap. "I'm not sure I follow you; the police don't usually get involved in medication errors. There are so many things that can go wrong with that..."

Christina now really felt that she was not able to convey her concern, "My aunt died from complications of a very low blood sugar. She had been home alone. Shawn found her on the floor when he came in in the morning."

At this piece of information, Agnes became more attentive. "And he was here, because he comes here every morning?"

Christina nodded agreement.

"What are your thoughts about this?" The trooper's tone was cautious.

"Let me get the vial to show you. It may just be a mislabeling from the pharmacy. I haven't done anything with it."

Christina left the room to retrieve her purse where she had kept the vial since the night in the hospital. Only she and Kevin had spoken to the doctor at the emergency room. As she made her way to her room and back downstairs, she had glimpses what was happening outside.

The coroner and his team were working in one location on the patio. She caught a quick view of a stretcher and a black body bag, and her stomach turned. Reality came barreling in.

It had to be Annie.

She stopped her motion and took a few minutes to collect herself. This was surreal, after all the years of wondering what had happened. Her head swam with questions.

After a few moments, she reentered the room with the state trooper and handed her the vial. Agnes studied it for a moment. "I see what you mean." She examined the label where the paramedic had pulled it back to reveal what was underneath. "Looks like a label on top of a label." She paused and gazed directly at Christina. "What do you want to do with this? A medication error is usually approached by a lawsuit or the state boards for pharmacy. Medication errors are not treated as crimes, typically."

Christina hesitated. It was only a feeling that she had, there was nothing else for her to really say.

"What I would say is for you to have a conversation with your lawyer to see what steps you should take." Agnes looked empathetically at her. "I'm sorry to not be of more help."

CHAPTER 29

Kevin shifted in his chair, uneasy at the questions that the state trooper was asking. It wasn't guilt that made him uncomfortable; instead, he struggled to relay what had happened that morning without seeming like a complete nut job.

The officer questioning him was an ex-student of his and was clearly uncomfortable interviewing his old teacher. Kevin decided it might be advantageous to find out some more detail. "Have you been able to see the remains? I would think if it were Annie Stone that there would just be skeletal remains left by this time."

The trooper nodded in agreement. He seemed to relax a bit as Kevin moved the dialogue to be more of a conversation and not a police interrogation. "I haven't gotten too close; the coroner's team has to deal with the remains. But I was able to get a glimpse of the skull, which looks like it's been caved in. That's likely the cause of death."

At that piece of information, Kevin forced himself to not react. He wanted more details and assumed he'd get more if he kept his ex-student talking. "Not something you see every day, right? I bet you don't see that a lot."

"Yeah, nothing like this. Couple suicides and a shooting in a family dispute. A few overdoses, car accidents." He settled back in his chair, crossing his legs. "Coroners team was a little peeved about the backhoe. Mixed things up for them a bit."

"Interesting job they have," Kevin commented. His mind reeling to the crushed skull. *Who could have done that to her?*

"Yeah." He laughed, shaking his head. "Not something I would want to do. But not likely to see much of days like this 'round here."

Apparently, the blade of the backhoe had separated several bones in Annie's spine. It occurred to him then that if the backhoe had not stalled and lurched, spilling the contents of the shovel, w*ould anyone have noticed they were digging up human remains?*

His thoughts were interrupted when the formidable Agnes entered the room with Shawn trailing behind. Shawn looked squeamishly uncomfortable.

"Can you please excuse us?" Agnes asked of the junior trooper who exited the room quickly.

Shawn pulled a chair to sit next to Kevin and Agnes took the chair vacated by the younger officer. Kevin looked at them expectantly and Shawn cleared his throat.

"I wanted Agnes to hear this from us both," Shawn started. His voice was hesitant as he looked from Kevin to Agnes. "None of this can go into the record. I don't ever want to talk about it again."

It was clear that Shawn was shaken. Kevin assessed his old friend for distress, which was apparent. He was barely holding it together; he had known him for so long that he could tell. He was putting on the same tough façade that he used to wear years ago. Clearly, he wanted to be anywhere but here – just feet away from where the body of his first love was being examined – and he couldn't blame him.

Agnes studied the pair with her assessing cop eyes. Kevin could feel her scrutiny. He remembered her assessment when Annie had initially gone missing. Shawn had been the prime suspect. Being the recent ex-boyfriend, it was natural that he would be suspected as the culprit. He was well known to the local police at the time since he'd gotten into some scrapes early on.

Agnes had taken an interest in Shawn, or likely, she had been assigned to keep an eye on him. Back then, Shawn had been a distraught young man, who was scared and terrified for Annie. He had put those feelings above his concerns for what would happen to himself. Agnes had found Shawn to be a good kid who had a tough upbringing. He needed direction and purpose. She had introduced him to the idea that he could make a better life for himself, and he had. Shawn had gotten through community college and through the Vermont Police Academy while he waited for Annie to surface. As life moved on, he had been elected Sheriff for the county.

Kevin knew he still held out hope that one day Annie would return. They all did. But he also knew that Shawn realized the critical windows had long closed, and it was likely she would never return.

"Tell me what happened this morning," she started.

Shawn shoved his hands in his pockets and looked at Agnes. She looked up at him her gaze solid and steady. "Ok. So... you are in the habit of coming here every morning for coffee and a free breakfast, and just happened to be standing on the patio, close to dangerous machinery that was excavating a stone wall? Then they happened to dig up the likely remains of your ex-girlfriend, the same one you were suspected of killing?"

Shawn ran his hands through his hair, acting as though he was about to speak, and then stopped himself. He exchanged a pained look with Kevin.

"What do you need to tell me?" she asked, imploring him to be honest with her.

"I can't believe it happened. But I'd like to believe it did," he started and then caught the look on his fellow Officer's face. Intrigued, Agnes gave them her full attention. The two men leaned in closely, so only she could hear what they said, and they quietly reiterated the events of the morning and the vision of Annie with her charm bracelet.

CHAPTER 30

A knock sounded at the door and was then opened by a petite woman hesitantly entering the room. "Would you like to speak to me as well?" she asked, addressing Agnes.

Three pairs of eyes looked at her with wonder and skepticism. There were several beats of silence before Agnes was able to respond. "Well...thank you for being willing to talk to me. Actually yes, I would like to talk to you about this morning."

It was clear that Agnes was curious – very curious – about what Shawn had reluctantly shared. She had assured the men that she was not planning to include their information in her report.

Layla had apparently been cleaning, as she held a duster, cloths, and furniture polish in her hands. There had not yet been guests, but they were preparing for the opening. Of course, the crime scene tape out back might deter that from happening too soon.

"I'd like for them to stay, if you don't mind," she stated, pulling a chair from one of the nearby tables and sitting down facing the Officer.

"I know you spoke to the Deputy already. Thank you for taking the time in doing so," Agnes replied. A crease appeared between her eyebrows. "How did you know I wanted to speak to you myself?"

At Agnes's question, Layla became extremely ill at ease and didn't make eye contact. "You didn't want to follow up with me?" she asked.

The Officer hesitated. "I do want to speak with you, but these men and I just completed our conversation. How did you know to come over now?" She plowed forward, not waiting for an answer. "I wanted to ask you about this morning. Did anything occur... that was out of the ordinary?" she asked haltingly.

Layla continued to not make eye contact and kept her head downcast. "Shawn & Kevin told me what you pointed out to him...." Agnes started, hesitating. "He told me you saw her first."

"Well yes, I suppose," the petite woman answered haltingly.

"Can you tell me what happened?"

Layla made direct eye contact with each man and then rested her eyes on Agnes. The pure green brilliance of her eyes took Kevin's breath away. Her gaze was intense. "You don't believe them."

It was a statement, clear and simple. Her words hung between them as Agnes considered her answer. "Frankly, I don't believe anyone. It's my nature. I have been exposed to the Ghost Files on TV and other malarky such as that. None of this will go into the police report. However, I am most interested in who buried the body in the wall. If any of this gets us closer to solving that then I'm all ears." Agnes leaned forward and looked directly into Layla's eyes. "I guess what I'm saying is, I don't know what to believe. Someone I have known for a long time told me that something hard to believe occurred this morning. Is this a normal occurrence for you?"

Layla continued her steady gaze, taking her time to answer. "It's not something I talk about and no one here knows anything about me," she swallowed hard. "I'd rather they didn't know about this."

Agnes considered her words. "Is there anything that would cause harm to the people here? Maybe your new employer?"

Layla immediately shook her head emphatically. "Oh no, nothing at all like that. It's just... people treat you differently when they know," she said. "I was hoping for a fresh start."

"Is this a usual occurrence for you?"

Layla's gaze turned downward again, and she nodded.

"So, you see... ghosts?"

Layla laughed out loud at that. "I see people clearly who are on the other side. I see their energy and sometimes, I can hear them."

"Do they speak to you?" Agnes asked, curiously.

She hesitated. "Not really...It's hard to explain.... It's like... I *know* what they say. I hear it in my head."

Kevin nodded in agreement. It did feel like he had heard Annie in his mind. It wasn't something he'd like to have repeat, but he knew he would not forget it. "Is this something you work at?"

Agnes scowled at him. Evidently, she wanted to be in control of the conversation. "Sorry, science teacher...it's a phenomenon. That I saw too."

Layla shifted uneasily in her chair, not sharing Kevin's sense of wonder at her 'gift.' "I really don't work at it.... It's not something I pursue." She continued. "I really don't want people to know, especially with this new job... and all."

The two women looked at each other. Agnes looked as though she was trying to absorb what was being said. Layla was anxious to not have this be the catalyst that would cause her to move on. Again.

"I think we can keep this between us," Agnes assured her, glancing meaningfully at each man in turn. "What did this one say, the one you saw this morning?"

Layla hesitated, swallowing deeply. "She was calling for Shawn."

"Do you know who she was and what happened to her?" Agnes asked quietly.

Layla shook her head.

"Is that all she said?"

Layla hesitated again, rubbing her palms on her thighs. "She said she wanted them to be found."

"Them?" Agnes asked, surprised.

"The woman and her baby. She said she wanted them to be found so she could get her revenge on the man who killed her."

CHAPTER 31

Kevin sat stunned in his chair as Agnes escorted Layla from the room, thanking her for being honest with them and reassuring her that her secret was safe with them. Shawn sat next to him, watching Kevin's face closely.

"Did you know?" he asked. Kevin looked at his friend with concern.

Shawn's eyes teared up. "Yeah, I knew." He sighed deeply as a tear coursed down his cheek. "Told me after we broke up. I was young and stunned. Before we could figure out what to do, she was gone." He looked in his friend's anxious face. "No one knows. Not Christina, not Ada. Just Annie, me and the cops on the case."

"There was no way that Layla could have known that Annie was pregnant when she disappeared. The police had to get a warrant to get into Annie's medical records to see if she had disappeared for a medical reason. A young, pregnant, unmarried woman may disappear to have her child and reappear months later, after putting the baby up for adoption. That was the theory the police had hoped for. I just wanted her back. I couldn't imagine that she would have left because of the pregnancy."

But the cops still pursued it, as there was nothing else to go on. They looked into clinics and adoption agencies that were all cold. And when she didn't appear months later, they gave up on that theory. She just disappeared off the face of the earth."

A chill went up Kevin's spine. "If no one knew that, then...Layla...It was real?"

"I can't believe it either. But I saw it with my own eyes." Shawn rose from his chair, looking out the window onto the patio below. Agnes was outside, walking over the patios as if she were looking at the scene from their vantage points.

Who had done this? Kevin's mind reeled. How did Christina's plans to expand the inn's dining rooms put the inevitable discovery of Shawn's dead girlfriend's corpse into play? Would Agnes suspect that they had concocted a story to cover for when the corpse appeared, as Shawn knew it would? Was she thinking Shawn had been supervising the dig out there this morning on the patio, to help ensure the disposal of the bones with the rest of the debris, hoping no one would notice? It was farfetched, but not impossible.

Agnes made her way around the patio as Shawn watched her from the window. The remains had been removed by the coroner and his team, along with any further site evidence that may help to identify the body and the circumstances of death. Agnes scanned the area, observing the surroundings, and likely piecing together the stories of the four people in the vicinity.

She climbed into the cab of the bucket loader, which was stopped, just as it had been left this morning. She observed the vantage point of the operator. "I know I didn't kill Annie. I know you didn't kill her," Shawn stated. His hands clenched the window frame, fingernails digging into the wood. "Who would have done this to her?"

Kevin's heart went out to his friend. The anguish that this had caused him over the years was unimaginable. Keeping secret that the missing girl carried his child. The police were right to still consider him a suspect, the circumstances were supportive of a motive. Kevin wondered how the elaborate story of seeing the ghost of his dead girlfriend would impact their investigation. But he was confident in what he saw and heard.

Heavy footsteps came down the wooden hallway, followed by a knock on the door. The young trooper entered hesitantly. "Mr. McKinley, Sheriff...." The young man swallowed deeply as both men looked at him sternly. "The Captain is asking that you both don't leave town for a few days."

CHAPTER 32

For the second time this year, Christina found herself in the cemetery for another burial and memorial. This time, the sun was shining and the air was warm. There were few people in attendance for Annie's funeral. Not many had remembered her, or if they did, they didn't live nearby to attend. Her only family – Christina, Jeremy, and Daniel – were present, as well as those of whom remained in their small group of friends.

The pastor from Ada's church said a few prayers over Annie's coffin before it was lowered into the ground. A light breeze blew by, flapping Christina and Gina's skirts as they stood side by side at her graveside. Kevin held Christina's hand throughout the service, as Gina did the same for Shawn.

They had waited all these years for Annie to surface, or for a sign of what happened to her, and she had been in reach the entire time. It was heartbreaking to realize that whatever had happened to her, her killer had the thought to place her body in the stonewall feet from her home. The police were still silent about what they had found, explaining that they needed to complete their investigation before they revealed their findings.

For Christina, to know for certain the fate of her cousin and best friend, was oddly freeing. All the guilt and pain that had haunted her for years was slowly seeping away from her psyche. Her spirits were lifting and a heaviness that had followed her everywhere was easing. She still needed to know what the police thought, and that made her uneasy. When Annie had initially disappeared, they had theorized at the time that it was likely a random occurrence. If she had been abducted, it was most likely someone that was passing through who had found an opportunity when they saw a young girl driving alone at night on a lonely, uninhabited road.

She had held onto that for years – the randomness. It was not likely that anyone she knew could have been responsible. She could not imagine Shawn, Jeff or Kevin having the capability to do such a thing. It was also terrifying to think that it could have happened anywhere. Thankfully, it had not been a factor that added fear to her life. She had enough burden with living while Annie likely was not.

Victor made the brief service just near the end of it. He came and took her hand at Annie's graveside. Not one to show his emotions, he had gripped her hand as the casket was lowered into the ground. Christina was glad he had come all the way from London. He had some business to attend to in the city but would be able to stay with them for a couple of nights.

They had all gathered later back at the inn, except for Daniel and Jeremy, who left the cemetery together. Layla had served a luncheon that Gina had put together earlier. Christina's friend was always one to feed people in their time of grief.

"Are you doing all right, my dear? I haven't had much of a chance to catch you alone," Victor asked as they brought tea out to the patios. The outside patio space was nearly completed after the police released the area. The interior new dining space was well under way.

Christina sighed. "It's a lot to absorb. They haven't provided much detail about what they were able to piece together. I was grateful we were able to have a service for her."

"It's been too long of a wait," Victor replied. "I am glad as well. It feels like she is where she should be."

Christina nodded. She hadn't expected a positive outcome for years, so she understood his meaning.

He reached out and held her hand. "You do realize, my dear, that all of this is not your doing. Nothing you did, or didn't do, caused this for her."

Christina smiled sadly. He knew her well. "I know. It's getting lighter for me, just knowing what had happened to her for certain."

"I am sure Kevin has helped with that as well."

She nodded. "It feels…inappropriate… I guess is the word ….to have the inn when it should be hers."

He patted her hand. "I understand. But perhaps you could think of it in another way. What you are doing is honoring her and her family by preserving their history and their lives that they spent here."

"Your aunt worked hard on this place and tried to preserve it as best she could. Annie loved to live here, and she loved you."

Christina's eyes brimmed with tears. It was true. This had been their home. What she had done was to preserve the land around them, improve the inn's usable space by expanding the dining and patios, and bring back the building's heyday by fully operating.

They sat for some time, enjoying the peace of the afternoon and sipping tea. This was how Victor was able to share himself with his stepdaughter, by quietly offering his support. She had loved him for his tranquil and solid backing throughout her life. He had been her rock.

After a time, Victor broke the silence. "I would have expected to see Jeremy and his father come for lunch."

She shook her head. "I haven't had much interaction with Jeremy since I let him go from assisting me early on. He was upset over the change in accounts, and since then we haven't spoken."

Victor nodded, appearing to return to his tranquil thoughts; however, it was just the opposite. "I hadn't wanted to worry you, but there is something out of order in those accounts. There are inquiries being made. I'll have to find out where the investigation is now. You must keep this to yourself for now." He patted her hand. "Nothing to be of concern, I am sure."

Something was clearly awry, and she knew he would not have wanted Christina to worry about it with everything else on her mind. Her thoughts whirled with the information, or rather, the lack of it. She knew better to ask further details; he would offer them when he was ready. She had this experience with Victor before, always trying to protect her. It was simpler to let him.

It occurred to her there was more he should know. "Actually Victor, I had the attorney look at something for me. There was a medication of Ada's that was mislabeled. It looks like it could have caused her to have a very low blood sugar." She sighed, relaying the details of her findings. He listened attentively.

"That explains what he asked me to pass on to you, I had forgotten until you mentioned it just now. He said that the pharmacy where the insulin was filled does not carry the higher concentration. If a patient needs the higher concentration, they refer them to a pharmacy in Brattleboro that carries it. So she couldn't have gotten it there.

"The state pharmacy board is doing their own review, once they are done verifying those details, he'll let us know."

A chill climbed up Christina's spine.

She would need to let Agnes know once they got the final report. Something more sinister was at play than met the eye. *What had really happened to Ada?*

CHAPTER 33

Everyone was gone this morning and would be for the next few hours. She relished the silence after all the preparations for the soft opening scheduled for the following week. It had been noisy, with people hustling and bustling about over the past weeks. Once they had been cleared to complete the renovations, there was a surge of activity. Life had indeed flowed on.   Christina's thoughts briefly went to Annie. The police did not offer any further insight to what had happened to her, but it was obvious that she had died from a fractured skull, and her body had been placed in the rock walls that were being renovated at the time. Having her funeral and taking time to grieve her had been freeing. Knowing for certain what Annie's destiny had been had assuaged Christina's relentless wondering and guilt. The renovation of the inn – specifically, restoring it to be a prosperous community gem – was a kind of atonement for Annie. Annie had not lived to see her inheritance and to build her life. Christina was doing that for herself, but also for Annie.

Chipper laid his head on her lap and peered up into her eyes woefully. She grinned at the dog and scratched his ears. "Hungry boy?"

The dog responded with a doggy grin and a tail thump on the wooden floor. She rose and got them both something to eat in the kitchen. The morning light was bright. The days had been warm, but now that it was late August and the nights were much cooler, there was good sleeping weather. She had heard there would be an early frost this weekend. The weather in Vermont was ever changeable.

She shuffled through the new dining room. Her slippers whispered on the smooth wood as she admired the work that had been done there. It looked as though the added space had always been a part of the house, as it seamlessly fit the room. Sipping her coffee, she made her way to her office with the dog at her heels.

A loose paper on top of her desk caught her eye. She noted that it was the draft she and Jim had created. She stared at the handwritten map of the game cameras that Jim had left in the office from their work resetting the cameras the other day. There was something niggling her about the image. Something Gina had mentioned while looking at the same paper drawing...

A path? A line? No that was not it.

Alarm. That was it. No animal large enough would be close by the house without being noticed. It would set off the cameras and a photo would be texted out. That was the game camera alarm system, or a 'red neck' alarm system, as she had called it.

No animal large enough.

It was no coincidence that they all went offline all around the same time. The cameras had to be manually adjusted. Something or someone would have had to move them and turn them away, so they were useless. Something or someone.

Christina felt a chill run up her spine and the back of her neck began to prickle.

Fear.

She was alone in the inn. No one was around today, and it would likely stay that way until later this afternoon.

The bones of her long dead friend had just been recovered. The murderer was still unidentified.

The phone in her pocket vibrated indicating an incoming message. She slipped the phone from her pocket to check. It was camera #2. The 'money shot.' The image was of an animal large enough to set it off.

But the image was a human being. It was Jeremy, with a look on his face of pure rage. The hairs raised on the back of her neck; her heart rate accelerated.

It was him, and he was coming for her. He would get to her before help arrived, even if she called now.

The house was not safe. He knew all its hiding places too well.

Run! A voice in her head compelled her forward. Every cell of her body leapt to attention in the flight or fight response.

She chose flight. She knew the woods better than he did, and without a car in the driveway to escape in, this path was her only choice.

She ran, quietly closing the screen door so he would not hear her exit as she ran into the woods. Running past the woodshed, she grabbed the small ax from the stump, not fully knowing if she would be able to defend herself with it. But it felt better to have something in case she needed it.

Someone grabbed her arm and wrenched her around, a vice grip clutched both her arms and imprisoned her. She stared into the unshaven face of Daniel; his ripe alcoholic breath was hot on her face. "Now where you goin', missy?"

Her heart pounded as ice shook her belly, adrenaline rushed through her veins, and confusion clouded her senses. Where had Jeremy gone? What was Daniel doing there? Every one of her senses was flashing danger signs.

She heard the sound of running footsteps behind her and a low growl. Then everything went black as her skull exploded in pain.

"That damn dog bit me," Jeremy rumbled as Christina came back to consciousness.

She was lying on the floor in the front room of the inn. There was a horrible howling and barking coming from her office. Apparently, the dog had been shut in the room, and she could hear him digging at the door, his nails scraping the wood. Her head throbbed. She reached up and touched the back of her head and her fingers came back bloody. She had been knocked out by the blow to her skull. Immediately, her thoughts went to Annie and what the officer had said was the apparent cause of death. A fractured skull. Christina was overcome with fear, and realized she needed to get out of there. She attempted to get to her feet, but the room spun.

"Sit down," Jeremy commanded. "Dammit! Just stay down and do what I say!"

She froze, taking him in. He was in a state. His arm was dripping blood over the throw rugs and the shiny wooden floors. *He must have killed Annie*, she thought, *the same way that he had just hit her over the head.* Her head ached and the room was spinning, so she knew she wasn't in good shape. Fear clutched her heart.

"Shut up!" Daniel growled entering the room, yelling at the dog. "My shotgun is in the truck, or I would 'a shot that damn beast."

He kicked Christina's leg as he strode by her on the ground, as if she were a piece of dirt on the floor. He grabbed Jeremy by the collar of his shirt. "What business do you have coming here after me, you shithead moron? You need to leave this to me."

"You don't know what kind of trouble you are getting into! You can't keep doing this, it doesn't solve anything." Jeremy screamed back at his father as they tousled and shoved each other.

"I'm gonna take care of all this, for once and for all. She don't deserve nothing. She ain't family. The Stone house has always been Stone's."

"I can't let you do that." Jeremy screamed, as the two men wrestled and fought.

Daniel grabbed Jeremy by the neck and started to choke him. It was apparent that the older man was stronger than his son. Jeremy's face began to turn beet red as he struggled against his father and the two men crashed to the floor.

Christina tried to get to her feet again, but the room continued to spin. Was Jeremy trying to protect her? "Stop! You're going to kill him!" she shouted, as the room again went black before her eyes.

She became vaguely aware that she was in a moving vehicle. She was blindfolded and her hands were bound. There was another person beside her. She could feel their warmth against her side. They were still and unmoving, as the vehicle surged forward. The road beneath them was full of ruts and holes, they bounced roughly against the steel bed as the truck charged over the ground.

Terror flooded her veins. The person next to her was unmoving. It was likely Jeremy. He was probably dead. She knew she would be dead as well, as soon as the vehicle stopped.

What was it that they had been fighting about? Her addled brain tried to piece the conversation together. She was beginning to panic. What the hell was she going to do? How could she get out of this? She had never been in a situation like this before.

The figure stirred beside her, and she felt the movement. She was relieved and further terrified of her now shared situation. Her head continued to ache and spin. She could feel that her hair was matted with dried blood. How was she going to defend herself?

She had to live. She had to get out of this alive. A sob gathered in her throat.

They traveled for what seemed like a long time. Banging over the road, the other figure bumped into her again.

"Can you hear me?" a male voiced asked beside her. It was clearly Jeremy. His voice was hoarse. "Don't panic. We will get out of this. Just do as I say and don't make him mad."

"Why is he doing this?" she whispered.

Jeremy's answer was lost as the vehicle pulled to a stop. Moments later, the creak of metal and a loud *thunk* allowed a gush of air into her face. The smell of pine filled her senses.

"Get up, the both a' ya."

They shifted and scooted their way out of the bed of the truck. Her blindfold slipped from her eyes as she moved to stand before him. Daniel held a shot gun on them both in one large hand. His other hand held a shovel. He motioned them to walk a head of him to a stand of pine trees.

"Dad, come on." Jeremy pleaded, "this is really gone far enough..."

"Shut up," he shouted, taking a swig from a bottle in his jacket pocket. "You damn idiot."

They approached the stand of trees. Daniel demanded they kneel and face him. Christina could not believe that this was happening. She was terrified, and her heart was pounding in her chest. Her breaths were short. Tears clouded her eyes. She was certain he was going to kill her – and possibly kill them both.

Satisfied they were effectively hackled; he leaned his shotgun against the trunk of a tree behind him and began to dig with the shovel. The blade of the tool dug into the dirt. As it scraped the rock and dirt, realization came over her. He was digging her grave before her eyes. Tears began to course down her face.

"Please, please," she begged, "why are you doing this?"

"Shut up!" he shouted. He stopped and took another drink from the bottle he pulled from his shirt pocket.

"You have no right!"

The blade dug into the dirt as the stones pinged against the metal. She shuddered at the sound.

"You and your shit family! *You* have no right. That land and that house is a Stone property."

Scrapes, pings, and scatters of dirt emphasized his words as he ranted. "My stupid brother married that whore with her brat. He makes sure that she got the house when he died. He musta knew it was comin.'"

Scrape, ping, scatter of dirt. He took another swig from the bottle. "Shoulda been mine. I shoulda been able to give it to my idiot son." He motioned to Jeremy beside her, looking at his son with despair as he knelt in front of him. "I did this all for you. It should all be yours." Christina's legs were beginning to tingle as they fell asleep, furthering her anxiety.

Surprising her, Jeremy scooted closer to her so their sides were touching. "I never meant for you to do what you did," he said somberly.

Scrape, ping, scatter of dirt. "Yeah, I meant to scare that bitch, but I hit her too hard," he laughed grotesquely. "Your head is a lot harder than your cousin's. When I found out she was knocked up with that bastard's kid, something needed to get done. We'd never get it back."

He had killed Annie! Renewed fear surged through her body. She was about to die, and her life had just begun. Her thoughts shifted to Kevin. Would she ever see him again? Would he be safe from Daniel's unhinged rage?

Just when she thought all was lost, Jeremy's fingers groped at her wrists startling her. A renewed surge of hope coursed through her. "You hid her in the rock wall."

Daniel stopped shoveling and leaned on the handle. "I did." He smiled a self-satisfied grin.

He took another swig from his bottle, resting from his efforts. She felt the ropes fall from her wrists, effectively freeing her.

Hope rose in her chest.

Jeremy shot to his feet. Christina quickly followed suit, but her legs were wobbly and her head was still swimming from the earlier blow.

"What's this?" Daniel stumbled, shocked that his captives had broken their bonds. He stepped back to reach for his gun and stumbled.

Jeremy lunged toward Daniel, shouting back at Christina. "Run!"

She bolted. The world was swimming from her head injury. She had to live!

A gunshot rang out behind her. Certain the bullet shot past her; she ran as fast as she could. Her slippered feet were painfully cut on the rocks and roots of the forest floor as she ran.

Behind her, Jeremy lunged again at his father as he aimed at Christina's fleeing form. Another shot rang out and Jeremy's body fell to the ground. An other earthly scream emanated through the trees as Daniel realized he had shot his only child. Blood poured from the wound in Jeremy's chest as he hit the ground.

Daniel went to his son, forgetting his intended target. He had just killed his only child. Everything was lost – everything he had worked for and had killed for. It was all for his son, and now it was gone.

He couldn't bear the thought of life without him. He took his shotgun and placed it in his mouth and pulled the trigger. It was all over.

Christina heard the shots and ran as fast as she could away from them. She was sure he was being pursued by the man who had murdered her cousin. She tripped and fell on tree roots, scraping her leg badly. She hoisted herself and ran, limping through the woods. She had to keep going. He was coming after her. She had to live.

The trees and rocks all blended together as her vision swirled. She was running along a ridge, unsure of where she was. There were no trail markers and no evidence of humans anywhere. She needed to get away from Daniel, but she also needed to find help.

Suddenly, the earth beneath her feet gave way, and she slid into darkness.

CHAPTER 34

She felt something give way in her ankle as she landed in a heap in the deep darkness of the earth. The sodden smell of damp soil filled her nostrils, along with another odor that she couldn't quite identify. Bears immediately came to mind.

Christina had tried to not cry out when she fell into the hole to avoid alerting her pursuer of her whereabouts. She tried to not move, hoping her eyes would adjust to the darkness and she would be able to take in her surroundings. There was absolute silence.

She strained to listen for noises above the ground, such as the sound of running feet, but could hear none. There was a distant sound in the darkness of trickling and dripping water. No other noise was evident.

Her head throbbed. The fall had not done her head injury any good, and the darkness wasn't helping either. Her ankle ached, but it was the only other major injury she assessed as she tried to calm the pounding of her heart.

Controlling her breathing took significant effort as the adrenaline continued to course through her veins. She tried to concentrate and assess her immediate circumstances. If she were to survive, she needed to have her wits about her. The fall into the hole had to have been several feet. It had felt like diving into a pool and landing on the waterless bottom. Was those 6 or 7 feet? She had no idea.

One slipper was missing from her foot. She could not recall where or when she had lost that. *What ridiculous circumstances,* she thought. This morning she had been glad to have a few hours alone to catch up on paperwork in peace. When she had left her slippers on, she wasn't thinking she would need her hiking boots to protect her feet while she tried to escape being murdered!

Slowly, her heart stopped pounding. She tried to think of what time it was. She had been unconscious for a while, so she knew her perception was off. Based on the light, it seemed like it may be later afternoon. *Everyone should have started to come back to the inn by now,* she thought. She wondered if they would know she was missing. They may guess that she went on a walk or a hike. They may not even know to miss her until much later in the evening.

She dropped her head into her hands in despair. It would likely be hours before anyone even suspected she was in trouble. By then, Daniel would likely locate her hiding place, and she would be dead in that shallow grave he had been digging before her eyes. And what of Jeremy? Had he become his father's victim as well?

Her head swam from the movement and the hopelessness she felt. Clearly, she had a concussion, and she tried to recall what she should do in that situation. *Stay awake and stay alive,* she thought.

The late afternoon brought people back to the inn in small groups. The first to arrive were Jeff, Layla, and Kevin. Kevin watched as the couple pulled around to the barn to check in on the horses. Kevin followed them into the barn deep in conversation with Jeff about his plans for horse driven amenities. Jeff concentrated on the care of the horses, while Layla kept him company as he moved from stall to stall.

The door to the barn blew open and banged against the wall. The horses shifted nervously in their stalls. "Hey, grab that, would you, Hon?" Jeff called out to Layla. "Must be a rainstorm or something coming up."

Layla went to the barn door to pull it closed. As she did so, the front door to the inn came into her sights. "Jeff," she called into the barn, "you'd better come here. Something's not right at the inn."

At her words, Kevin felt pin pricks tingle on the back of his neck, and his stomach dropped. Jeff looked at his companion, annoyance clear on his face. There were chores to be done with the horses and with the remainder of the animals in the other barn. "Ayah, just a minute. I'll be right there..." he called back to her.

"I'll go see." Kevin reassured his old friend. He had some things to do anyway and was eager to see Christina. As he exited the barn, the door to the inn blew open, as if a burst of air from inside threw it open. He exchanged a sideways glance with Layla.

"Something is very wrong." Layla stated somberly. She joined him as they both made their way cautiously to the front door.

The inn door had been left flung open. It was still and quiet inside. "No one here?" he asked of Layla.

She shrugged her shoulders.

As they stepped into the doorway, they immediately saw the dried blood smears on the floor and across the rug of the front room. There were additional drops of blood along the floor and smeared on the smooth boards of the hall. A chair was overturned. Hearing them, the dog began to howl from behind the closed office door. A deep feeling of dread crept into his heart. "Christina!" he bellowed running through the building desperate to locate her. He knew in his soul he would not. She wasn't there. "Don't touch anything," said Kevin. He yanked out his trail radio as the Sheriff cruiser pulled into the lot with Gina in the passenger side. Layla and Jeff rushed out to meet the pair as they got out of the vehicle. Kevin joined them, dread weighing his steps, grateful to see Shawn who would know what to do. Kevin's mind was muddied with anxiety. *What had happened here, where was Christina?*

Jeff quickly relayed what they had seen, Shawn curtly asked them a few brief questions, and checked his firearm. "You two stay here. Kevin, Jeff, come with me."

They entered the house. Shawn cautiously walked around the room, taking in the details as his trained eye permitted. The dog began howling again and pawing at the door. "Can you find a leash? I think they keep it hanging back by the kitchen door. Don't touch anything else if you can help it. I'll want to keep the dog out of the blood on the floor."

He followed Jeff in through the dining room. It looked normal. There was nothing broken or out of place, just as the front of the house had been. But it was apparent that something had occurred there. He had an instinctual sense that something was off. Logically, there could have been a simple explanation, but to his naked eye, it looked like someone who was injured had been dragged out the front door. The hair on the back of his neck began to bristle. "Christina?" he bellowed, his deep authoritative voice echoing through the empty house.

No one answered.

Jeff came back with a leash. "He's really going nuts in there. It's going to take us both to grab him."

Together, the men gingerly opened the office door as the dog lunged and barked at them, eager to get out of the office and frantic to help his mistress. They managed to hook the leash on the animal, and they realized he was injured. His paws were bleeding, apparently from digging at the office door and trying to get out. The sight of the attempts of the dog to get out of the office sent chills down Kevin's spine. That dog had been at Christina's side since they found him on the stagecoach road her first day back. The animal was frantic, and it made him further solidify that something sinister had happened.

"I'm calling Agnes," Shawn said, reaching for the desk phone. They had all promised to let her know if anything came up in the Annie Stone case. This sure seemed like something and he would need reinforcements. "The line's dead."

On the side of the desk, Kevin picked up Christina's cell phone. "She would have never left the house without her phone," Kevin stated as his stomach dropped.

CHAPTER 35

Kevin sat at one of the dining room chairs with his head in his hands. The police were still gathering details in the front of the house. Christina had not been missing more than twelve hours, but the concern was coupled with the suspicions raised toward Jeremy and his father, Daniel. The police had been watching them since the discovery of Annie's remains.

Jeremy's car was parked off the road to the inn, where he could have accessed the inn on the path that they used to sneak in and out on when they were younger. Daniel was not home and was seen leaving pulling out of his driveway earlier that morning. Neither of them had shown up to work that day. No one had seen them all day.

Further details had Kevin's stomach reeling. A game camera had captured Jeremy coming through the orchard, the phone line to the inn had been cut, and long hair and blood were found on the butt of an axe. The latter was the information that had his stomach in knots. Someone had hurt her badly.

He was feeling helpless as the clock ticked on. They had nothing to go on yet. Jeremy and Daniel could have taken her far from here in the hours that had passed. They could be in Canada, Boston, New York, out in the Atlantic...or lost among millions of people. His heart sank as he thought of what she was going through, and what they might be doing to her if she was still alive.

Jeff had taken Gina, Layla, and the dog to his place. The dog's paws were raw from digging at the door for so long. Jeff wanted to see to them to ensure the animal would be all right and the police were glad to not have the dog wandering through any evidence.

Law enforcement had put out an APB on Daniel's truck to all surrounding areas and states. A state police helicopter was coming in, but so were heavy rainstorms. Soon a weather front would be passing through bringing thunderstorms, heavy rain and cold. An early frost was predicted for the weekend. The rain would hamper the collection of any evidence.

Kevin heard the police radios buzzing and there was a renewed flurry of activity in the house with the officers gathered there. He watched as there was a commotion. Shawn hustled into the dining room, looking for Kevin. "A truck matching the description of Daniel's was located by a group on four wheelers up around the Somerset ridge."

He hesitated before adding more, taking a deep breath before speaking. "They found a male matching Jeremy's description that is severely injured, but alive. It appears one of the four wheelers is a thoracic surgeon. They found another male who is dead. No one else was found."

Kevin let out his breath. He was dizzy and unsure how to respond to the news. He was obviously elated that she had not been among the injured, but where was she? What had happened to her?

"Mountain rescue is on the way. Dartmouth hospital is looking for a place to land their chopper."

Shawn looked soberly at his friend. "You are part of mountain rescue, so technically I can let you go to the site...."

Kevin bolted to his feet, stopped short and turned back to his friend. "Let's take my truck."

Both men bolted for the door, blowing past Agnes as she instructed a young officer to accompany them. "Stay with them and stay in contact with me," she shouted as the men left.

Another team of troopers was on the way as well. Jurisdiction was a little vague in the area, but with town and state police, rescue and now the Sheriff, they would be covered. The immediate need would be to take care of the injured man. If this was a kidnapping, they would need to call in the FBI as well.

As the men raced onto the old logging road, they encountered mountain rescue and their four-wheel truck. Letting the ambulance ahead of them, they followed the emergency vehicle over the rough terrain. It was a slow and treacherous ride as they swerved to avoid deep ruts and huge potholes. Kevin's patience was tested as they slowly made their way. Overhead, they could hear the helicopter and the communications between them and the ground crew. The state police had taken charge of the situation. They understood the case and details that Shawn apparently had not been engaged in, due to his relationship to the deceased.

Kevin's mind whirled with his thoughts as his anxiety grew. He prayed that she was safe. He also prayed that the injured man who was still alive would know something about where Christina was and if she was hurt or injured. Deep in his thoughts, he really wanted to pummel whoever was responsible for this situation.

Finally, after what seemed like hours over a barely passable old logging road, they arrived at a clearing where several four-wheelers were parked near Daniel's truck with its covered bed. The tailgate was still opened. All three men bolted from the vehicle after pulling it out of the way.

Kevin's stomach dropped as he noticed Christina's fuzzy slipper laying in the bed of the truck as they walked past. "Look here," he called hoarsely to Shawn, "it's her..."

Shawn directed the young officer to take photos of the bed as he pulled his friend aside. "We'll find her."

The two men exchanged meaningful looks. Both were aware of what they were up against. They moved their attention to a group gathered nearby, watching the rescue take over from the four wheelers. Jeremy's shirt was soaked in blood. His face was ashen, and he was unconscious. There would be no questioning him about Christina.

Under a stand of pine trees nearby was another figure. The head was covered in a jacket, and the ground was soaked with dark blood. Kevin took in the surroundings. There was a shovel on the ground near the body. Dirt had been dug and moved. His brain slowly permitted him to realize what he was looking at, and his stomach fell. It was meant to be a shallow grave. A pair of troopers were taking photos of the area and gathering pieces of evidence.

He scanned the area for any indication that Christina had been there. Shawn was already addressing the small group of law enforcement and relaying Kevin's identification of the slipper. They murmured among themselves with Kevin picking up only pieces of their conversation.

As he stood, he took in every tree and bush. He scanned the area for anything that would lead to her whereabouts. He wanted to see her coming out from the trees unharmed with a smile on her face. But the hope evaporated as he took in the situation in front of him. Daniel was dead, and Jeremy was nearly. Where was she?

"Hey, you're mountain rescue, right?"

The address jarred Kevin from his thoughts. "Yeah I am."

"Can you guide us up to the ridge where the chopper can land? They say it's not far and we need to move quick. It would be great if we didn't get lost."

"Let's go!" Kevin shouted, running on his way to the squad.

He hopped into the back of the large 4-wheel drive ambulance. Jeremy lay still under a blanket with an IV in his arm. One EMT and another man dressed in camouflage tended to him. Kevin gave the driver directions and they bumped off through the woods on the logging road.

As they sped as fast as they could through the ruts and holes, Kevin realized that this man must be the doctor. "I don't know too many docs that are into four wheeling," he said, introducing himself.

"Ha, yeah, I was trying to get away from it all for a bit," he shook his head as he looked down on Jeremy's prone form. "I guess it wasn't to be. This guy is incredibly lucky."

Kevin looked at Jeremy's ashen face. He wanted to throttle him for information about Christina, but he restrained himself. "How so?"

"Looks like an attempted murder suicide to me. Guy who shot himself fell right onto him, which slowed his bleeding out. Looks like he tried to kill him and then inadvertently saved his life!"

"He conscious at all? Say anything to you?"

The doctor looked at him intently, rubbing his blood-stained hands on his pants. "When we moved the other guy off him, I think he said something like 'ran away' or 'got away.' We didn't see anybody around at all – so not sure what he was talking about. Maybe he was surprised that he was still alive..."

They had arrived at the rendezvous site for the medical evacuation. The helicopter was hovering overhead and landed in the clearing once they were finished unloading the patient from the gurney. Kevin had done this routine a few times over the years, so the guys in the chopper were familiar to him. "Better get rolling. Big storms are coming in from the west. Just made it in here before the weather started up."

His gut clenched at their words. The heavy rain meant that any evidence or sign of Christina would virtually disappear. If the police would commit to a search for Christina, they could pull in teams, but it would take precious time. If it was storming, they would have delays and challenges getting the search teams organized.

They arrived back to the group in the woods shortly afterward. The ambulance would remove the body of the deceased with the permission of the coroner. Shawn approached Kevin immediately on his arrival back to the scene. "Tell him what you told me," Kevin directed the doctor before he rejoined his group.

The physician told Shawn and a few other officials what he had told Kevin about Jeremy's confused words. "Rescue can pull a search party together quickly; we've got a storm coming in so we'll need to move. It's going to get cold tonight and the next few days. If she's out there, she's not prepared for it. Plus, she's injured."

"There's a lot of woods out there. Any idea or evidence as to which way she would have headed?" Shawn immediately began barking orders at the group of law enforcement.

A pad of paper was produced, and an urgent search area was established in the perimeter around the immediate scene. It would be imperative that they get started as soon as possible to establish a solid area to search, and then expand that further when more help arrived.

Shawn and other officers began to organize a formal search party. They used their radios to call back down to the captain, fire, and rescue. Kevin paired with other officers, and they began to establish a perimeter for the immediate search. They paired up with radios and a search plan.

Kevin and the young trooper worked together, systematically searching the immediate area. They worked in a lane type search to cover the entire location around the immediate scene. This would permit them to establish some evidence about which way she had run. With the four wheelers and the other vehicles coming into the area, there was a chance that any signs that may show her path would have been erased.

Far in the distance, they could hear thunder. The weather front was fast approaching with heavy rain. They would need to find something soon to indicate her direction or they would end up searching a large area and could miss her.

Kevin began to feel desperate. He prayed to himself as he tried to concentrate on the details he was trying to locate. His heart pounded in his chest as he thought of all the scenarios that could put her in danger.

His radio crackled, startling him out of his reverie. "Got a footprint."

He rejoiced! A lead! He and his young escort rushed to their search partner. Indeed, there was a footprint in mud and tall grass, leading away from the scene. Kevin bent to closely examine the impression. Christina had been booking it, by the indentation of the print. She'd likely been running because her life depended on it. Dismay filled him, as he realized this foot was bare. She had been fleeing a killer with one bare foot and one fuzzy slipper. The terrain was rough, and she would have been further hampered by the bare foot. It was likely that she would have injured herself.

The path she was headed was directly into the wilderness area. There was miles and miles of unpopulated, dense forest. The same forest from the local legends – the Bennington Triangle. The same forest that several people had walked into and never had been found.

She had been gone for hours, so she could have made a lot of progress to get away from here. She could be hiding as well, thinking she was being pursued. She was also likely injured, possibly with a head injury and all the challenges that came with that. She could be disoriented and unsure of what to do. She could be unconscious and in need of medical attention.

Locating her would be like finding needle in a haystack.

"How long before the dog team gets here?" he barked into his radio.

She couldn't end up being one of those lost people. He had to find her.

CHAPTER 36

The rain came as it was predicted with heavy downpours and localized flooding. The cold front that the rain ushered in also lived up to the forecast. The early cold front brought temperatures into the 40's for the evening. There was a danger of frost before sunrise, the coldest part of the night.

As of sunrise, they had not located Christina. Kevin was distraught and had not slept all night. They had searched the afternoon and evening until the rain became too much. The dogs had arrived, but by then, the heavy rain had impacted their effectiveness. They would head out again once it was daylight.

Christina had moved deeper into the cave as the rain poured down to avoid getting soaked and further exposed to the elements. She tried to capture some fresh water from the rain fall in the palms of her hands. She knew she was becoming dehydrated since she'd had nothing to drink but coffee. She was very hungry and very scared.

If Daniel found her, she had no way to escape from her spot in the ground. She had thoughts of him firing his shotgun into the cave until she was dead. Her head and ankle throbbed. The passage of time was sketchy due to her head injury and the darkness in the cave.

The entry to the cave had not been easy to spot. She had clearly not seen it as she was running through the woods. But her panicked mind may not have taken in the details clearly, and Daniel was an experienced hunter. He had a better chance of locating her hiding place. And the rain would hamper any effort to find her.

Her eyes had begun to adjust to the extreme darkness. The light from above was very dim with the rain, and with the onset of nightfall, the cave was cloaked in complete blackness. She had decided that there were no other animals with her in the cave, as she reasoned she would have heard them move around by now. There was still that odd odor, but she couldn't smell anything that resembled the musky smell of fur. Minimally, there were at least no other creatures that would want to eat her.

She felt along the solid rock wall and had found a spot that seemed higher and away from where the rain was pouring in the hole above. The higher elevation of the floor would keep her dry in theory. As the temperature dropped with the rain, she began to shiver. The cave was in complete and utter darkness.

She knew she needed to get warm and stay dry. She felt her surroundings for leaves or pine needles to make a shelter, or at least, a cushion against the cold rock. She felt the floor and area around it, shuffling on her bottom to avoid crashing her injured head into something. It also kept her off her hurt leg.

She found a smattering of dry leaves and other items as she scooted. She piled them in her lap to keep them where she could find them. There were few, but it did not feel like enough to give her any kind of shelter. Disappointment and further worry filled her mind. She was going to be exposed to the elements and it was going to get cold. The cards were stacking against her.

She continued to move around her dark surroundings, feeling blindly along the rock. Surprisingly, her hands came across something that felt like some kind of material. It was dirty and matted with who knows what, but it was manmade, nonetheless. Some of the material felt as if it was stuck to the ground. As she felt around her hands came across a bag. She felt around further and realize that it felt like a backpack. It was full of something!

She hoped it wasn't some animal nest she was digging into with her bare hands as she located the packs zippers and opened the pockets. One pocket held what felt like a shirt, and the other larger pockets contained what felt like a small comforter or a light sleeping bag. It was not adult sized, but it was a godsend! It would keep her warm or at least, give her a chance at warmth.

She felt around further and pulled on the material that seemed to be buried in the floor of the cave. It gave way under her hands and separated. She realized it wasn't anything useful to her and so she stopped her efforts. The additional clothing and light blanket were a blessing.

Further inspection of the backpack revealed a flashlight. Hopeful, she banged it against her leg and attempted to get it to work. Expectations were not realized as she grasped that this pack had likely been in there a long time, considering the condition of the materials inside and the musty smell.

They were dry at least and would help to keep her alive as the temperatures dropped. As she tried to settle into a dry patch, under enough coverage to help her keep warm, her thoughts went to Kevin. He had taught her how to survive in the woods. Admittedly, she did not pay so much attention to the serious topic, but he had been adamant that she learn at least the basic survival skills and some level of first aid. They had frequently gone camping and hiking when they were together before Annie went missing. It was mostly an excuse to be together alone. Thankfully, she had listened to some of what he had said.

Now she may never see him again. Her heart fell as she realized how far they had come in the past few weeks. She loved him and had never really stopped. The time they had together was priceless and it made her feel how fortunate they were to at least have had that. Tears coursed down her dirty and bloodied face. Hope that they would be together again rose in her. She had to live, if just to see him one last time. She had to.

She wondered if they realized she was gone, and what had happened. Surely people were coming home now. She tried to recall the events at the inn, the frantic dog barking and what had been said. Her head injury made the details unclear. She tried to piece together the course of events and the evidence that would help any rescue efforts.

She settled herself into what felt like a corner of the cave, where she would not be exposed to cooler air from the entrance. Draping herself in makeshift bedding to protect her skin from the cold rock, she wrapped herself in the small blanket. As she placed the shirt over her head to capture her body heat, she realized the wound on her scalp was still oozing blood and hurt immensely. Tenderly wrapping herself in the shirt, she worried about her head injury. Her thoughts went back to what the coroner has said was the probable cause of death for Annie. Her skull had been fractured. She wondered how badly her own skull was injured and thought about how close she had come to death. She could still die if

Daniel were to find her. She may die if no one were to find her at all.

How long could she last in here? No food or water, no clothing to protect against the cold. She pushed the thoughts from her minds.

As she wrapped herself in the materials, she knew they would not be enough to keep her warm. She needed to stay awake and keep breathing and hope – hope that someone would come along and find her.

The cave was black as night. She thought she could see shadows occasionally, but knew it was her eyes trying to adjust to the light. It almost made no difference to her if her eyes were opened or closed due to the absolute darkness. She knew it was going to be a fight to stay awake. So, she started to think about the details of that morning.

Jeremy had been the one coming through the orchard. It was his picture that popped up on her text messaged from the new game cameras. She wondered if it had been him that had been messing with Jim's cameras all along – but why would he do that? He had access to the inn until she had fired him, and that had not kept him fully away. Daniel had grabbed her in the back as she was fleeing Jeremy, so it was likely Daniel that hit her in the head with the axe.

But Jeremy? He had told her to stay down in the front room and to not anger him further. Daniel? And then Jeremy untied her while Daniel was digging her grave. She shivered, pulling the blanket tighter. What was it he had been spouting while he dug? She tried hard to recall his words.

He had killed Annie.

He really had hated her and the fact that Ada and Annie had inherited the inn and not he and Jeremy. He had killed Annie so Jeremy would inherit the inn, but then Ada had left it to her. He was planning to kill her as well for the same reasons. Jeremy appeared to have been involved in the whole sickening thing, but it was not clear to what extent. Her head swam with the thoughts and her injury compounded the spinning sensation.

There was something that came back to her from when Daniel was sputtering – something about killing Annie when he found out she was knocked up. Had Annie been pregnant when she died? Daniel referred to Shawn as 'that bastard,' as it was likely his child. Shawn caused a load of trouble when they were younger and may have vandalized some of Daniel's equipment at one time or another, which had clearly sealed Daniel's dislike for the boy.

Christina's thoughts whirled to back just before Annie had been missing. She had been so in love with Kevin, and Annie and Shawn had recently broken up. She recalled that the circumstances of their breakup were a little vague as Shawn had been the initiator. Annie had been withdrawn and not herself.

A sudden realization hit her. She'd found Annie early one morning, vomiting in her bathroom. She had blamed it on the wine coolers they routinely consumed over the summers and complained about being awakened early from the construction equipment in the yard working on the rock walls. The very walls where her body had been found.

Christina's thoughts whirled. No one had mentioned that as a possibility of a child when they were searching for Annie. How did Daniel find out? Did Shawn know? He had never mentioned it at all. How awful that not one, but two young lives had been wasted. So many lives ruined for greed.

Tears slipped down her dirty face in the deep darkness of the cave. Outside, the rain poured down, and the temperature began to drop.

CHAPTER 37

Kevin was back in the clearing, organizing another search party now that the early round had come back empty handed. A couple of trained search dogs and their handlers had been engaged in the search since dawn. They wanted to catch the best scent they could while the ground was still damp. They were fighting the heavy rain and the other environmental factors. They had picked up Christina's scent apparently, but had lost it. They were going to give it another try after some rest and water.

He was impatient, he knew, but as time ticked on with the colder weather snap, the more likely she would die from exposure to the elements. Hypothermia was a killer. Even in moderately cold temperatures, people died. Kevin pulled his jacket closed and shivered. It had dropped to 32 degrees overnight and was now hovering at 40. The day would warm up into the 60's, but it may be too late for Christina. He prayed that she had found some shelter somehow, and that she was not injured enough to be unable to care for herself.

His stomach fell every time the radio squelched, or another search team came in. More volunteers were on their way, and they would have enough people to do a full grid search and expand it from their targeted searches with the dogs. They would start in the area that the dogs had lost her scent.

It was likely they would have picked it up again if the rain had not washed everything away.

A jeep pulled into the clearing that he recognized as Layla's. She and Jeff likely came to volunteer in the search party. He hoped Layla was well enough to participate and was glad when he saw she had brought food and water for the volunteers.

"Glad to see you guys!" he called over to them.

Jeff opened the door and the dog bounded out to greet Kevin. "Oh, sorry man. I didn't know what to do with him. He's been frantic all night."

The dog licked Kevin's hands eagerly in a greeting, and then proceeded to bark at him in earnest. "I see what you mean," Kevin said. "Better get a leash on him. We've got some other search dogs in the area, and we can't have him running wild through the crime scene."

Jeff grabbed the dog by his collar and hooked a leash on him. "Crime scene? Sorry man, but what's happened? I can only really guess, between the chopper evac, coroner and now a ground search for Christina."

"How'd did you know we were searching for Christina?" Kevin asked.

At that moment, Shawn joined them. He had been side by side with Kevin the whole time, guiding his team and coordinating the incident command that the state troopers had organized. The FBI was on its way, which was something that he wasn't sure they needed, as it wasn't exactly a kidnapping and more in line with an abduction. Shawn reacted at Kevin's question and immediately, they knew how Jeff knew they were searching for Christina.

"Hey Jeff. Do you mind unloading that water and food over by the squads?" Kevin asked. Jeff nodded in agreement, leaving Layla with the two men.

Shawn turned to Kevin to diffuse the intensity of his question. "Heard it on the scanner, like the rest of the county. You okay to be out here?" Shawn asked. She nodded her reply.

"Do you know something that would help us?" Kevin murmured so that no one else would overhear.

"I really don't know anything definite, but I think the dog may be able to help." She whispered.

Both men looked at the dog being held on a leash. The mangy mutt had tried to protect Christina and from the looks of Jeremy, he got a good bite in before they shut him in the office at the inn. Kevin knew Shawn couldn't get over the resemblance to the dog Annie had when they were little kids. They were running out of time, and they knew it. It would be at least an hour before the fresh search group would be there. They may already be too late. They would take whatever help was offered.

"Here, let me hold the dog. He seems pretty worked up," Shawn said.

The dog immediately responded to Shawn's command over his leash and gave him his full attention. Shawn appeared to think better of letting the dog lead him through the rough terrain. It was not his usual place to be in the woods, and he likely felt a bit out of his element. Instead, Shawn took the dog's leash and shoved it into Kevin's hands. He put a police radio in his other hand. "Trust me," he said to his friend, "I've got the search well in hand, so radio me if you find anything."

Kevin looked surprised, but grabbed his pack at the last minute as Shawn urged the dog, "Show us where she is boy!"

The dog took off in a solid direction, pulling Kevin along behind him. They moved quickly, past where they had found Christina's bare footprint. The dog did not hesitate. He kept his forward momentum and did not stop to sniff a single tree or bush. Kevin saw he was following along a ridge, moving in and out of the undergrowth. If she had been following this route, it was clear she was trying to evade someone behind her. He realized with a chill that she had been trying to evade being killed as she was being shot at. The trail they were following zig zagged from cover to cover. *It's harder to hit a moving target.*

What horror she had been through, he thought as he kept moving behind the dog. He prayed she was still alive. That was all that mattered to him – that she was not dead. He did not think he could face it if she were dead. It would destroy him. They had to find her.

They went through the woods. The dog pulled him further and faster over rises and boulders. His tongue hung from his mouth as he ran without stopping. His injured paws left bloody pawprints as his wounds reopened from the activity and still, he did not falter. Kevin begged the powers that be that she be all right, as he struggled to keep up with the animal's pace.

They must have traveled about a half mile or more through the woods at a breakneck speed, and then the dog slowed his pace. Kevin took the break to swig some water and offer the dog some. He noticed then what had gotten the dog's attention. It was the other two search dogs and their handlers.

The dog barked to them with short, pointed barks that were returned by the other dogs. Kevin waved to them to acknowledge their presence as they took a brief break. The others moved toward them as Kevin watched. The other search animals appeared to be excited by Chipper's presence.

"Hey, I didn't know you had a search dog," said one of the handlers Kevin recognized from other searches on the trail.

"Yeah, he's a stray. Christina's been watching him," he replied, taking a swig of water.

He felt a bit ridiculous now, letting the crazed animal lead him on a wild trail at top speed through the woods. There were other animals that had training and gave them a better chance at finding Christina. *What the hell was he doing?*

"Hey, your dog is pointing."

They all looked at the dog. He had one paw up and his nose directly pointing in one direction. "What?"

One of the handlers reached down and unhooked Chipper's leash. The dog bolted forward, and they all followed suit, chasing him for a hundred yards or so. He ended his run at a gathering of bushes and rocks. He stood there, barking, and waiting for the men and dogs to reach him.

At first, they could not see what he was barking at, but he was relentless. He barked and urged them to action as he dug into the rock beneath. At further study of the area, Kevin could see an opening hidden in the terrain. "Christina?" he shouted down the small opening, but only silence followed.

The dog suddenly started howling. It was an eerie, soul-wrenching sound. Goosebumps rose on his arms.

"I'm going in there," Kevin announced to the handlers.

They took charge of the dog as Kevin lowered himself gingerly down the hole. He knew this was reckless, relying on a stray dog and going sight unseen down a hole in the ground. He landed hard on his feet into the cave and immediately flashed his flashlight around, shouting her name.

He almost missed her. She was just a small figure wrapped in a filthy blanket, covered with leaves. His heart leapt as he approached her. She was so cold, and his heart dropped as he felt for a pulse. At his touch, her eyes flickered open, and he rejoiced.

"Oh baby!" he shouted as he carefully examined her, shouting up to the dog handlers that she was found.

He knew he immediately needed to warm her up, and he proceeded to take off his clothes to wrap around both their bodies as he got her skin to skin. She was barely conscious as she resisted him taking off her clothes to expose her skin to his. He murmured to her as he did so, thankful she had been found alive.

Above ground, rescue was getting organized. It would be a challenge to get them both out of the hole in the ground. As he felt her body start to absorb some of his warmth, he flashed his light around the room. She was covered in a dirty old Power Rangers blanket and wrapped around her head was a sweatshirt with a familiar school logo. A dirty backpack lay on the floor, and a pile of dirt lay against one wall.

He jumped as his light hit what appeared to be a half buried human skull on the other side of the cave.

CHAPTER 38

"Come back to bed," she murmured to him.

It was early morning and the sun was just coming up. The early morning fog was lifting from the fields. It was quiet and peaceful; at this hour, everyone was still asleep getting those last few winks before their big opening day.

He got back into the warm bed, snuggling up to her naked buttocks. Her cast dragged heavily across the sheets as she settled into his arms. It was the only outward evidence of the past few weeks. He pressed his lips against the back of her neck and inhaled her scent. This was the compass for his life. He felt truly blessed to have her in his arms after all they had been through, not only in the past few weeks, but in the years they were apart.

Recalling how close he had been to losing her forever had shaken him. He shivered and she pulled the blankets more closely around them.

She had been lucky that they had found her when they did. She had been hypothermic and barely arousable. He pulled his arms more tightly around her. The events of that day replayed clearly in his mind.

Daniel had shot himself, apparently after he thought he had killed Jeremy, his only child. Jeremy had attempted to help Christina get away and had stepped into the line of fire. Daniel's intent that day was to kill Christina and pave the way for Jeremy to inherit the inn. He had admitted to killing Annie.

According to Shawn, off the record of course, the evidence was being compiled against Daniel, but the police did not have probable cause for an arrest. Apparently, he, Jeremy and Shawn were their main suspects in Annie's death. They had been keeping tabs on all of them but hadn't expected what happened that day.

Jeremy was recovering in the County Jail from his wounds. It had been discovered that he was involved in a money laundering scheme connected to a local drug ring. He had been running money through his father's construction company and the inn, as Ada had left him in charge of the business as her health and interest in the property declined. When Christina had come and hired her attorney, they found some suspicious activity and had alerted the bank, who were still conducting their investigation, but things did not look good for him. He was looking at several years in jail.

Jeremy did provide additional information on his father, saying when his father started drinking again, he told Jeremy about murdering Annie. He also said his father had tampered with Ada's insulin, and that he'd caused the accident that killed his brother. He had always been so envious of not inheriting the inn, he felt it was his to own and he had wanted to pass it to his son. It had been a deadly inheritance for everyone else because of Daniel's jealousy.

There had been a vindication for Jeff in the whole ordeal. The backpack Christina had found in the cave had been Jeff's from all those years ago, when he was lost on a camping trip. The skull they found in the cave was part of an entire human skeleton that had been there for many years. There was speculation that it could have been Paula Weldon, who had gone missing in the 1950's from Bennington College. They would have hard evidence soon.

It was all over now. The past was the past and would no longer define their lives going forward. They were together and that was all that mattered to him. He would follow her anywhere if she chose to leave this place. He was glad that she had decided to stay for the time being. She and Gina had a wonderful business plan and would do well with the inn and the restaurant. With Jeff's horses added to the mix, they would offer further amenities to attract patrons.

Life was looking up for all of them. There was one more thing however – one last step that would solidify their future. He reached in front of him to slip a ring on the left hand of the dozing woman in his arms.

She stirred. "What are you doing?"

She looked down at her hand, waking from her dozing and saw the diamond ring on her finger. She was speechless and turned in his embrace to face him. "Is this what I think it is?" she whispered finding his mouth with her lips.

Tears slipped down her face as she pulled back from the kiss.

"Is that a 'yes'?" he asked.

She laughed as she felt him stiffen against her thighs as he covered her body with his. She smiled as she gazed into his eyes. "I love you so much. Of course, it's a yes!"

His heart soared. Happiness filled his soul. He watched her face change from love to passion as he gently entered her. Together, they moved toward ecstasy as joy filled their hearts and they rejoiced in the promise of their life together.

FROM THE AUTHOR

Thank you for reading Deadly Inheritance! I hope that you've enjoyed it! Please consider leaving a rating or a review on Amazon or Goodreads. It would be greatly appreciated!

If you'd like to receive EXCLUSIVE insights to new books and sneak peeks at my work in progress, sign up for my newsletter at

Jeulia Hesse's newslettter or at www.jeuliahesse.com

Keep reading for a preview of the next book *Killer Recipe*

PREVIEW

CHAPTER 1

He hadn't been in town long before he realized just how much he hated it. Rural communities gave him the jitters. Small town residents paid too much attention to what was going on, and were always looking at him with long, slow glances. They had the potential to identify him as someone who didn't quite belong, someone they couldn't place and give him the attention he didn't want or need.

The gun felt warm from its recent use, its weight heavy in his hand as he cleaned it carefully with a rag. The black metal glinted in the streetlight; he had no fear that anyone would notice his being there. The sole occupant of the only house on the lonely road was dead and recently deceased at that. There was no one to alert law enforcement of his presence.

Not that he liked to kill. He took no pleasure in the act itself. It functioned as the means to the desired end; the "no longer here" factor. The dead man deserved his destiny, after failing time after time to do his job. And his final slip up, that he had considered running to the police, drew his last straw.

He laughed to himself. *Really?* Going to the cops would not raise the threat intended. He was not afraid of the police and what they may do now that his operation had come so far. They moved a lot of merchandise through the town; it was a perfect setup. A couple of hours to the border, a couple of hours to the city with a lot of eager takers along the way.

The dead man inside the house would draw pressure from the local cops. They asked too many questions and got too close to the action. The police apparently worried about the increased volume of drugs in tandem with the heightened overdoses. They had the dead man in their sights. His nerves and anxiety about their attention had him thinking of flipping on the entire operation. What he knew of it, anyway. No one understood what he actually did to make a living. And he liked it that way, thank you very much.

The dead man had not been performing up to standard, his work had been dropping off. They'd been for a while, and he'd taken no action to make them to rise again. School was in session, creating ample opportunity to grow more users in that vast field of green. Kids in high schools and the nearby colleges offered abundant opportunities that the deceased dealer failed to capitalize on.

The man dropped his gun into his bag, wiping off his hands and checking his own reflection in the rearview mirror. He acknowledged he would need to stick around and make sure things ran how they should. If you want a job done right, do it yourself!

He would identify someone else to install locally to be in charge and keep business rolling. Then he could step out again and go back to his way of life as usual. Arrangements could be made for what he needed to not draw attention to himself. In fact, word was that *she* was in the area. He would need to discover more about what *she* was doing here.

Maybe it would work into his plans to include a little relationship building.

He turned the ignition on and pulled the rental out of the driveway and down the long uninhabited road. He'd left no evidence behind, of that he was certain. Meticulousness always his strong suit. He would drive the car back to counter at Logan, and it would be lost among all the same standard cars with the identical make and model.

He would go back to his life as if nothing happened.

CHAPTER 2

Maybe the idea of moving here was a big mistake, Gina thought as she drove through the tiny town of Wilmington, Vermont. There was little to do. The offering of very few social activities was making her restless.

The weather was beautiful with clear air and sunshine, and it was a lovely Thursday afternoon in October. She was just coming from the farmer's market where she'd met new people who shared her interest in food. A basket of fresh vegetables and bread sat on the passenger seat, along with the best cheese she'd ever eaten from a goat farm in the area. Gina had plans to use it as part of an appetizer for the small gathering planned for Saturday, otherwise known as Christina and Kevin's wedding.

A smile crossed her face, thinking of her friend and her beau. They were marrying after a brief engagement and would be taking their honeymoon directly after. The bride and groom had known each other for years, although there had been a several years' gap in their relationship. The quick union was unquestionable. They were so happy there was no reason to wait.

A deep sigh escaped Gina's lips as she drove through the quiet town. The delight she felt for her friends' marriage was heartfelt. It didn't mitigate the sting of jealousy. She still wondered, where was *her* prince charming? The events of her life, up to this point, had not exactly led to her storybook ending. She wondered if it was in the cards to even consider, and if a man from this quiet place could live up to her expectations.

The streets were silent. She passed only a couple of other vehicles on her way back to the inn. The locals had told her that this time of year between foliage season and the holidays was typically quiet. Tourists were no longer in town to clog the roads or eat at her restaurant. It was the perfect time for Christina to escape for a few weeks, and to plan out the festivities for the upcoming season.

The inn had an opportunity to offer Thanksgiving dinners and holiday parties. Capitalizing on that potential would be paramount for their first year in business. They needed to do what they could to grow as a company. In addition, Gina had some loose plans for both a holiday cookbook and another specialty recipe book. It had always been her dream to have her own restaurant and a catalog of cookbooks.

She was halfway to achieving her dreams, but a small part of her wished that the restaurant and tavern were not in the Vermont woods, as she craved excitement. Her original dream restaurant had been something upscale and metropolitan. She wondered if she would grow disenchanted with the historic inn and rural location. It was worrisome she felt that way already. More of a social life was what she needed. She'd been so focused on the business that she had little time to have any fun.

Clearly, she was experiencing buyer's remorse. Coming here had been such a straightforward decision after Christina inherited the inn. Gina jumped at the opportunity to partner with her best friend. They planned for Christina to run the inn and Gina would run the restaurant and tavern.

The promise of success in the business remained; they'd already done better than projected for the foliage season, and they were just getting started. But she missed city life the most, the noise and the sheer multitude of things to see and do. It was lovely here, but a little too quiet.

Over-eager to do *something,* she shifted her position as she drove her car, reflecting on the purchase with its all-wheel drive. Supposedly she would appreciate the feature once the winter came, and she had to drive the rural road up the mountain. With the leaves mostly gone from the trees, everyone seemed to focus on when the first snow would arrive. It sounded cold, but beautiful. Snow in the city lasted only until the plows and traffic cleared it away. Looking forward to the snow and cold was something she never thought she would do. It definitely would slow down her usual pace of life.

There was no one around. As she came closer to the turnoff for the inn, she passed no other cars on the road since driving out of town. Yet the only traffic light on the road for miles turned red as she approached it. It wasn't apparent at this time of day, but the light's purpose was to provide a safe turning lane for the entrance to the ski resort. In winter, it served its purpose well, but not so much in late October when there was no traffic to speak of. Frustration grew in her belly as the seconds ticked by, even though she had no pressing need for the light to turn green. It simply seemed like a waste of time to be waiting unnecessarily.

Fidgeting, she put the car in neutral and revved the engine. It was oddly satisfying to hear the machine's roar. A mischievous idea rose in her mind as she waited. Double checking the area to ensure that no one was around, she stepped on the gas. The car lurched as she shifted into drive, speeding through the red light, squealing tires as she shot forward. A thrill rushed through her veins as she stomped the accelerator and sped up the abandoned highway, laughing aloud.

Maneuvering the car well above the speed limit, she turned onto the dirt road to the inn, hitting the loose dirt so fast, it caused the car to slide. She struggled briefly to regain control. Dust, dirt, and stones flew wildly into the air. It wasn't Manhattan, but it was a bit of fun.

A siren blared, startling her. Dread immediately took over her thrill. In her rearview mirror, she saw the Sheriff's cruiser, its lights flashing. Swallowing hard, Gina slowed and pulled over, chagrinned that her little burst of fun was going to end in a ticket and embarrassment.

Shawn Johnson stepped from his cruiser. Gina was relieved to note it was him and climbed gracefully from the driver's seat. But her relief that a friend had pulled her over evaporated when she saw the stern look on his face. The stupidity of what she'd done rose in her gut and combined with her guilt. Shawn had his own share of struggles with the growing drug and crime problems in town just yesterday. He had other more important things to do than to deal with her getting her jollies by speeding, she realized.

"What the hell, Gina?" Shawn asked. He took off his hat, tossing it on the hood of her car. He ran a hand through his tawny hair and looked menacingly down at her. "What were you thinking? You ran a red light *right* in front of me. Just took off like Smoky and the Bandit..."

"Smoky who?" she asked.

His eyes glared down at her as he contemplated his next steps. "Never mind!"

As he scowled, something stirred in her. She looked at him as though she had never seen him before, despite seeing him nearly every day since she moved here. He was tall and muscular, likely imposing to someone who didn't know him.

He wasn't a stranger to her. They had become friends gradually as Christina and Kevin rekindled their relationship, often leaving them with each other as company. Shawn had a habit of coming to the inn daily, but his visits had dwindled after they found the remains of his old girlfriend buried on the property. He had sobbed in Gina's arms after that happened. They had been acquaintances at the time, but the incident had brought them closer, and they'd become friends. Their friendship had grown as Gina worked to start up the restaurant. Shawn became a willing participant for taste-testing for her menu creations and would show up at the inn regularly.

He was a very good-looking man. Now, as he stood over her imposing and authoritarian, something in her shifted and all at once, she found him immensely attractive. Confusion and shock streamed through her veins as she stood looking up at him, she found herself looking at him as if she had never seen him before. Her heart pounded against her ribs, surprising her with her response to his close proximity. Compulsively, she stepped forward bringing their bodies closer. She found herself wanting to press her body against his; it was an unexpected wanton need. *What was happening?* Stopping her forward momentum, she inhaled sharply.

He froze at her advance, an absolute statue. Her sharp intake of breath had garnered a response from him. She looked up into his eyes, finding surprise and something else. A heat simmered in his gaze. A flash of electricity sparked between them as they stood on the abandoned roadway inches apart. Compulsively she drew herself closer, her eyes focusing on his full lips. He inhaled deeply, still unmoving.

Her common sense kicked in at the last moment, she pulled herself back. Her body and brain battling over what her body wanted and what her intelligence warned. Kissing him now would seem like she was doing it only to get out of a ticket. But she really wanted to press her lips on his. She swayed. Shawn responded reaching out to steady her, his large hand on the curve of her hip. Both their bodies froze at the contact. It was clear that in those seconds, he wanted to kiss her as badly as she wanted him to.

The energy that ran between them was unlike anything she had ever felt before. It was random and completely unexpected. A deep need rose in her. She wanted this man. But right now, when he had rightly pulled her over for a traffic violation, was not a good time to throw herself at him. Breaking away from his grasp, Gina opened the car door and slid into the driver's seat. Shawn straightened himself up, replacing his hat and straightening his shirt. His eyes never leaving her.

"Okay then?" she asked, starting up the car.

"I'll see you around," he answered hoarsely stepping away from the car, waving his hand dismissively.

She guided the car onto the dirt road and drove away, this time minding the speed limit. She gazed in the rearview mirror at the figure standing in the road, looking after her. A puzzled expression filled his face.

Things just got interesting.

Made in the USA
Middletown, DE
02 June 2025